I0775714

The Night of
the Dead Boys

a 509 Crime Story

by Colin Conway

The Night of the Dead Boys

Copyright © 2023 Colin Conway

ISBN: 978-1-961030-03-9

Cover Design by Rob Williams

Original Ink Press, an imprint of High Speed Creative, LLC
1521 N. Argonne Road, #C-205
Spokane Valley, WA 99212

What is the 509?

Separated by the Cascade Range, Washington State is divided into two distinctly different climates and cultures.

The western side of the Cascades is home to Seattle, its 34 inches of annual rainfall, and the incredibly weird and smelly Gum Wall. Most of the state's wealth and political power are concentrated in and around this enormous city. The residents of this area know the prosperity that has come from being the home of Microsoft, Amazon, Boeing, and Starbucks.

To the east of the Cascade Mountains lies nearly two-thirds of the entire state, a lot of which is used for agriculture. Washington State leads the nation in producing apples, it is the second-largest potato grower, and it's the fourth for providing wheat.

This eastern part of the state can enjoy more than 170 days of sunshine each year, which is important when there are more than 200 lakes nearby. However, the beautiful summers are offset by harsh winters, with average snowfall reaching 47 inches and the average high hovering around 37°.

While five telephone area codes provide service to the westside, only 509 covers everything east of the Cascades, a staggering twenty-one counties.

Of these, Spokane County is the largest with an estimated population of 506,000.

"Vengeance is in my heart, death in my hand,
blood and revenge are hammering in my head."

William Shakespeare, *Titus Andronicus*

The Night of
the Dead Boys

Chapter 1

Tremaine Brown slammed on the brakes, and the tires of his Monte Carlo squealed in protest. The traffic light had been red for too long, and the opportunity to blast through the intersection was gone. The Chevy's rear end shimmied as the car struggled to stop on wet asphalt. Tremaine's sweaty hands gripped the steering wheel tighter, and his body stiffened in preparation for a collision.

Even though it was shortly before midnight, the traffic at the Hamilton Street and Mission Avenue intersection remained heavy. It was often like that because it lay in the shadow of Gonzaga University. Growing up, Tremaine spent a lot of time working outside the bars in this area—college kids had a lot of disposable cash and wanted what he had sold.

Heavy rain fell at an angular trajectory through the radiance cast by streetlights. Neon signs reflected off standing puddles in nearby parking lots as the raindrops peppered the ground.

Tremaine rode low in the driver's seat with his eyes barely above the dashboard. It was an uncomfortable position for a man of his size. He didn't glance left or right but instead took the whole picture in at once as a camera does—a snapshot of a moment. That was all the time he had.

His goal was on the other side of this intersection. Roughly a mile ahead—through another traffic light and over the bridge—was the entrance to the freeway. There was also an off-ramp to Second Avenue, which could lead him back to his South Hill apartment, but he couldn't go there—not while he was being followed.

The night sounded alive inside Tremaine's Chevy courtesy of the recently exploded rear window. An aroma of exhaust invaded the compartment, as did the smell of the night's storm. The car's wiper blades hastily flicked away the rain—*fwip, fwip, fwip.*

A motor roared a moment before Tremaine's world erupted. His head snapped back and hit the seat. Someone had collided with the rear of the Monte Carlo. The dashboard lit up in protest, but the engine didn't stop. The Chevy slid through the crosswalk, the tires failing to hold their grip on the slick asphalt.

Tremaine was on his way into the intersection against the red light. He had only a fraction of a second to act. He stomped the gas pedal, and the heavy car leaped forward. Horns honked, and vehicles jerked out of the way. A pickup collided with the Chevy's rear and forced Tremaine off course. He yanked the steering wheel in the opposite direction and fought to straighten his path.

The Monte Carlo cleared the intersection and raced ahead.

Tremaine made the second light as it turned green. Soon he was barreling up the Hamilton Street bridge. The howl of the night came through the missing back window.

He pulled himself upright in the driver's seat to brave a look into the rearview mirror. His pursuers were still there—two cars. One with its headlights busted out now. They had made it through the previous intersections. He had to find a way to ditch them.

The steering wheel jiggled in his hands, and he clutched it tighter as if to stop its motion. The alignment was off, or perhaps the car now had a bent frame. The dashboard warning lights remained on, and the engine sounded like an old man in the last throes of a smoker's cough. Maybe a piston was misfiring, but that didn't stop the motor from chugging.

Rain dropped in large sheets, and the wiper blades sounded panicked now—*thwick, twhick, thwick.*

Tremaine became aware that something was dragging on the car. He checked the driver's side mirror—nothing. In the passenger's side mirror, he saw it. The bumper had ripped off but hadn't detached. It slid left and right like a wayward skier.

Thunk.

Tremaine slid down in the seat.

Thunk thunk thunk.

They were shooting at him again. He had no idea who they were, and now wasn't the time to figure that out. He needed to get to safety. Once he did, he could work on the question of his pursuers' identities. Maybe he could plan some retribution, too, but that was getting ahead of himself.

Right now, he had to survive.

Tremaine raced over the bridge. He swerved past a slow-moving Subaru and accelerated. The Chevy's engine sputtered and backfired, which caused the car to slow briefly as if taking a deep breath.

"C'mon!" Tremaine yelled, slapping the steering wheel.

The Monte Carlo lurched forward in a burst of renewed confidence.

Tremaine's eyes snapped toward the floorboard of the passenger compartment. In the furthest corner was his gun. It had tumbled there earlier when the Chevy bounced out of the shopping mall's parking lot.

This whole time his gun was less than a foot out of his reach. He'd been a man running instead of a man fighting. It pissed him off, but he couldn't entirely lose his temper. Doing so would cause him the ultimate failure. He'd seen too many associates go out that way, and he wasn't making that mistake tonight.

At least he still had his cell phone tucked between his legs. He'd made three calls since the chase started, but none of his crew had answered. Had something happened to them? Was someone hitting them all at once? Those were questions for later, but for now—

Thunk. Thunk.

Tremaine's shoulders rose to his ears. He jerked the wheel and took the eastbound I-90 off-ramp. It looped down past the Office Depot toward Liberty Park. When he reached the interstate, Tremaine didn't merge with traffic. Instead, he remained in the far-right lane and soon exited onto Third Avenue and into the East Central neighborhood.

The engine whined unexpectedly.

"The fuck?"

A horrendous chunking sound came from under the hood. Tremaine had never heard such a noise but imagined the motor had seized. The dashboard lights mocked him, and the wiper blades quit throwing rain away from the windshield. The car coasted as it approached the traffic signal at the Altamont intersection.

Tremaine grabbed his cell phone and crawled into the passenger seat, where he collected his Smith and Wesson. He heard more gunshots and felt some of them hitting the trunk. He yanked the passenger door handle and dropped out of the car just as the Monte Carlo was rear-ended.

The car wasn't rolling fast when he fell out. However, slamming into the asphalt startled him. Tremaine expelled all his breath upon impact, but he didn't lose his senses. He rolled away and clambered to his feet just in time to see a Dodge Durango pushing his Chevy beyond the intersection.

Tremaine lifted his gun to fire at the SUV, but he heard the approaching roar of a second engine. He spun and fired at an oncoming Chrysler 300. Tremaine kept shooting until the car veered off to the left and into the tunnel of the Altamont underpass. It ran full speed into the concrete wall. When it hit, the hood buckled, and the car's horn blared.

The tires of the Durango spun on the wet ground as it backed up. Tremaine quickly aimed at the rear window and where he thought the driver was. He fired once, and the slide of his gun locked back. The Durango continued in reverse for several more feet before the brakes were applied, and it slid to a stop.

Tremaine sprinted south into the neighborhood. He didn't bother looking back as he ran. He knew the Durango was following him because its engine growled. An occasional *pop-pop-pop* of a gun fired, too.

He sprinted until his lungs hurt. Tremaine zig-zagged through yards and cut between homes. He heard the rumble of the Durango's engine above the blood pounding in his ears and the thundering storm above. Tremaine sucked for air as he ran and fought against the searing pain in his side.

Stopping now was certain death.

A new sound entered his consciousness—one he'd heard many times before. He couldn't determine how many there were, but more than one police siren had entered the neighborhood. Tremaine didn't take comfort at the arrival of the cops, though.

A fox doesn't quit running when more dogs enter the hunt.

It runs harder.

Chapter 2
2349 hours PST

The black GMC Denali skidded across the wet asphalt of Third Avenue before stopping at the intersection of Altamont Street. The other three officers in the vehicle hopped from the rig before Corporal Kurt Botzon could slip the gear shift into Park. He snatched the dangling microphone and waited for his turn to enter the excited communications on the police radio.

Rain splashed the SUV's windshield, and the wiper blades worked diligently to flip it away. The emergency flashers inside the front grill clicked back and forth and struggled to bath the neighborhood in blue and red through the slashing rain.

When there was a break in radio chatter, Botzon squeezed the transmit button and said, "Sam-38, show us out at Third and Altamont."

A male dispatcher responded, "Sam thirty-eight, copy. On scene. All units be advised Fire is responding to Mission and Hamilton with the report of a car fire."

Mission and Hamilton was the intersection the running gun battle had recently gone through. Patrol units had already been dispatched to the multiple collisions there. Could this night get any worse?

Botzon grabbed his portable radio and entered the storm. Even though he never wore baseball hats, he wished he had one for tonight. He hadn't even moved around the front of the Denali before the rain soaked his longish hair and matted it against the back of his neck. He stopped and assessed the scene.

The two north corners contained supports for the

freeway overpass—a tunnel provided north and south access for Altamont Street. The southwest corner was now a vacant lot—it had been a gas station back when Botzon was a kid. The opposite corner held a California split. There were no witnesses outside on any of the corners.

Multiple calls had come in over the last ten minutes about a running gun battle that started at NorthTown Mall. Supposedly, there was a dead woman up there. Callers reported the mobile gun battle came down the Hamilton Street corridor until the last witness claimed seeing a crash and an exchange of gunfire at Altamont and Third.

Right now, no one stood outside watching.

Botzon couldn't blame anyone for not waiting around. He wouldn't be outside in this thunderstorm if he weren't working. His father once told him that weather was easy to deal with if the elements—rain, wind, or cold—came one at a time. Once those elements doubled up was when the situation became miserable. All three worked together tonight, and his light windbreaker wouldn't keep him warm if they had to be outside for any length of time. He should have planned better.

Across the intersection sat a 1987 Chevrolet Monte Carlo with a crumpled rear-end, missing back window, and a barely attached bumper. Bullet holes riddled the trunk. Its headlights pointed down Third Avenue and through the falling rain.

Botzon didn't need to run the license plate to find the registered owner; he knew the man from repeated contacts—Tremaine Brown, leader of the local sect of the Dead Boys, a notorious street gang that had originated in Los Angeles.

A uniformed patrol officer stood near the open passenger door of the Monte Carlo. He held a flashlight in his hand and searched the interior.

In the freeway underpass was a mid-2000s burgundy Chrysler 300. Its crinkled hood was up.

The car sat almost perpendicular to the wall as if it had run directly into it. Botzon imagined its path originating from the point where he stood now. He didn't know the Chrysler's owner, but it was a ubiquitous vehicle and a favorite of gang members due to its look, size, and weight.

A second uniformed officer stood near the 300 along with Botzon's teammates.

He took a couple of steps but stopped when he noticed a lamp on in a window of the California split. A heavy curtain fell, and the light disappeared. Botzon considered the house for another moment before continuing toward the Chrysler.

The rain stopped hitting him when he entered the tunnel. He welcomed the respite. A rumble of freeway traffic overhead now competed with the noise of the rainstorm.

Rachelle Walsh intercepted Botzon before he could make it to the Chrysler. "Two dead inside the car," she said. "Both black males. Maybe mid-twenties. And before you ask, I don't recognize them."

"You're sure?"

She frowned.

Rachelle had been in the Special Investigation Unit for five years. She wore a Harley Davidson baseball cap and a heavy-duty, black rain jacket tonight. Rachelle hated the gangs and made it her mission to know everyone who was affiliated. She was a human computer.

"I'm not saying they're not in the game," Rachelle said, "but we've never had contact with them."

"Out-of-towners?"

"Could be." Rachelle pointed to the Chrysler. "The car

has Washington plates, so maybe Seattle or Tacoma? Hernandez is getting us the registered owner info now."

Botzon motioned toward the Monte Carlo. "Tremaine had a shootout with these fellas and got the better of them. Even if he claims self-defense, we can nail him as a felon in possession of a firearm. We'll put him back inside."

Rachelle shook her head. "I don't like it."

"Why not?"

"It's sloppy. He'd never be so obvious as to get into a running gun battle. He's smarter than that."

Botzon appreciated her assessment of Tremaine Brown, but as far as he was concerned, an intelligent criminal was inherently an oxymoron. "Maybe the Dead Boys have an out-of-town beef that made it to our turf. Someone caught him off-guard, and he did what he had to do to survive."

"I haven't heard anything about an interstate grudge. You think CTF caught wind of anything?"

The Criminal Task Force was a sister group within the department. While SIU's mission was gang related, CTF's objective was murkier. Botzon didn't like organizational politics, so he never understood why CTF remained viable, especially since the two groups often stepped on each other's toes. It seemed like CTF should have disbanded long ago, and their mission—however opaque as it may be—rolled into SIU's.

Botzon thought of SIU and CTF as similar organizations. They both had ships, cannons, and men, but his group was the Navy, while the Criminal Task Force was a bunch of pirates.

"You want me to consult with Morgan?" Botzon asked. "Maybe invite his team to the party?"

"No" Rachelle said, "that's not what I was asking."

"Then fuck CTF."

She smirked. "Oh boy. Bad touching."

Botzon pointed toward the California split. "Grab Peterson and Swezey and check the house on the corner. There's a light on over there. See if they saw anything."

"C'mon, Kurt. I was only playing."

"Check the house."

She rolled her eyes before hollering to her teammates, "Hugh. Jay. Let's go."

The other SIU teammates turned toward her. Rachelle headed off toward the house. Hugh Swezey and Jay Peterson looked at Botzon, who motioned after Rachelle. The two men trotted away.

Botzon approached the Chrysler then. The closer he got, the more he could see that the front window was shot to hell. The front doors were opened.

Officer Josh Hernandez nodded his greeting. "Helluva mess."

"Was it like this when you found it?"

"I opened the doors to check for vitals. Both occupants were DOA. Then I wrenched the hood open because the car alarm was blaring. Took some effort to do that, I'll tell you what. I cut the speaker wires to shut the damn thing up."

Botzon squatted inside the passenger door. The airbags had deployed but now hung like limp plastic bags. The man in the passenger seat slumped forward with his head pressed against the glove box. It appeared he had taken a round to the throat. Blood dripped down the airbag and soaked into the floor mat between his feet. A 9mm Sig Sauer and a cell phone also sat there.

He studied the dead man for several moments but couldn't identify him. Like Rachelle said, this guy wasn't a known subject to the SIU team.

Botzon walked around to the driver's side and squatted inside that door. A seat belt strapped this man in.

The left side of his face was gone, so Botzon leaned further inside the car to get a better look at the side that remained. He felt positive that he'd never seen this guy before. Blood had spattered onto the car's ceiling, and another 9mm Sig Sauer lay on the floor between the dead man's feet.

He stood and looked at Hernandez. "Did you get the info on the registered owner yet?"

"I did. The car was reported sold one week ago but not registered by the buyer."

It was a common tactic among the criminal underworld—buy a car in an off-market transaction but fail to record it. The state required both sides to report the activity, but often only the seller did so. The transaction would show incomplete in the system until the buyer reported the sale. If the license plate tags were still good for the current year, the new owner could drive it without fear of being stopped for bad tags. The car would remain in paperwork limbo, and the law enforcement community would stay unaware of who the true owner was. Like many aspects of the government, it was an imperfect system.

It was Friday night. The Department of Licensing's main office wouldn't open again until Monday morning. If they wanted answers, SIU would have to do it the old-fashioned way and request a copy of the seller's Report of Sale.

"Do me a favor," Botzon said. "Ask dispatch to send someone to contact the previous owner. Maybe they kept a record of who they sold it to."

Hernandez nodded. "Will do."

"Is a supervisor enroute?"

"Been requested. K9, too. He's a couple minutes out."

A dog could track in the rain, but Botzon didn't have much faith it would be successful in this downpour.

Besides, if Tremaine Brown had a lengthy head start, who knew how much ground he might have already covered?

Botzon stiffened. He lifted the portable radio to his lips but waited until Hernandez finished transmitting his request to dispatch. When the airwaves were clear, he spoke. "Sam-38."

"*Sam thirty-eight. Go ahead.*"

"Look up the last known address for Tremaine Brown. Should be an apartment off Hartson and Arthur. Send a unit to make contact. Also."

"*Go ahead.*"

Botzon paused as a burst of thunder sounded above them. He was about to transmit his request when he noticed Hernandez looking upward with his eyes closed. The guy mumbled something, then crossed himself and kissed the tips of his fingers. Botzon pressed the transmit button. "If Brown isn't there, have the unit remain on scene. I believe our guy is headed home."

"*Copy. Available unit to check?*"

Botzon lowered the portable and headed toward the edge of the tunnel. There wasn't much he could do now at this crime scene. He wasn't a homicide investigator, so this case wouldn't be handed to him.

The Special Investigations Unit currently had ten members assigned to it—a sergeant, a corporal, two detectives, and six officers. The team often broke into smaller units like the one working tonight. They were on the street in hopes of finding incidents just like this.

Kurt Botzon was excited his group was on the clock. A gun battle and chase had led to three dead people and Tremaine Brown on the run. He didn't care why it jumped off; Botzon only cared that SIU was in the mix.

He shoved his hands into his pockets and smiled. It might be cold and rainy, but it was still a good night to hunt a bad guy.

Chapter 3

Tremaine Brown ran into a cluster of trees lining the Ben Burr Trail. He was sure he'd lost his pursuers by weaving through the East Central neighborhood. He'd cut through many properties—hopping over fences, sprinting through yards, and sneaking past the windows of houses with their lights still on. The thunderstorm helped hide his movements. A couple of times, lightning flashed across the night sky and exposed his position. However, it was brief, and no one seemed to notice him.

If his pursuers managed to follow him to this cluster of trees, they would have to ditch their cars and follow on foot. The Ben Burr Trail ran northwesterly through the neighborhood, and Tremaine had caught it at Eighth Avenue.

As for the cops, the sirens had stopped a few minutes ago. He was now worried about them bringing in a tracking dog. A member of his crew had been bitten by one before, and the animal had torn a nasty chunk from his friend's calf muscle. The hospital treated the wound, but it became infected in jail. Tremaine's friend almost lost his leg because of the dog's dirty mouth. He did not want that experience to befall him.

Tremaine stopped and searched the darkness for anyone who might be following. Not finding anyone, he put his hands on his knees and gulped for air. His breath came in ragged drags. He lifted his head to fill his mouth with rain but only found an occasional droplet hit his face. The cover provided by the canopy of branches protected him from the continuing shower. Tremaine leaned a shoulder against a nearby tree and slid into a squat.

He struggled to hear anything, but the thunderstorm covered the night like a sonic blanket. Tremaine closed his eyes and relaxed for several moments. He wanted to believe he had escaped and could let his guard down. Yet Tremaine jumped when a truck roared southbound on Altamont, its engine quickly muffled by distance and the rain shower. He exhaled when he realized he was still safe. He fell into the nearby tree and wrapped his arm around it for stability.

Tremaine's clothing was soaked completely through. He wore a fleece sweatsuit which now felt like a wet towel draped around his body. His new basketball shoes were ruined. They were covered in mud and squished whenever he moved.

He rested his cheek against the tree. I'm alive, he thought. *Not like Emily.*

She'd been shot when they walked out of NorthTown. He hadn't stopped to check on her, but she was dead. She was hit in the head; no one survived that.

Who could have known they were there?

No one, Tremaine decided. He hadn't told anyone in the crew that he was going to the mall. Even if they saw him there, what would they have said? Nothing. He'd been with a well-dressed woman before. They'd have figured he was making a play and left him alone to do his thing. Maybe some of them might have lingered in the distance to signal their approval, but they surely wouldn't have come up to ruin the moment. No one would have done that to him.

He pulled his cell phone from his pocket. The screen brightened, and he quickly covered it with a hand. Tremaine scanned the road and the walking trail but didn't see any movement. From somewhere in the neighborhood, a dog barked over the constant roar of the falling rain.

Tremaine needed help. The first call he made while fleeing the mall was to Jaxson—his lieutenant. He hadn't answered then and still hadn't called him back. That bothered Tremaine. Jaxson always replied, and he was quick with a call back; he was good that way.

He called Jaxson again. Still no answer.

Tremaine now sent a text to the man. CALL ME 911.

He selected a number for one of his soldiers—Denzelle. Tremaine had called him while running from the mall, too. He'd gotten no answer then.

There was no answer now, either.

Tremaine shook the phone. He wanted to holler, but doing so could alert someone to his position. If his pursuers had left their cars and were following him on foot, losing his cool would cost him his life.

He clutched his phone and looked around. Tremaine still didn't see any activity. He needed to start moving again, but he had time to attempt one more call. Tremaine activated his phone and found another soldier—Keenan.

No answer.

Shit.

Tremaine shoved his shoulder against the tree and straightened himself. Three men and no answers. No return calls either. That wasn't a coincidence. His men answered when he called or, at least, they quickly called him back.

Something terrible had occurred.

He was out of time. He needed to go. Staying in one place for too long was asking for trouble.

Tremaine shuffled through the dense clump of trees. Water sloughed off the foliage and drenched him anew, but he didn't care. Tremaine followed the paved Ben Burr Trail. He knew where the path would eventually dump out—Liberty Park. It was at the bottom of the hill underneath his apartment. Perhaps he could go home, grab a change of dry clothes, and get out of this rain. That thought gave him pause.

If the cops identified him through his car, they knew he was involved. The first place they would go looking for him would be his apartment. He never tried to hide where he lived. Doing so with the police was a losing proposition. Better for the cops to always think they had the upper hand with him.

No, he couldn't go home.

He stayed near the edge of the trail and the rain found him again. With his breathing stabilized, something new emerged in Tremaine's consciousness—a chill. He shivered, and his thoughts returned to his apartment. Maybe the cops wouldn't be there. He could sneak inside, take a hot shower, and get warm. There were times when the police didn't do what he assumed they would. Maybe tonight would be one of those.

Tremaine glanced over his shoulder to make sure no one was tailing him. The trail was clear, and he was alone.

Emily was dead because of the ambush. Someone had chased him through the city and shot his Monte Carlo all to shit. And now he likely killed someone. The cops couldn't ignore any of it. They would come after him, and they would spy on his apartment. That was from the patrol cop playbook.

Therefore, he couldn't go home. It was a childish impulse anyway. He pushed it aside and hurried along.

It wouldn't just be patrol cops after him. If he had killed someone in the Chrysler, homicide detectives would soon be involved. They weren't stupid. Tremaine didn't know how they operated. He'd have to be smart and careful if he wanted to stay free.

He knew a cop. Maybe that man would be working tonight. Or perhaps they would call him in to help find Tremaine. If that happened, it could be a lucky break.

Detective James Morgan and Tremaine had a relationship much like the United States and Russia. Their dislike ran deep, but they realized there was a benefit to occasionally helping the other. Tremaine knew Morgan would never enrich himself, but he did things that no other cop would do. Yet, he was still a cop, which meant the guy couldn't be fully trusted.

If Tremaine reached out to Morgan to explain what happened, Morgan would likely demand a face-to-face. It was highly likely Morgan would snatch him up then and turn him over to the homicide detectives. Essentially Tremaine would have turned himself in.

No, he couldn't call Morgan—at least, not yet. Not until he understood the situation and where all the players stood on the board.

Tremaine needed to work this problem out on his own. He rubbed his hands together and blew into them as he shuffled along.

First, he needed to get dry and warm.

Chapter 4
2359 hours PST

Kurt Botzon huddled with his team in the tunnel of the Altamont Street underpass. The others had just returned from chatting with the owner of the house on the southeast corner.

Nearby, two uniformed officers strung a line of yellow caution tape. Due to its proximity to the Chrysler 300, Botzon expected this to be the start of the inner perimeter. They were locking down the scene and preparing it for the arrival of the Major Crimes detectives. No one except the investigators and the forensic team would get inside that area now.

"Who'd they call?" Rachelle Walsh asked.

Botzon shrugged. "Didn't ask." His gaze swept toward the patrol car now parked in the intersection.

K9 Officer Trent Whitmire opened the back door of his patrol car, and a sleek, black Belgian Malinois jumped out. Lazer yipped with excitement as it bounded about Whitmire.

Jay Peterson said, "Who's running with the dog?"

Hugh Swezey waved a dismissive hand. "I sprained my ankle on the last one. One of you take it."

"I'd rather not," Rachelle said, watching Whitmire and Lazer with a frown.

Jay barked a laugh. "Is there anyone on this department you haven't slept with?"

"You."

Hugh covered his mouth to stifle his chuckle.

"I don't know why you think it's funny," Rachelle said. "You haven't made the honor roll either."

"True," Hugh admitted. "But the difference is, I'm not trying."

In the intersection, Whitmire and Lazer headed for the Monte Carlo. The dog hopped into the car.

"I got it," Botzon said. He left the cover of the tunnel and entered the pouring rain.

Next to the Chevy, Whitmire issued commands to the dog to smell the driver's seat. The K9 handler wore a black jumpsuit and baseball hat with the SPD logo.

Botzon patted Whitmire's shoulder twice but didn't speak. He didn't want to interrupt the man's communication with the dog.

Whitmire eyed him. "You look like a drowned rat."

"Man overboard."

"Any idea on which direction the suspect ran?"

Botzon pointed at the California split on the southeastern corner. "The homeowner there heard a loud bang from a crash and went to her window. She saw a black male standing in the intersection shooting at the Chrysler. Afterward, the male ran southbound." Botzon pointed down Altamont Street. "A little SUV chased him. She didn't know the make."

"And we're assuming the black male is Tremaine Brown?"

"This is his Monte, so that's who we're going with, yeah."

Whitmire quickly appraised the neighborhood. "Wish we could have gotten a perimeter set up."

"Not enough support. There's another body up at NorthTown."

"I heard, but, with the rain and no containment, our chances of success go way down." Whitmire shrugged apologetically. "Sorry I didn't get here quicker. Was coming from far north."

Botzon raised an eyebrow. "Want to skip the track?"

"And miss an opportunity to let Lazer run? Forget about it." Whitmire clicked his tongue.

The dog hopped out of the Monte Carlo, and Whitmire attached a lengthy leash to him. Lazer was well-trained but letting him run untethered through a residential neighborhood was a legal nightmare. Anything might happen.

"You my six?" Whitmire asked.

Botzon nodded. He would act as the handler's backup.

"Call it in."

He lifted the portable radio. "Sam-38."

"*Sam thirty-eight?*" a female dispatcher responded.

"Be advised K9-12 and I are starting a track."

"*Copy. Channel is restricted.*"

Whitmire patted Lazer's neck, and the dog whined with excitement. "Lauf," he ordered. Lazer sprinted through the intersection. The leash pulled tautly, and Whitmire ran with the dog.

Botzon stayed a few feet behind them. His job wasn't to worry about Lazer or what he might be doing; it was to keep alert for threats to him and the handler. Botzon ran with his gun in the low ready and scanned the area all around them.

Lazer bolted through a yard on East Fourth Avenue and went between two houses. Botzon lost sight of the K9 officer and hurried to catch up. When he did, he heard Whitmire utter positive-sounding grunts to the dog. For all Botzon knew, they were commands. The K9 officers trained their dogs with German words, and Botzon only knew a few of them.

Overhead, lightning lit the sky, but Lazer didn't seem to notice. He cut through another yard until he reached an alley and sprinted further east. Thunder boomed overhead. The dog skittered briefly but continued its search. Whitmire uttered another command. This one sounded oddly soothing in the middle of a run.

The rain continued its relentless pour, but the wily dog and the man following it did not slow. Botzon was no longer worried about being cold. The excitement of the track had his blood pumping.

"Update our location," Whitmire hollered over his shoulder.

The dog turned south again and raced along the sidewalk.

"Sam-38," Botzon called. He worked to keep his words even.

"Sam thirty-eight, go ahead."

"Southbound on Cook. Approaching Fifth."

The track continued like this for several blocks—Lazer cutting in and out of yards with Whitmire issuing his positive-sounding grunts. The dog stopped at a wood-slated fence and searched desperately for a scent. Whitmire guided him around to the alley in the back. Lazer caught the scent again, and the two men struggled to keep pace.

The dog ran southbound along Cook Street until he entered a cluster of trees.

"The scent's better in here," Whitmire shouted. "Less rain. Look at him go!"

Botzon couldn't discern any difference in behavior, but the excitement in Whitmire's voice was unmistakable. The handler uttered something in German, and the dog wagged his tail.

The three of them crossed Altamont Street and entered another patch of woods. The dog moved like a guided missile until he popped out on the Ben Burr Trail.

Botzon updated dispatch of their position. Whitmire flashed a thumbs-up sign over his shoulder and continued running.

They hurried along the asphalted trail for several

minutes before Whitmire shouted, "What do you wanna bet he's hiding in Liberty Park?"

Botzon figured Tremaine Brown would be smart enough not to head home. However, he might have decided to hide in the park until the cops left the area. Lazer might flush him out and push him in that direction if that were the case.

He activated his radio. "Sam-38."

"Thirty-eight?"

"Advise the unit watching Brown's apartment that we're tracking toward Liberty Park." Botzon held the transmit button as he gulped air. "The suspect might be heading home."

"Copy."

A thought occurred to him then. "Brown is to be considered armed and dangerous."

Officers searching for Brown should already be aware of that since the man was involved in a shooting. However, Botzon had been on the department long enough to know it was human nature to let one's guard down at inopportune times. His warning was to keep everyone alert.

"Copy," the dispatcher said. *"Armed and dangerous. David four-seventeen, did you copy?"*

The three of them arrived at Liberty Park in less than five minutes. Lazer didn't slow, though. The dog cut through the grass, crossed the one-way Third Avenue, and ran up toward the freeway.

Whitmire tugged on the leash. *"Phooey!"*

The dog jerked back but struggled to get to the interstate.

"Phooey!"

Lazer whined, yipped, and barked at the end of its leash.

"Heir!" Whitmire rolled the leash around his elbow to

bring the dog closer to him. "*Kommst du!*"

The dog stopped tugging and turned toward its trainer. He lumbered over.

"*Braver hund.* Good dog." Whitmire pulled a tennis ball from the fanny pack and tossed it into the park. The leash unraveled from around his elbow.

"Tremaine went up on the freeway," Whitmire said.

Botzon pointed to a nearby underpass that connected to Perry Street. "Why don't we go through to the other side and give it another try?"

Whitmire shrugged. "We can, but why? The tunnel is right there, and Tremaine would know that. He lives up on the hill. For him to go over the freeway to get to the other side doesn't make any sense either. No, he jumped on the interstate to make sure a dog couldn't track him."

"How would he know to do that?"

Whitmire smirked.

Then Botzon understood. "You've tracked the Dead Boys before."

"Not just me. Tremaine knew what he was doing, and I'm not risking my dog on the freeway. We know who we're chasing. Call it in."

Botzon lifted the radio. "Sam-38."

A female dispatcher quickly responded. "*Sam thirty-eight?*"

"Cancel the track. Our suspect appears to have jumped onto I-90. Also."

"*Channel is unrestricted. Sam thirty-eight, go ahead.*"

"Broadcast Tremaine Brown's description. Include the county and state with that information."

"*Sam thirty-eight, copy.*"

Whitmire patted the side of the wet dog's face. "This is the worst part of the job."

"What's that?" Botzon asked.

"The long walk back."

Chapter 5
12:07 a.m. PST

Running along the freeway's ramp was a risk Tremaine didn't want to take.

He didn't like dogs, and he especially wanted to avoid their attacks. That's why he hopped the chain link fence and sprinted along the Interstate 90 on-ramp. He wasn't foolish enough to actually run along the freeway.

The rain continued. Headlights played over him, and a horn blared as an old pickup rumbled by. Tremaine lifted a hand to shield his eyes.

The irony of the moment wasn't lost on him. He had sped down this on-ramp as he fled from whoever chased him. Now, he trotted up it in hopes of escaping the cops that were surely searching for him.

Tremaine's shoes squished with each step, and his wet clothing provided no warmth. His hands hurt from the cold, and he balled them hoping to gain heat. He couldn't worry about his discomfort now. There was only one goal on his mind—getting out of the public eye as quickly as possible.

He worried about a passerby calling the cops and reporting a black man running up the on-ramp. Even though he hated the police in this town and sometimes questioned their intelligence, he knew it wouldn't take them long to put together the pieces.

If it wasn't a do-gooder citizen alerting them to his position, it might just be a cop with dumb luck who stumbled upon him. Even on a typical night, this neighborhood was usually littered with officers from the Spokane Police Department. Troopers from the

Washington State Patrol covered the freeway in this stretch, and deputies from the Spokane County Sheriff's Office worked the area because the county jail was only a couple of miles away. All those agencies might be aware of Tremaine's shootout and could be searching for him right now.

That was bad because Tremaine knew he would have to answer for what happened on Third Avenue. If he killed anyone in that car, those cops would not let him walk on a self-defense plea. That's not how things happened in his world. Prosecuting attorneys didn't give breaks to guys like him.

Carrying an empty gun in his pocket right now was tantamount to handing them his head on a platter. It bounced and banged against his leg with every step. Tremaine had wanted to throw it away in the woods along the Ben Burr Trail, but he was afraid a dog tracking him might alert to it. Throwing it away along this on-ramp was also a terrible plan. It could be found if anyone reported him running near here. No, he needed to wait and take his chances. He was already in deep. What was a few more feet of water over his head?

Tremaine knew where he wanted to get rid of it, so he mentally crossed his fingers and ran harder.

A large semi pulling a trailer with a regional grocery chain's logo splashed him with puddled rain. Tremaine turned his head, but the brunt of the water hit him in the chest.

Ahead the ramp curved and began to elevate. If Tremaine followed it, the road would lead him back to Hamilton Street. He wondered if the pickup that hit him earlier was still in the intersection further up the road. He doubted it. It would likely have pulled into a parking lot and waited for a cop to arrive. If that were the case, an officer might be with that driver now.

To the east was a small cluster of trees. On the other side of it was the rear of the Office Depot. Second Avenue lay just beyond that. He could follow that street into downtown and hopefully find someone there to help him.

Overhead, lightning brightened the sky for an impossibly long moment. Thunder followed as if it were an afterthought. Maybe this crappy weather would work to his benefit and continue to hide him.

Tremaine left the on-ramp's shoulder and darted into the trees.

Chapter 6
0032 hours PST

Detective Quinn Delaney drove up the NorthTown Mall's parking garage ramp. When he reached the second floor, he slowed.

Ahead, a uniformed officer stood in front of a patrol car. He sported a baseball cap and the black jumpsuit most graveyard cops wore. The car's emergency flashers splashed blue and red across the garage's concrete pillars. The cop waved for Quinn to continue up to the next level. He seemed bored by the whole situation.

Quinn gunned the Chevy Impala's engine, and the sedan accelerated onward. He didn't bother acknowledging the posted officer. Quinn wasn't apathetic, but he was no longer excited by the prospect of a homicide investigation.

When he reached the upper deck, it didn't take long for Quinn to determine where he was needed. A gathering of Spokane Police Department vehicles waited at the far end. Two mall security trucks were there, too.

The wiper blades flicked rain away from the windshield. Now, Quinn categorized the problems he would encounter due to the weather. The evidence destruction. The lack of enthusiasm from patrol members to stay on task. His own comfort would constantly nag him from the back of his mind. Cold, rainy nights were near the top of his list for worst conditions to work under.

But beggars couldn't be choosers, and neither could homicide detectives.

Quinn found a spot and parked. He might have considered waiting for his partner, but she was attending a continuing education course in Chicago this week. It ended today, but she'd extended her stay through Sunday to do some sightseeing. He grabbed a Seattle Seahawks baseball hat from the passenger seat and left the car.

Pole lights bathed the parking garage in a yellowish glow. The ground shimmered in the falling rain. Beyond the massive structure, the north Spokane neighborhood was covered in soggy darkness. It was shortly after midnight now. Quinn checked his watch for the exact time, and rain droplets immediately found its digital face.

He headed for the cluster of vehicles. Several officers he'd never met before eyed him with a mixture of suspicion and reverence. They moved out of his way but only enough to let him by. Patrol officers didn't look at Major Crimes investigators with awe. That was Hollywood make-believe and perhaps detective hubris.

Patrol cops respected what Quinn did but they also carried a healthy dose of resentment. They were on the street while he usually sat in a climate-controlled office. Working in the cold rain tonight was an outlier, and it wouldn't validate him in their eyes. Instead, they'd take comfort in knowing he suffered just a little as they did. It was departmental schadenfreude, and everyone felt it at times.

Sergeant Heath Stockton approached. He was an athletic man with broad shoulders and thick arms. Stockton was a member of the department's SWAT team and took great pride in the team's unofficial motto, "You're either SWAT or you're not." Quinn's previous membership with the team held little sway with a man like Stockton. Being a former member simply landed Quinn in the category of not SWAT.

Rain washed over the brim of Stockton's SPD baseball hat. "Look at you, Delaney. Out braving the elements like us common folk."

Quinn ignored the jab. "What have we got?"

A flash of lightning zigzagged in the distance, and a nearby officer said, "Count it."

Sergeant Stockton moved out of the way. As he did, he motioned with his arm like a used car salesman presenting the latest arrival to his lot.

About five feet away was a line of yellow CAUTION—DO NOT CROSS tape. Twenty feet after that was a second line. And ten feet beyond that lay a body covered by a white plastic sheet. The two lines of tape represented the inner and outer perimeters. No one was inside either perimeter, and only investigators were to be inside the tape closest to the body.

Several orange cones represented the location of spent shell casings. Those were inside the outer perimeter. The patrol team had done an adequate job of securing the scene.

"We haven't been able to identify the victim," Stockton said.

A rolling burst of thunder interrupted the night, and an officer announced, "Four seconds. Four miles."

Stockton's eyes narrowed as he turned to the officers. "Make yourself useful. Levitt, you're on the log."

Embarrassment crossed several faces, and the nearby officers faded away. Levitt remained, however, as he would now be responsible for recording whoever moved in and out of the perimeters.

The sergeant faced Quinn. "You'd think they'd never seen a thunderstorm before." He lifted the line of outer perimeter tape, and Quinn ducked under it.

The two men walked silently until they got to the tape marking the inner perimeter. Quinn stepped underneath and moved toward the woman. Stockton stayed outside.

"We called Forensics," the sergeant said. "They should be here soon with a canopy."

Quinn raised a hand in acknowledgment as he squatted next to the body. He pulled back the plastic sheet. Typically, covering the victim with anything would be tantamount to contaminating a crime scene, but the officers were trying to protect the victim from the rain. Given the circumstances, they did their best.

The woman lay on her stomach. Wet, blond hair was matted to the side of her face. Her arms were by her sides, and her feet were tangled together. One of her high heels had come free during her fall. On a dry day, there may have been a puddle of blood underneath her, but the accumulating rain ran toward a drain several feet away.

Water dripped from the brim of Quinn's baseball hat onto the victim's back. Usually, this would be cause for great alarm. He could be polluting a crime scene, but the rain had already done a fine job of that. He lowered the sheet.

"Any witnesses?" he asked.

"Plenty but none that stuck around." Stockton motioned to a group of security guards. They stood away from the officers and chatted amongst themselves. Their attention remained on the body. "The shooting was caught on video." Stockton pointed at a camera mounted on a nearby light pole. "That one. A guard is searching for additional footage of our victim inside the mall. You should see their system. Pretty impressive. They can email you a copy of whatever they find."

"Have you seen the footage?"

"Only the shooting." Stockton nodded. "The guards are searching for additional footage now, but this outside camera will not do you a lot of good, though. The shooters were masked."

Quinn lifted an eyebrow. "A planned hit?"

"That's what it looked like." The sergeant waved at the dead woman. "The guy she was with was Tremaine

Brown."

Quinn looked over his shoulder. "The name sounds familiar."

Stockton laughed. "It should. He's the leader of the Dead Boys."

"Is he one of the bodies down at Altamont?"

"You're not that lucky. From what I heard, he's in the wind."

Chapter 7
0035 hours PST

Detective Andrew Parker stood under the freeway overpass and watched the rain fall into the intersection of Altamont and Third. A flash of lightning occurred in the southwest. Out of habit, Parker started counting.

One thousand-one. One thousand-two. One thou—

Boom. Thunder rattled through the night. He wondered if his little girls would sleep through the storm or if each would soon crawl into bed with his wife.

"What a night for something like this to go down," Jessie Johnson said.

Parker's eyes slid to his partner. He was tired and didn't feel like engaging in conversation, so he grunted.

Johnson wore a department-issued raincoat with large SPD letters across the back. He also wore an SPD baseball cap, the type the patrol guys wore. Parker sported the same raincoat, but his hood was over his head. He shoved his hands into the pockets of his jeans so he could keep warm.

Parker hated calls like this. Not the homicide itself, as it didn't seem overly complicated, but the time of day. He was a creature of habit. Parker tried to hit the rack every night at ten sharp and get up at 4:30 a.m. to start his workout. It allowed him to achieve his goals while still meeting the duties of a father.

The job of a Major Crimes detective wasn't conducive to bodybuilding. Getting a call shortly before midnight was worse than a call at three in the morning. At least the latter allowed him several hours of sleep. The former felt like a short nap, and Parker would no doubt need to keep working through the day. He would feel like a zombie by the time he got home, and he'd have no energy for his wife or the kids.

Overhead, the interstate traffic rumbled by. Another flash of lightning lit up the sky to the southwest.

One thousand-one. One thousand-two. One—

A long roll of thunder hit, but this one sounded like a stuttering motorboat. Parker was sure this one wouldn't have interrupted the girls' sleep.

Johnson stepped forward and looked east along Third Avenue. "How long do you think before the evidence geeks arrive?"

Parker rolled his eyes. "How would I know?"

His partner smirked. "What crawled up your butt?"

"Forensics." He threw a hand in the air. "We gotta wait for them because they're thin? Why's that our problem?" Parker didn't bother to hide his frustration from Johnson. He might have if anyone else was around.

"I don't know."

"It's because of the Glory Hounds. You know they'll go up to Northtown before they come here."

"It's not like Quinn has the power to make them do that."

"Whatever."

Parker's face warmed, and he didn't look at his partner. He was acting emotional and starting to feel out of control. Some of it was because of the situation, but a lot was because he was tired. Making eye contact with Johnson would only make him feel foolish.

Besides, Parker knew the real reason they were in the queue. Dispatch had already briefed him on the phone. Half of the county forensics unit was investigating an unrelated murder/suicide in the small town of Fairfield. The other half was dispatched to Quinn Delaney's location because it was the first homicide to occur tonight.

The department could turn to Washington State Patrol's forensic team for additional support, but that was as good as inviting a vampire into one's home. The city didn't want the state involved for various reasons, the least of which was the superior attitude WSP brought to everything they did. He was sure the brass had some political reasons for avoiding it, besides.

So that meant Parker and Johnson had to wait their turn for the evidence team, but it still didn't make Parker feel better. He longed for the city to have its own forensics unit, however, that would likely never happen. The evidence team was a joint venture between the city and county but administered by the latter. The records unit was much the same—a joint venture but it was managed by the city. Somewhere in the past, Parker imagined a backroom deal was made and the city got the worst of it. For the two entities to split them and go their separate ways meant a slew of political and budgetary issues he didn't comprehend, or entirely believe.

"Fuck this," he said and headed toward the Chrysler 300.

"Where you going?" Johnson hurried alongside him.

Both men ducked under the line of yellow caution tape marking the inner perimeter. Officer Josh Hernandez stood there with a clipboard. "Forget something?"

Parker and Johnson had already checked out the Chrysler upon their arrival. They didn't do more than visually inspect the bodies and the car. Going further than that would require disturbing the bodies too much, and the best practice was to wait for the forensics team to photograph and search.

Both detectives flipped Hernandez their middle fingers.

Hernandez laughed. "Double-barreled. Nice."

Parker tugged a pair of blue latex gloves from his pocket. "Let's figure out who these guys are."

"You want to move the bodies?"

"We'll put them back when we're done." Parker arrived at the open passenger door. He motioned for Johnson to step closer. "Take a video of this guy."

His partner hesitated. "We should wait. We're getting overtime."

"To stand around and hold our dicks? No, thanks."

Johnson reluctantly pulled his cell phone from his pocket. "Why can't you chill out?"

"Who's going to complain?" Parker motioned at the officer holding the clipboard. "Hernandez? He's not going to give a shit." Parker spun his hand in a hurry-up motion. "Let's go."

Johnson started the camera on his phone and squatted near the car.

A black male sat in the passenger seat with his head pressed against the dashboard. The deployed airbag hung deflated and covered in blood. Between the passenger's feet lay a Sig Sauer handgun and a cell phone. Blood covered both items.

After a moment, Johnson stood. "I'm good."

Parker moved by his partner and reached into the passenger's back pockets. "Nothing." He grabbed the body by the shoulder and pulled him upright into a sitting position. The head flopped back against the seat. The man had been shot in the throat, and blood had leaked down his chest. For a moment, Parker wondered why more wasn't on the shirt then his gaze flicked to the puddle on the floorboard.

He pressed a hand against the man's chest as he probed into the front pockets of his pants. The first pocket contained only a wad of cash. Parker lifted it so Johnson could see it then he shoved it back into the pocket. He moved to the other and found what he was looking for—a wad of cards wrapped with a rubber band. A California driver's license was on top.

"Rashard Foreman," Parker said.

Johnson scrambled to pull his notebook from his pocket. When he was ready, Parker repeated the name, then read the man's date of birth and California address.

"Got it," Johnson said.

Parker returned the wad of cards to the pocket. He was about to set the man back into position when he considered the glove box. He carefully moved the airbag out of the way and then opened the glove box. Inside was a box of 9mm ammunition and a set of folded documents.

He handed the papers to Johnson, who opened them. "It's a registration for a room at the Status Stay under Foreman's name."

"How many nights?" Parker asked.

"Two. He checked in earlier today."

Johnson folded the documents and handed them to Parker. With a single hand, he tucked them back into the glove box, closed the lid, and dropped the airbag. Carefully, he set Rashard Foreman into place and let the man's forehead rest against the dashboard.

"Look right?" Parker asked.

Johnson studied the body against the picture on his phone. "Close enough."

The cell phone on the floorboard between Rashard Foreman's feet lit up. Parker cocked his head to read the words on the display screen. It showed a California number but no name. Parker wasn't going to answer it. There would be time to investigate that later.

He stood and moved around the car to the driver's side. Johnson followed.

Without prompting, Johnson videotaped the body, which remained upright due to his seatbelt. "Got it," he said and stepped back.

Parker found a wallet in the first back pocket he searched. He never had to move the body. "Spencer Anderson," Parker said. "Also from California." He recited the man's birthday and address.

When Johnson nodded he'd gotten the info, Parker tucked the wallet back into the pocket he'd taken it from.

"He's probably got the room key on him," Johnson said. "Check his other pockets."

Parker shook his head. "We'd still need a search warrant to go in. Better to ask a clerk for access for health and safety reasons." He stepped back and peeled off the latex gloves. "We got what we needed."

Johnson dialed a number on his cell phone.

"Calling dispatch?" Parker asked.

His partner nodded. "Hey, this is Detective Johnson. Run a couple names for me."

A figure walked in from the rain. Corporal Kurt Botzon stepped into the underpass and stomped his feet. The guy looked like he'd just taken a shower. His longish hair was soaked, as were his jeans.

In the middle of the intersection, K9 Officer Whitmire secured his dog in the back of his patrol car.

Botzon noticed Hernandez standing at the inner perimeter tape and waved. As he walked over, several SIU members exited a GMC Denali and entered the tunnel.

Parker hadn't realized the officers were sitting in the SUV the entire time. He left Johnson to finish his conversation with the dispatch operator and approached the group.

Botzon held out his hand, and Parker shook it. This led to the rest of the team shaking his hand. This surprised Parker because he had never had friendly interactions with the SIU team while on patrol.

"Hernandez said you identified the guys in the car," Botzon said.

Parker nodded. "Couple of Golden Staters. Rashard Foreman and Spencer Anderson. Johnson is running their names now."

Botzon looked to Rachelle Walsh. "Those names ring a bell?"

She shook her head.

"Me neither," Botzon said.

Jay Peterson and Hugh Swezey watched Parker with intense interest.

"They've got a room at the Status Stay under the name of Foreman. Just checked in today."

"They came into town," Botzon said, "so they could shoot up Tremaine Brown? What are we missing?"

"The car," Parker said. "Where did it come from?"

Hernandez pulled out his notebook. "Dispatch found the previous owner."

Parker lifted an eyebrow.

"Kurt asked me to look into it since it was sold, and the new owner hadn't recorded it yet."

"Nice work," Parker said.

Botzon turned a palm upward. "It's the game."

"The previous owner," Hernandez said, "is Nichelle Brunt. She's got an address in the Valley."

Johnson approached them now, and everyone turned in his direction.

"Dispatch ran our guys through NCIC. Extensive history with drug and violent assaults. Both are suspects in murders in Los Angeles."

"Any gang affiliation?" Botzon asked.

Johnson nodded. "The Vice Row Kings."

"The fuck?" Walsh said. "Who the hell are they?"

"Don't ask me," Johnson said. "You're the gang cops."

Botzon turned to Parker. "What's the plan?"

"Forensics isn't going to be here for a while." Parker eyed his partner. "How about I run over to the Status Stay, and see if maybe I can talk a clerk into opening their room?"

"You?" Johnson asked.

"I don't care. You can run over there, and I'll wait for forensics. Either way, one of us needs to stay here with the scene."

Johnson's eyes narrowed. "I think you're trying to Tom Sawyer me. I'm staying."

Parker shook his head. "You're weird."

Botzon laughed. "How about we roust some of the Dead Boys? Maybe we can find where Tremaine has gone to ground. And Rachelle will check into these Vice Row Kings and find out who the hell they are."

Parker pointed to Officer Hernandez. "Did dispatch send anyone out to contact the previous owner of the Chrysler?"

Hernandez shrugged. "I asked them. Who knows what they did beyond that?"

"I'll follow up on that," Johnson said.

"Thanks," Parker said. "We've got three dead bodies. I'd like to know how that car fits into it."

Chapter 8
12:42 a.m. PST

Tremaine Brown left the Second Avenue arterial as soon as he could. He had to hide among some bushes for a time after he noticed what he thought was an approaching patrol car. He wasn't confident it *wasn't* a cop when it passed. Perhaps it was a trick of the weather that made him think the SUV was a patrol vehicle. However, he remained there for several minutes until he felt it was safe to move.

When he finally stood, he faced a passing cop car. Tremaine froze—a statue among the overgrown landscaping. The vehicle proceeded slowly by as if the cop behind the wheel was searching for something—searching for Tremaine.

The officer should have seen him emerging from the bushes—there was no way the cop could have missed him if he was looking.

But he wasn't.

Tremaine saw this as the car crawled by. The cop's attention wasn't on the passing scenery. It was locked onto the computer inside his car. It gave the officer's face a faint bluish glow. Tremaine's heart pumped with fear. He expected the brake lights to flash at any moment. If they did, he would bolt in the opposite direction. The brake lights remained dark, and the cop car proceeded over the horizon.

Tremaine jumped free of the landscaping and ran westbound toward Scott Street. He turned northbound and left the arterial. He stayed on that road for only a block before heading east again on Pacific Avenue.

Downtown lay straight ahead. Tremaine still didn't have a plan except to get rid of the gun in his pocket.

The rain continued to fall as he hurried. At times, he ran. At others, he walked with his shoulders hunched and his head bowed. His hand often touched the Smith & Wesson as it bounced against his thigh. He repeatedly hugged himself in hopes of keeping warm. His teeth chattered now that the adrenaline was gone, and the cold had set in.

A bum slept in the darkened entryway of a vacant building. Tremaine stopped after passing the stoop and returned to steal the man's sleeping bag. He thought wrapping himself in its warmth would ease his discomfort. When Tremaine bent to grab the sleeping bag, he smelled urine and feces. He immediately stopped—his hand hovering inches from the end of the bag. Tremaine's self-respect denied his immediate comfort. He couldn't wrap himself in something that reeked so badly. He stepped away from the snoring derelict and moved on.

Tremaine's clothes and shoes were so wholly soaked it was as if he had fallen into a swimming pool. In a moment like this, he wished his mother were still alive. He could have gone to her and asked her for help. It was a childish wish for many reasons. She'd been dead for more than a decade. Cancer had gotten her—eaten her from the inside. Had she not been dead, she wouldn't have welcomed him into her home. She knew what he had become and cursed him for it. That was when he was only a soldier for the Dead Boys.

What would she think of him now?

Recalling his mother led him to ponder other women. He hadn't had a steady one since Regina was killed in a drive-by. Tremaine had gotten his pound of retribution for that, but he hadn't taken up with anyone since. Of course, there'd been casual hook-ups, but he'd never claim anyone as his again. It was too dangerous to get that close to someone.

However, maybe he could call one of the hook-ups, and they'd give him a place to hide.

Tremaine opened his phone while he walked. His hands trembled from the cold as he tried to protect the screen from the rain. Tremaine found a number—Amber. She was a plump girl with a pretty face who did things most girls wouldn't. Nearly all the guys in the crew had pinned her to a mattress. She wasn't the type any of them wanted long-term, but Amber more than did the trick on a slow weekday night.

The phone rang twice before it went to voice mail. She had denied his call.

"The fuck?" Tremaine whispered. He wanted to shout but doing so would call attention to himself. He already knew he looked strange enough. Hollering like a maniac would only bring more interest.

A lightning bolt flashed across the sky, and Tremaine lifted his head. He noticed others scurrying about the neighborhood—other shadows like him who didn't want to be seen.

Thunder rumbled, and Tremaine returned his attention to his phone. He continued walking as he redialed Amber's number. It rang only once before being sent to voice mail.

"Son of a bitch," he muttered.

A car drove slowly by. Tremaine lowered the phone and prepared to run. He glanced sideways and noticed the driver of the BMW scanning the neighborhood. It was then he remembered he had walked into prostitute row. With the recent upgrades along Sprague Avenue, the whores moved to the side streets where he walked now.

His teeth had stopped chattering. Perhaps it ended

from his anger over Amber's dismissal of his calls, or maybe it was the small surge of adrenaline at preparing to run. Whatever it was, the shaking made him feel weak, and he was glad a portion of it had ended.

Tremaine's attention returned to his phone, and he searched for another girl. He quickly found one—Brooklyn. She was a tall girl with long blond hair and an overbite. Her phone rang five times before going to voice mail. Maybe she didn't hear the ringer. It was late, and Brooklyn did have a day job at an accounting firm.

He searched his phone contact list until he found the next one—Chloe. That freaky bitch had been passed around by the crew like a cold. He called her, and it went to voice mail after the first ring.

"Shit," he muttered.

Tremaine redialed, and it again went immediately to voice mail.

He stopped walking and stared at the screen. What the hell was happening?

"Hey, baby," a woman with a husky voice said.

Tremaine looked up and searched the darkness.

"Over here."

She stood in the entryway of a cabinet-making business. He could barely make her out due to the shadows. A cigarette ember glowed. When the woman stepped forward to give him a better view, Tremaine knew her truth.

"Not interested," Tremaine said.

"I could change your mind."

She couldn't even if she started her life out as a woman. He didn't have time for any of this. He needed to get safe. He ached to get warm. Tremaine took off without another word.

"Fuck you, too," the woman hollered after him.

Tremaine zigzagged down a block to First Avenue and

started calling members of his crew again. Jaxson was his most trusted lieutenant, yet he still hadn't returned his calls from earlier. The phone rang five times before going to voice mail. Frustrated, Tremaine tried Jaxson's number again with the same result.

He then called Tariq, Sidney, and eventually DeWayne. All their numbers rang five times each before going to voice mail.

Something must have happened to them all, Tremaine decided. Otherwise, one of them would have answered. For a moment, he considered the impossible—a revolt within the ranks. Could the club have turned against him? It was certainly possible some of the men would think about it but not all of them. There was always dissension in any organization and the Dead Boys were no different. Some considered him too harsh at times while others thought him too soft. He couldn't please all the men all the time. That was the burden of the crown. He pushed the worry aside. No, something else had happened.

He turned at Division Street and passed underneath the train tracks. He continued northbound.

If he couldn't go to his crew for help and he couldn't go to one of the girls, who could he reach out to for help?

Tremaine's brother wasn't an option—he was in custody again. Even if he wasn't, he was no longer in town. Dontari was forced out of Spokane about a year ago due to some bad decisions he'd made. He had moved to California and hooked up with the Original Dead Boys. Dontari and Tremaine had barely talked since the move because it was Tremaine who pushed him out of town. It was for his brother's good. Otherwise, Dontari would have gone to prison.

Perhaps Tremaine was only prolonging the inevitable, but that's what he had done since they were kids—kept his younger brother out of trouble. Tremaine would love to reach out to Dontari and get his input on what happened, but he didn't know how to get a hold of him now.

Right now, Tremaine needed to find someone who could help.

He latched on to a name he hadn't thought about in some time. It was a man who once helped a mentor of Tremaine's. The two were never close—their ages and stations in life dictated as much. However, maybe this man would be the one who could help Tremaine make it through the night.

Tremaine felt a surge of hope because he now had a plan. First, he still had to get rid of the gun in his pocket so it could never return to haunt him.

He approached Borracho, a nightclub he'd partied at many times. A group of smokers gathered in front, their backs were pressed against the building and coats were pulled up over their heads in an effort to avoid the wind and the rain. It was nearing one o'clock now. Other clubs were on the block, including Boom Box Pizza, The Globe, and The Blind Buck. Those joints weren't closed yet either, but the sidewalks were busy with folks heading home. Someone in this area was certain to recognize him.

Tremaine thought about approaching the crowd. Maybe he'd find a girl he'd met in the past. But if the police were looking for him, the word might already be out. Perhaps they'd contacted some bouncers—many of them were wannabe cops. Tremaine believed his best bet right now was to keep a low profile, especially since he had no idea what was happening with his crew or the girls who hung around them.

He crossed the street and went east. Tremaine was moving further away from where he wanted to go, but he figured the fewer people from bar row who saw him, the better. Tremaine walked over to Pine Street before heading north again. He crossed Spokane Falls Boulevard, avoiding prying eyes as he did so, and entered the satellite campus of Washington State University.

Tremaine didn't know anyone who had ever attended class there. He knew enough about the university's football program to understand the main campus was in Pullman, about ninety minutes south of Spokane. There would likely be a roaming security guard tonight. The government did that to protect their stuff. Therefore, Tremaine avoided the parking lot lights by trotting from one patch of darkness to the next. Even rent-a-cops could cause him trouble.

The lump in his right pocket banged on his thigh, and he grabbed it with his hand. He made his way to the Centennial Trail, an asphalted path along the Spokane River. Tremaine looked left and right before slipping into a small group of trees. He moved closer to the water.

Tremaine unzipped his pocket and pulled the gun from it. He held the Smith & Wesson by the barrel and lifted it above his head. For a second, Tremaine imagined himself a Native American warrior throwing a tomahawk at an advancing Calvary soldier. He refrained from hollering a war cry.

With a whip of his arm, the gun disappeared into the night. A moment later, it splashed into the middle of the river.

Tremaine turned away and ran with renewed energy.

Chapter 9
0056 hours PST

"Hey," a male voice hollered. "Detective!"

Quinn Delaney looked around until he found a mall security guard waving at him. A younger man stood at the edge of the outer perimeter. Quinn raised a hand to indicate he would be over in a minute, then returned his attention to Geri Utley, the head of the Spokane County Forensics Unit.

She wore a baseball hat with the team's logo and a rain jacket. The hood was pulled up over her head.

Nearby, two members of her team assembled a white canopy. They would erect it over the unidentified body when finished.

The rain continued, and its intensity hadn't lessened since his arrival. Due to the weather, the press was assembled under an awning over a second-floor mall entryway.

"Going to be a long night," Geri said. "Once we clear this, we've gotta run down to Altamont and process that scene. Wouldn't be so bad if the other half of our team wasn't on that murder/suicide."

"Fairfield, right?"

She nodded. "Some nights, you slay the dragon." She trailed off wanly.

"Yeah, this won't be one of those nights."

"Hey, Detective!" the security guard hollered again.

"Excuse me," Quinn said to Geri.

The guard motioned for him to hurry.

When he neared, Quinn read the guard's name tag—*Koza*. He was a tall guy who might have been twenty years old. Even though his short, dark hair was plastered to his head due to the rain, the guard didn't seem bothered by the night's elements.

An excited grin grew on Koza's face. "We got them."

"Who?"

"Her!" The guard pointed at the body. "And the guy she was with."

Quinn cocked his head.

"We found them, just like the sergeant asked. Got 'em coming and going through the mall." Koza smiled broadly. "Wanna see? The sergeant told me to tell you."

Quinn looked over his shoulder. The canopy wasn't set up yet. It would still be a few minutes before they could process the body. He needed to be there when they did. "Geri," he called. "I'll be back."

She nodded and headed toward the evidence van.

The security guard hurried in the direction of the mall's entrance. "C'mon."

Quinn fell in behind him.

Koza stopped at a service entrance door and pulled a key from a ring attached to his belt. "Let's go this way. Keep you away from those fake news types."

Several reporters left the dry comfort of the awning and moved toward the two men.

The security guard yanked open the door and stepped inside. Once Quinn was in the hallway, Koza jerked the door closed with a loud chunk.

"Follow me," Koza said. He was obviously enjoying this moment.

The two men jogged down a corridor Quinn imagined snaked behind several stores. They burst through another door and entered a large corridor. Storefronts were on both sides. It was eerily quiet inside the mall. No shoppers moved about, and the movie theater had long ago let out its last patron.

The security office was in the northeast section of the mall, near what used to be Sears. The huge department store now sat vacant.

Inside the security office were three other guards—two men and a woman. All were roughly the same age as Koza, and each bore an identical expression of excitement.

Koza said to the two men, "You guys go back up to the crime scene. The evidence team is here. See if they need anything from us."

Both men nodded and hurried from the office as if given a special assignment by the president.

Koza moved next to the seated woman and pointed to the far-right monitor. "Look at that one, Detective. That's the woman and the guy she was with right before she was shot."

Quinn leaned in closer for a better look. A white woman and a black man stood frozen in mid-step. The woman carried a briefcase in her right hand. The two were on the upper deck of the parking garage where Quinn had just been talking with Geri Utley. In the lower right corner of the screen was a time stamp, and it read 11:33 p.m.

Sergeant Stockton said the male was Tremaine Brown. Quinn was now sure he had seen the man before.

Koza turned to the young black woman behind the control panel. "Norah, start with number three."

On the screen Quinn was watching, Tremaine and the woman continued walking. There was no sound. Two masked men stepped out from behind a car and fired several rounds. Tremaine ducked as the woman was hit. He ran toward the stairwell as she crumpled to the ground. One of the shooters chased Tremaine while the other ran to the fallen woman. Once he reached her, he stole her briefcase. The case in hand, the second shooter sprinted off.

Norah paused the video.

"There's nothing more on that one," she said. "People rush over to help her, but she's already dead. We called the cops and kept everyone back until one of your patrol units arrived. I can let it keep running if you want to watch all that."

Quinn shook his head. "What else have you got?"

Koza pointed at another monitor. "Show him that one."

Norah nodded. "This is the male victim getting into his car and driving off. Can't say as I blame him. I wouldn't stick around either if someone just shot my girlfriend." She smiled up at Quinn. "Boyfriend, I mean. If I had one."

Koza smirked. "Just play it, Norah."

She laughed nervously. "Right. Okay."

The next screen came alive. Tremaine ran toward a late '80s Chevrolet Monte Carlo. He backed out of its parking stall before spinning the tires and launching it forward. The rear window exploded, but the Chevy didn't stop. It continued around the corner and disappeared.

Norah paused the video. A shooter stood frozen in the stairwell with his gun leveled at the back of the Monte Carlo.

"We got the other two cars, also," Norah said. "The shooters each caught up with a different ride. Look here." She pointed at a screen as it started.

One of the shooters hopped into a burgundy Chrysler 300. It zoomed out of the parking garage.

Quinn reached for his notebook.

Norah backed up the video until he could read the license plate of the Chrysler. She watched Quinn until he said, "Got it."

"And here's the other."

The second shooter climbed into a black Dodge Durango. Norah paused the playback when there was a clear shot of that license plate. After Quinn recorded the numbers, she started the video again, and they watched the vehicle run out of the frame.

Quinn straightened. "Do you know if they arrived together?" He pointed to the screen, which held a paused photo of Tremaine and the blond woman.

"They came in different cars," Norah said, "but they met in the food court."

Another screen started. Tremaine and the blond woman sat at a table in the middle of the quiet food court. Hardly anyone else was nearby.

"What time does the food court close?" Quinn asked.

"Ten," Koza said. "But some movies run until after eleven, so people wait in the food court seating area. You know, parents and whatnot. People giving others rides. That sort of thing. We don't kick them out until the last movie is done."

Quinn studied the screen again.

The woman's briefcase lay on the table between them. She and Tremaine made an odd pair. She wore a business suit—slacks and jacket—while he donned a fashionable fleece sweatsuit. Perhaps he could have been a rap star in another world, and she was his agent.

However, Tremaine Brown was the leader of a criminal organization, so the woman was… what?

Quinn ran through possibilities in his mind.

His attorney? It was possible, but it was a strange time of night for them to meet.

His accountant? Again, it was possible, but why meet at the mall on a Friday night?

His girlfriend? This was the most believable, but their interaction seemed less than personal, especially with the briefcase involved.

While the video continued to play, the woman reached into the case, removed some documents, and handed them to Tremaine.

"This goes on for a while," Norah said. "It's kind of boring watching him read. Like watching paint dry."

She sped the video forward as Tremaine appeared to study the papers. When he finished, he handed them back to the woman, and she tucked them into the briefcase. The two of them talked a while more.

When they stood, Norah returned the video to normal speed. Tremaine and the well-dressed woman walked out of the picture frame. Norah stopped the video then. "We got them walking toward the exit. They're only talking. It's nothing romantic. No kissing or hand-holding. Not even any laughing. Just talking. You can see that if you want."

"Just walking?" Quinn asked.

"And talking," Norah said.

Quinn frowned. Who was this woman and what was her relationship to Tremaine?

"You can see if you want," Norah offered.

Quinn dismissively waved his hand. "Can you make me copies of what you got?"

Both Koza and Norah nodded.

"When you were watching them, did you notice anyone following them?"

"No," Norah said, "and we were looking for it. We thought maybe the shooters were inside, you know, spying on them, but there were no dudes anywhere nearby."

"Would you mind going back through the camera feeds and, this time, look for a woman? Maybe she was on her cell phone. Someone called the shooters and told them those two were leaving the mall." Quinn paused for a second.

Someone must have known Tremaine and the woman were at the mall; therefore, they were followed. Or one of them was. If that was the case, who were the shooters following?

Quinn's eyes went to the monitor of the shooting. Was Tremaine the intended target, or was it the woman? She was the one killed, and her briefcase was stolen. Maybe she was the one they really wanted?

But the shooters chased Tremaine across the city and left a trail of destruction.

Quinn felt like he was missing something—he was sure of it. His gaze swept across the monitors, and an idea occurred to him.

"What about her car?"

Koza pointed to the far-left monitor on the lower row started. "It's on the middle deck. Zoom in."

The camera was frozen on a dark Ford Escape.

Quinn felt a burst of excitement now. "All right. Let's go find it."

He took off without looking back.

Chapter 10
0003 hours PST

"Spokane Police," Parker said. He flipped open a wallet that contained his identification card and a smaller version of the SPD badge. His regular badge was clipped to his belt and under his rain jacket.

The Status Stay desk clerk's expression soured and he rose from his chair to consider him. Parker wondered if it was because he was a cop or dripping on the lobby floor.

Parker continued. "What room are Rashard Foreman and Spencer Anderson staying in?"

"Sir?"

Being assigned the graveyard shift in any profession often brought out the oddballs—even law enforcement. For this hotel, it meant the clerk was a throwback to the rockabilly days of the 1950s. He was white and in his mid-thirties. His dark hair was slicked with some type of greasy product. He wore black horn-rimmed glasses, a white short-sleeved shirt, and a thin black tie. A teal and yellow tag attached to his breast pocket announced his name as *Buddy*. Parker wondered if that was indeed his name or if he was paying homage to the crooner of "That'll be the Day."

"Foreman and Anderson," Parker said. "What's their room number?"

The clerk stiffened. "We don't share information about our guests." His face slackened as if he might have said too much. "*If* they are guests to begin with."

Parker frowned. "They're dead."

"Dead?"

"Just like Buddy Holly."

"Who?"

This gave Parker pause, and he reconsidered the clerk's hair. He couldn't remember if Buddy Holly had short hair or a ducktail like this guy. Perhaps he had misread the clerk's getup, which was a hipster outfit.

Parker waved a contemptuous hand. "Rashard Foreman and Spencer Anderson were involved in an altercation earlier this evening and were killed. We found registration paperwork for your hotel. I'd like to see their room to know if anyone else is staying there. You know, to make the notification."

Buddy mashed his lips together. "How do I know they're dead?"

Parker leaned an elbow on the counter. "You think I'd lie about that?"

"I don't know."

"Are you impugning my character or just the police in general?"

The question seemed to confuse the clerk. Or he may have been surprised that Parker used the word *impugn* conversationally.

Parker didn't have a warrant to get the information about Foreman and Spencer's room. He could always go and get one, but it was better to talk his way into what he wanted right now. The clerk didn't seem impressed by the badge, so he used a different tactic.

"Maybe I should skip all this and just go to the press."

"What for?"

"To tell them Foreman and Anderson stayed here. I'll wind them up—just a little bit, not too much—and encourage them to camp in your lobby until they get some answers about why your hotel rented a room to a couple of murderers."

Buddy's face tightened. "Murderers?"

Parker nodded. "I wouldn't lie about that either."

"You said they were dead."

"But not before they killed a woman."

The clerk tapped the spacebar on the keyboard. "Well then." His fingers jumped across the keys. "They were in room two fourteen." Buddy looked up. "I can't let you go in unsupervised. Policy, you understand."

"They checked in yesterday, correct?"

The clerk's eyes went to the computer and then the clock on the wall. "Yesterday afternoon. Friday. Correct."

"Who paid for the room?"

"Mr. Foreman. He paid with cash."

Parker cocked his head. "He didn't put down a credit card?"

"He didn't have a card. He paid with cash."

"Isn't there a policy?"

Buddy seemed embarrassed. "Our occupancy is lower than the industry average, so cash beats policy."

"He check in with anyone else?"

"Looks to be the only room." Buddy cleared his throat. "Would you like to see it?"

Parker nodded and then followed Buddy to the elevator.

The clerk stabbed the Up button. "How'd they die?"

"What's that?" Parker asked.

"You said they were killed. I was just wondering, you know." He looked down at his hands and an embarrassed smile creased his lips. "If you don't mind."

"They were shot."

Buddy's grin faded. "Oh."

"A couple of very bad men," Parker added.

"We didn't know."

That stopped the conversation.

Parker realized there wasn't any music in the small box. He was thankful for that, even though it was only a short ride. The doors opened, and the two men stepped out.

"We're to the left," Buddy said. He led Parker about half the way down the hall. When he arrived at room 214, the desk clerk knocked on the door. "Housekeeping." He didn't announce it very loudly.

Parker removed his Glock and waited patiently.

Buddy's eyes widened at the sight of the gun, but he knocked a second time. "Housekeeping," he muttered. This time was softer than the first.

Buddy slipped a key card into the lock when there wasn't an answer.

Parker gently pushed the clerk away from the door, then turned the handle. "Spokane Police." His voice was loud and clear. "We're coming inside."

He paused before entering, though. After several seconds no one came to the door, and no sounds were made, so he stepped inside.

Two small gym bags sat on the floor near the beds. Neither was opened. A crumbled ticket from Los Angeles to Spokane via Southwest Airlines lay on the small writing desk. It had belonged to Rashard Foreman and showed the man arrived earlier on Friday.

Parker lifted both gym bags onto the nearest bed and opened them.

Inside the first bag were a pair of jeans, two shirts, two pairs of underwear, and two pairs of socks. The contents of the second were much the same.

Parker closed the bags and returned them to the floor.

"Their beds don't look slept in," Parker muttered.

"No, sir," the clerk nervously replied.

He looked toward Buddy.

"Sorry. I suppose that was a rhetorical observation."

Parker frowned. Perhaps the clerk *had* understood his use of impugn.

He returned his attention to the crinkled airline ticket.

Foreman had come in yesterday. It was likely Anderson came with him. The two men flew in from L.A. and checked into the hotel. That meant someone got them the car. He supposed they could have rented it themselves but that seemed too dumb even for gangsters. Someone definitely had to supply the guns, since they couldn't have brought them onto the plane. All that coordination so they could ambush Tremaine and the woman.

Who the hell were the Vice Row Kings and what did they have against Tremaine Brown?

Parker's phone buzzed in his pocket, and he removed it. The caller ID screen read DELANEY. He answered it. "Parker."

"How's Altamont?"

"Fine. Johnson's down there now." Parker walked over to the circular trash can. Inside was a crumbled piece of paper. He pulled it out. It was Spencer's plane ticket. He dropped it back in. "I'm at the Status Stay on Fourth."

"Why are you there?"

"It's where our shooters were staying."

"Find anything?" Delaney asked.

"Two gym bags and a couple airline tickets from Los Angeles. Our guys came in on Southwest yesterday afternoon."

"Anything in the bags?"

"Just clothes. What about you? I heard you got a dead woman up there."

"Yeah." Delaney's voice echoed as if he were walking through a hallway. "But there's something weird."

"Weird, how?" Parker checked the pad of paper on the writing desk. It hadn't been used. He flicked it away. He'd seen many movies where someone wrote a note, then ripped off the top sheet. Later, an inspired detective would break the case open by rubbing a pencil over the remaining pad. That had yet to happen in any of Parker's cases.

Hollywood lied. What else was new?

"The woman was with Tremaine Brown," Delaney said, "but it looked like business."

"How so?"

"She brought her briefcase."

"Like she was his attorney?" Parker asked. "It was a little late for a meeting, don't you think? Have you identified her?"

"Not yet. Still working on it, but we've identified the cars of the shooters."

"Let me guess. One of them is a Chrysler 300."

"You got it at your scene?" Delaney asked.

"That's right. Also got a Chevy Monte Carlo registered to Tremaine Brown."

"We saw that one, too."

"How'd you see it?" Parker nodded. "Security footage or something?"

"That's right," Delaney said. "What about a Dodge Durango? Is that down there, too?"

"That one we don't have."

"Okay. So, here's what we saw on the cameras. There were two shooters and two drivers. They went after Tremaine and the woman. They killed her and stole her briefcase."

Parker spun around and scanned the room for a case. "Which car did the briefcase go into?"

"The Durango," Delaney said.

Even though this room was rented to the guys in the Chrysler, it was still worth searching for the case. Parker dropped to his hands and knees and looked under the bed. It had a wooden frame that stopped anything from sliding underneath. "Did you get a plate on the Dodge?"

"I did, and we just ran it. Shows up as sold last week but not registered by the new owner."

"Funny," Parker said as he stood. "That's the same story with the Chrysler. We asked dispatch to send an officer out to the last owner of record."

"We did the same." A door banged open, and Quinn sounded distracted. "I've got to go. Stay in touch." He hung up.

Parker next dialed dispatch and requested an officer to guard the hotel room until the forensics unit arrived.

"No units are available," the dispatcher replied.

"Can you call in a volunteer?"

"We'll give it a shot."

He hung up without saying thank you and immediately regretted it. Yet he wasn't going to call back and apologize. Dispatchers had been treated far worse than being abruptly hung up on.

This created a problem for Parker. Technically, he should remain with the room until he was relieved, or the evidence team arrived. However, there was still too much to do. He wasn't going to sit on the sidelines tonight.

Parker scanned the room again before making a decision. He dropped his phone into his pocket and turned back to Buddy. "Secure this room. No one else comes in. Not until the forensic team arrives. Got it?"

Chapter 11

"Well, well, well," Kurt Botzon said. "Fast Freddie Gilmore. How you doin', buddy?"

The man gripped the steering wheel tighter. He kept his eyes straight ahead. "You got no right to stop me, Botzon."

"Sure, I do. You're a felon in possession of a moving vehicle. There's a law against that."

Freddie cast a sideways glance. "That's profiling."

"There's no profiling when it comes to you, Freddie. We got history."

They were in the middle of downtown on Riverside Avenue. The Bank of America building loomed high above. Behind them, the Spokane Transit Authority Plaza was quiet as no buses ran now. Streetlamps bathed the sidewalks in yellow light. Puddles shimmered curbside. Overhead the thunderstorm continued its rage. Among the tall downtown buildings, however, it seemed less menacing than out among the residential neighborhoods.

On the passenger side of Gilmore's Ford Explorer, SIU Officer Rachelle Walsh peered through the window. She used her flashlight to examine the floorboard. Behind her, Jay Peterson did the same to the rear of the vehicle. Hugh Swezey stood next to Kurt Botzon as his back-up.

Frederick Gilmore slammed the palm of his hand against the steering wheel. "This is some bullshit."

Botzon chuckled. "Of course it is, Freddie. I'm just playing, but for real, you didn't signal your lane change. Why make it so easy?"

"I signaled."

"Hand to God, you didn't."

Freddie turned to him now. His face pinched, and his eyes hardened. "Motherfucker, I knew you were back there. I ain't stupid. I signaled."

"Then your turn signal is out. That's driving with defective equipment. That's another charge, and still a good stop. Step out of the car, and let's have a look."

"You ain't suckering me out of this car."

"What's that?"

Freddie's gaze shifted to Hugh, who used his flashlight to peer into the rear windows of the SUV. "If I step out, you're beating me down."

"Have we ever done that to you?"

"Hell yeah, you have."

Even in the cold and wet, Botzon's neck warmed. He hated being accused of criminal assault. "The only times we roughed you up, Freddie, you started it. Tell me I'm wrong."

Freddie clicked his tongue against the back of his teeth. "Man, that was an accident."

"You elbowed me in the face."

"When you were arresting me for some bullshit!"

"You broke my nose, Freddie."

"Shit, maybe I was wrong then, Botzon, but I went to jail for that. You can't hold that over my head. What about that time when you—"

Botzon flicked his hand. "Enough of this, Freddie. Get outta the car." He shined his light directly into the man's face.

Freddie squinted and turned away. "All right, all right, but I want it on record this is some major fucking bullshit." He started to climb out of the car.

"Turn on your blinker," Botzon said.

"Huh?"

"Do it. We're going to perform a safety inspection and

show you that I'm not a liar."

Freddie activated his right turn signal, then climbed out of the car. He wore a gray jacket, low-slung jeans, and white tennis shoes.

"Turn around," Botzon said. "I need to pat you down for safety."

"For *your* safety, maybe—not mine. I didn't do nothing wrong." Freddie put his hands on the Ford and spread his legs. "Go on, man, grab my nuts. Find out what your girlfriend keeps dreaming about."

Botzon tucked the flashlight into his back pocket. He ran his hands over Freddie's arms, chest, waist, and down his legs. He felt a rectangle in Freddie's front left pocket that he easily identified as a cell phone. There was no need to have the man pull it out as this was only a quick check for weapons. When he was satisfied the man wasn't carrying any, he stepped back.

"You're good."

Freddie turned around. "No shit, I'm good. I'm not dumb enough to carry a gun."

Botzon pulled his flashlight from his back pocket and waved the beam toward the vehicle's rear. "Go to the back."

The SIU team assembled around Freddie Gilmore. The right turn signal was dark.

"See?" Botzon said. "It's not working."

Freddie bent toward the light. "You musta broke it."

Botzon tapped the end of his flashlight against the hard plastic cover. "It's still intact, you ding-dong. How could we have broken it?"

Freddie straightened, but his look of defiance remained. "I don't know, but you did. That's how you cops do."

"Mind if we search your car?"

"Why for?"

Botzon tucked his flashlight into his armpit, then crossed his arms. The beam of light was centered on Freddie's chest. "You got something to hide?"

Freddie shuffled his feet and looked over his shoulder at the SUV. "No."

"So you don't mind?"

"Fuck yeah, I mind."

"We're not looking for drugs," Rachelle said.

Freddie eyed her. "What do I care? Ain't nothing in there I can't have."

"Then let us look," Botzon said, "and we'll be on our way."

"That's what this is about? Drugs? You all want to get in my ride and see what I got? Fine. Help yourself. But you won't find nothing."

Swezey and Peterson moved toward the SUV.

Freddie watched the two SIU officers climb into the vehicle. His attention returned to Botzon, and he threw his hands into the air. "You know you ain't gonna find anything."

"We stopped you for an improper lane change," Rachelle said.

"Nah. If that's all it was, you wouldn't be searching my vehicle."

"You consented," she added.

"Whatever. You're harassing me." His eyes narrowed. "It ain't for some drugs. What's the real reason?"

Botzon asked, "What're you doing out so late?"

Freddie *pshawed*. "It ain't late. I'm just leaving the club."

"Which one?"

"All of them." Freddie waggled his hand. "I bounce from place to place. You know how it is." His eyes traveled Botzon's length. "Maybe not you." He considered Rachelle. "But ol' girl here would know."

"Where were you heading now?" Botzon asked.

"Nowhere. I was just driving around. Seeing what's what."

"Right," Rachelle said.

"Believe it or not," Freddie said. "That's what I was doing."

Botzon shrugged. "Let's say I believe you. Tell me where Tremaine is."

Freddie's expression flattened. After a moment, he looked away. "What do you want with him?"

"I want to know where he is."

"Why?"

"Because I miss him."

Freddie turned back to Botzon. "You miss him?"

"Like I missed you."

"You want to check his car for broken equipment, too?"

Botzon spread his arms wide. "It's what we do. We're full-service cops at SIU."

"I can get my oil changed while my rights are being violated?" Freddie rolled his lower lip down and shook his head. "How would I know where the man is at?"

"You're telling me that you haven't heard from Tremaine tonight?"

Freddie nodded emphatically. "That's what I'm saying."

"Frederick Douglass Gilmore," Rachelle said. She sounded like a scolding teacher.

"That's my name."

"Your mother is an English professor at Eastern."

Freddie glanced at Botzon. "The fuck is she doing bringing my mother into this?"

Rachelle continued. "You think she's proud of what you're doing?"

Freddie abruptly stepped toward Rachelle. "Better

watch yourself, bitch."

Botzon held up a hand to stop Freddie's advance, but Rachelle didn't seem concerned.

"Threatening an officer," Botzon said. "Not smart."

"I wasn't threatening her." Freddie lifted his hands in the air. "But she shouldn't be bringing my mother into anything. It's not right. There are rules to the game."

"Don't you get it?" Botzon said. "She knows everything about you. Who your mom is, where she works, even what her favorite restaurant is."

Rachelle nodded. "That pizza joint in the valley."

Freddie rolled his eyes. "Bitch, please. There're lots of pizza joints."

"Brothers Office. Not the one in Liberty Lake but the one off Highway 27. You know the one I'm talking about?"

Freddie's eyes narrowed. "Whatever."

Something caught Rachelle's attention, and she turned her head. She whistled softly and lifted her chin toward the roadway. Botzon turned to look.

A bright red Chevrolet Suburban slowed as it passed in the opposite direction. The city's lights reflected off the vehicle's hood. The driver's window was down, and a black male sat behind the steering wheel. His attention remained on the SIU team's interaction with Freddie Gilmore.

"Keenan Mack," Rachelle said.

Botzon knew who it was before she said it. He'd had run-ins with Mack before. A Dead Boy driving by their traffic stop of Freddie Gilmore was problematic. Botzon stepped forward and put his hand on his Glock. "Go on!" he yelled. "We'll find you soon enough."

The Suburban sped away.

Botzon looked at Freddie. "What was that about?"

"How would I know?"

Rachelle asked, "Why are you guys traveling alone tonight?"

Freddie kicked at a stone. "I don't know what you're talking about."

"You guys never travel alone. It's not safe. That's like Dead Boy 101."

Botzon leaned into Freddie. "Stop playing games, man. Where's Tremaine?"

"How should I know?"

"Call him."

Freddie's face pinched. "No."

Botzon snapped his fingers. "Gimme your phone, and I'll call him."

"No." His hand covered his pants pocket. "I don't have to."

Peterson and Swezey returned from the car. "It's clean."

A wry smile hinted at the corner of Freddie's mouth, but it quickly disappeared.

"The hell was that?" Botzon said.

"What?"

Rachelle snapped her fingers and pointed at Freddie. "I saw it, too."

Botzon said, "Your poker face is for shit, Freddie." He turned to Peterson and Swezey. "You guys missed something in the car. Go back and look again."

"We searched good," Swezy protested.

"Look for a hidden compartment this time."

Peterson and Swezey shuffled backward.

"No!" Freddie said. "I don't consent anymore."

Botzon cocked his head. "What?"

"You searched my car and didn't find anything. What's it called? I revoke my consent. Either gimme my ticket or let me go."

"Where's Tremaine?"

Freddie grimaced. "Ticket me, or I'm walking."

"Someone tried to kill him tonight."

Freddie's gaze bounced from Botzon to each SIU teammate in turn before landing back on Botzon. "Yeah, well, I don't know what to tell you about that."

"He's the leader of your crew," Botzon said. "Aren't you worried about him?"

"Tremaine can take care of himself." Freddie pointed toward his vehicle. "Am I free to go?"

"Who are the Vice Row Kings?" Rachelle asked.

"How the fuck should I know?" Freddie said. "Am I free to go or are you gonna break something else on my truck?"

Botzon frowned. After a moment, he said, "Yeah, Freddie. You're free to go."

Freddie Gilmore pushed through the SIU officers and walked toward the Ford. He climbed in and drove away. Botzon watched him go, unsure what to make of their encounter.

Chapter 12

Tremaine knocked on the screen door but didn't bang too hard. The aluminum door bounced and rattled with each rap of his knuckles. Perhaps the doorbell had worked, and he just hadn't heard it over the rain pelting the side of the house.

He didn't want to pound on the door and call further attention to himself. The house was the last on Spofford Avenue. Next door was an additional parking lot for the West Central Community Center. Tremaine remembered a house had once stood there but couldn't recall what type it was. Even though he grew up in this neighborhood and often played ball at the center, he could only visualize the parking lot.

To the south was A.M. Cannon Park. At this time of the morning, it was quiet. Once the sun went down, the families went home. Only those with plans out-of-step with society stayed behind. This weather made sure only the truly crazy were out now.

Tremaine opened the screen door and hit the main door this time. He dared to be a little louder. When he closed the aluminum door, he noticed the fabric was missing. He might have laughed if the circumstances were different.

The door jerked open, and a white man in his early fifties leveled a Glock at his head. He wore only a pair of running shorts. Although the man had wide shoulders and a broad chest, he carried a soft middle. His short hair was messy.

"Cutler," Tremaine said.

"Why are you here?" The gun didn't lower.

"I need some help."

"Call the cops."

"I can't."

Cutler's face tightened. "Whatever this is, you got the wrong guy." He stepped back and shut the door.

Tremaine knocked on it again. He still avoided being too loud, but this time he was persistent. He didn't stop tapping.

Cutler jerked it open. "Move along, Tremaine."

"Let me explain."

"No. You had plenty of chances to come around. This isn't the time."

"Some guys tried to kill me tonight."

That gave the man pause, and he eyed Tremaine suspiciously. "Was it the cops?"

"What? No." Tremaine hadn't even thought of the possibility until that moment. Maybe some rogue cops *had* made a run at him tonight. Things like that happened in other cities, but not this one. He shook his head. "At least, I don't think so."

"Then who?"

"I don't know, but I might have killed one of them."

Cutler studied him. "So the cops will be after you now."

"Maybe."

"Is there anything you know for sure?"

Tremaine turned away. "I'm messed up, man. I've been running for I-don't-know-how-long, and I got everything screwed up in my head. I just need a place to get warm and think."

"And you thought of me?"

Tremaine turned his palms upward. "What can I say? I don't have many friends I can trust."

Cutler leaned slightly to look beyond Tremaine. "You

better come inside."

He stepped into the front room, which served as a small office. A metal desk with a laptop stood a few feet away. Two folding chairs sat on the visitor's side. A couple of unframed pictures of a young woman were tacked to the wall. Lots of official-looking documents were also pinned up.

"Wait here," Cutler said. He walked toward the back of the house.

John Cutler was never Tremaine's friend. Their connection was far more tenuous. Cutler had been his mentor's acquaintance. Before that man died, he asked Cutler to keep an eye on Tremaine. That never sat well with him—two older white men deciding he needed looking after. Tremaine immediately pushed back on Cutler, but he had to give it to the man—he'd been persistent. Cutler had come around to check up on him, even though Tremaine remained steadfast in his refusal of any relationship—often without any grace.

Now, here he was, asking for the man's help.

Cutler returned to the living room. He wore a black T-shirt, jeans, and black boots. He carried another pair of jeans, a second black shirt, and a towel. "Try these." Cutler motioned to the neighboring bedroom.

Tremaine nodded his thanks and stepped into the other room. He didn't bother to shut the door since the two men couldn't see each other.

"Tell me what happened," Cutler said.

Tremaine retold the events of the night as he removed his clothes. He peeled off the sopping-wet sweatsuit. He stood in his underwear and thought about putting the pants on over them but realized they were soaked, too. He stripped them off before rubbing the towel over his body.

The jeans were the right length but a couple of inches loose around the waist. The T-shirt was extra-large, so it was a size too big. It drooped from his shoulders.

Tremaine continued to tell the story of his night as he gathered his clothes, shoes, and wet towel. He returned to the living room.

Cutler reclined in the chair with his feet on the desk. He had a notepad in his hand.

"What're you doing?" Tremaine asked.

"After you threw the gun in the river, you came here?"

"That's right."

Cutler finished writing, then tossed the notepad onto the desk. "The clothes fit?"

"Close enough, except now I look like an old white man."

"At least you're warm." Cutler sat upright. "There's a dryer in the basement." He thumbed at the door behind him. "You can dry your clothes while you wait. Shoes, too."

"Thanks."

"Why did these guys jump you and your girl?"

Tremaine shrugged. "No idea."

"You never saw them before and have no idea who they were?"

He shook his head.

"Lucky you got away."

"Not so much. My girl died."

Cutler studied Tremaine. "Why didn't you protect her?"

"They shot her in the head, and I moved. It was instinct."

"Maybe she was okay, and you left her laying there."

"She wasn't."

"I'm thinking she must not have been that important."

Tremaine's hands balled, and Cutler's gaze flicked to them.

"Or maybe she was." Cutler leaned forward and rested

his forearms on the edge of the desk. "Or maybe you don't like me pointing out the truth of the matter."

"Which is what?" Tremaine said. "That I got scared."

Cutler stared at him.

"Fuck it. I was scared. That doesn't happen to you? Or am I the only one who ends up ashamed of himself?"

Cutler flopped back in his chair. "I've done plenty that made me ashamed."

"Well, maybe do me a favor and don't rub my nose in my shit. She was dead. I'm sure of it."

"I apologize." Cutler waved a hand. "What else do you remember?"

Tremaine relaxed his hands. "Nothing I haven't told you. The shooting happened, and I ran. They chased me across town until I ditched them and came here."

Cutler inhaled deeply as he continued to think. When he decided something, he stood and grabbed a raincoat from a nearby rack. His Glock was tucked into the back of his jeans.

"Where you going?" Tremaine asked.

"You need to know what's going on. Maybe I can help. I haven't been a favorite around the police department in some time, but there are still ways of getting information. Seems we have two questions. First, if the cops are looking for you. Second, who the shooters were."

"You'd do that for me? Check with the cops, I mean."

"Whether or not you believe it, kid, I've been trying to keep an eye on you for a long time. You don't make it easy."

Tremaine nodded his thanks.

"Stay here until I get back." Cutler moved toward the door.

"You got an extra gun lying around?"

"You don't need one. No one knows you're here. Just

relax and get warm."

Cutler stepped outside and closed the door behind him.

For the first time since the shots rang out at the mall, Tremaine felt safe. He also allowed himself to feel something else—hope.

Chapter 13
0107 hours PST

Deputy Ryan Lockman checked out at his location on his Mobile Data Computer. This wasn't a priority call, so there was no need to notify dispatch via radio. The MDC beeped with an updated location status. He slipped out of his patrol car, silently closed the door, and walked up the block.

Even though this was a low-risk contact, Lockman didn't park in front of the home he was supposed to contact. Out of habit, he scanned the neighborhood. The thunderstorm had little to do with the lack of activity. It was always quiet in the suburbs at this time of the morning.

Rain dripped from the curled brim of his baseball hat as he ascended the steps of the Lenora Avenue home. It was a trilevel house, common for this part of Spokane Valley.

A newer Honda Accord sat in the driveway.

Lockman rang the doorbell and waited. It was shortly after one a.m. He would give it a few minutes, but Lockman fully expected to knock. He'd done the job long enough to know most folks slept through the initial bell ring. Yet lights were on in this house, so perhaps someone was awake.

The knob turned, and Lockman stepped down a stair. His hand instinctively rested on the butt of his gun. Overhead, thunder rolled in the distance.

The door opened, and an attractive woman in her mid-thirties stood there. Her blond hair was cut short with side-sweeping bangs, and she wore a sleeveless white shirt and black slacks. A toothbrush stuck out of her mouth and white paste foamed around her lips. She kicked her head back and mumbled, "Hello?"

"Nichelle Brunt?"

She tilted her head further back as if to control the paste. "Uh-huh."

"I'm Deputy Lockman with the Spokane County Sheriff's Department. Can I come in?"

"For?"

"I need to ask about a Chrysler 300 you sold."

Her brow furrowed, and she lowered her head. "My car?" A dribble of paste ran down her chin. She lowered her head and covered her mouth. "Hold on." She ran from the room.

Lockman stepped into the house but didn't close the door behind him. He would step back out if she returned and fussed about him being inside. However, it felt psychologically closer to getting the information he wanted.

He surveyed the living room. It was tastefully decorated, but the pieces of furniture all showed wear. The sofa and chairs didn't match. The television sat on a stand that Lockman was sure he'd seen for sale at Target. The artwork on the walls wasn't anything special and he was pretty sure he'd seen one of the pieces at Home Depot.

There were a few pictures scattered around the room of Nichelle and various women her age. Perhaps they were her friends. Maybe one of them was a former lover. He doubted anyone lived with Nichelle, or she would have been quieter when she ran to the bathroom.

Near the door was a medium-sized suitcase.

In the other room, the faucet stopped, and Nichelle Brunt soon returned. She seemed surprised Lockman was in her house, but she didn't tell him to step outside.

She leaned her hip against the couch and crossed her arms. "What's this about my car?"

Lockman pushed the door closed behind him and the storm quieted. "You sold it recently."

"That's right. A couple weeks back." A smile had started to form, but it quickly vanished. "I didn't do something wrong with the paperwork, did I?"

"No, ma'am. You did fine."

"Ma'am?"

Lockman cocked his head.

"We're the same age," she said.

"I'm trying to be polite."

"If you want to be polite, don't call me that." She smiled and revealed bright white teeth. "The guys at work do it, and I put up with it because they're old."

Lockman nodded. He had expected a groggy citizen rousted from bed, yet he was dealing with a wide-awake woman who jokingly nitpicked at how he addressed her.

"You can call me Shelley if you want. All my friends do."

"Shelley."

"That's right." Her gaze flitted up and down Lockman's length. She seemed to approve as her smile returned. "So, my car?"

"Do you remember who you sold it to?"

"Some black guy."

"That's all you remember?"

She shrugged a single shoulder. "It's not like we were going to be friends. Besides, I hated that car. I bought it a couple of years ago on my boyfriend's advice." Nichelle's eyes briefly widened. "Ex-boyfriend. He liked that kind of car and said it would be good for me to get because it was big and safe. So I got it. I guess I shouldn't complain because it drove all right, but I'm glad to be rid of it."

Before Lockman could ask a follow-up question,

Nichelle added, "Rid of them both, I should say." Her smile broadened further.

He shifted his position, which caused his leather duty belt to creak. "Did you keep a copy of the paperwork?"

"The sale paperwork? Oh probably. I think I've got it around here somewhere." She checked her watch. "Do you normally come by people's homes at this hour?"

"The car was used in a murder tonight."

"Oh." Sadness crossed Nichelle's face. "Geez. Really?"

"It's important we know who you sold the car to."

"I can see that. But doesn't the state already know? I filled out the Report of Sale paperwork like I was supposed to and mailed it in."

He nodded. "I'm sure the state has it on record, but the buyer never filed his side. So, all it shows in the system is sold. We could call the state but since it's Friday night."

"Ugh. I understand. You'd have to contact DOL, right? And you probably can't contact them until Monday."

"That's right." Lockman wanted to ask what she did for a living, but that was more about her, who she was as a person, and it had nothing to do with why he was there so early in the morning. He needed to stay on task. "About that paperwork."

Nichelle thumbed over her shoulder. "I'll go get it." She started toward the back of the house but stopped. Her eyes went toward her luggage, then returned to Lockman.

Now, he reconsidered the bags. Surely no flights were leaving at this time of the morning.

"I'm not weird or anything," she said. "I've just got a flight to Denver in a few hours, and I can never sleep the night before a trip. I get all nervous." She laughed self-consciously.

It was a sweet sound, and Lockman felt a surge of

excitement that had nothing to do with the job.

"It's stupid," Nichelle continued, "but since I wouldn't sleep anyway, I get ready super early and go to the airport. I finally get some sleep out there in the terminal."

Lockman didn't think it sounded stupid at all.

"But you don't need to hear about that." She motioned toward the hallway again. "I'll go look for that paperwork."

While she was gone, Lockman listened to her rummage through papers. He noticed her apartment smelled of perfume. Was it the scent she had put on for this morning? Or was it the brand she wore daily as sort of a calling card? They were silly thoughts, and Lockman pushed them away. He needed to stay focused.

The calls were steady tonight; he shouldn't dawdle with this one. He listened to radio chatter courtesy of the microphone tucked into his left ear. Several deputies were still in Fairfield, assisting in a murder/suicide investigation. The city had two major incidents that depleted most of its resources, so a couple of priority calls were dispatched to county officers—like this one.

Had this been a slower night, Lockman might have tried to make a different kind of impression on Nichelle Brunt. Perhaps he would spend a few minutes chatting her up, trying to make her laugh, that sort of thing.

"Found it," she called from the other room.

Nichelle didn't return right away. It sounded as if she might have spent a few seconds tidying up a mess she had made. When she reappeared, she smiled. "I'm not the best record keeper but I do keep them." She gave the copy of the transaction to Lockman.

The buyer of the Chrysler 300 was Jaxson Reader. The document provided his address.

He photographed the Report of Sale with his phone. Lockman checked the quality of the picture before returning the paperwork to her.

"That's it?" Nichelle asked. "Is that all you needed?" Disappointment filled her voice.

"We're lucky you kept a copy," Lockman said. He wished he had something wittier to say. Usually, he was pretty good at expressing himself.

She checked her watch. "Ugh. Still hours to go. I was hoping this might distract me for a bit."

"How long are you going to be out of town?"

Nichelle's eyebrows rose. "A few days. Why?"

Lockman pulled a business card from his pocket and handed it to her. "Would it be out of line for you to call me when you get back?"

She held the card with both hands. "For follow-up or something?"

"No, ma'am."

Her eyes snapped to him.

"Shelley."

"Not business, then?"

"I'm thinking you can call me and tell me why you can't sleep before a flight."

Her eyes softened. "Oh, it's not that interesting. It's because—"

He held up a hand to interrupt her. "Let it be a mystery until you call. That way, we'll have something to talk about over coffee."

Nichelle smiled and waggled the business card. "All right. Until then."

Chapter 14

0109 hours PST

"Do you like being a cop?" Wesley Koza asked. Even at this time of the morning, the excitement in the security guard's voice was hard to miss.

"It's a job," Quinn Delaney said.

Koza shoved open an outside door and exited NorthTown Mall. Quinn remained close on his heels. The two crossed the walkway to the upper deck of the garage. The rain continued, and a flash of lightning brightened the sky. A formation of clouds was illuminated from behind.

The crime scene was roughly fifty yards away from the two men. The white canopy was up, and one of the side rails flapped in the wind. Geri Utley noticed Quinn, and she waved. He held up a hand and spread his fingers wide.

"Five minutes," he hollered.

She nodded her understanding.

"I took the test," Koza said, "but didn't score high enough to make it to the academy."

The guard hurried down the parking garage stairwell. Quinn followed.

Koza looked up over his shoulder. "Got any advice?"

"About the academy?"

"The test."

"Retake it. You'll do better next time."

Koza stopped and looked at Quinn. "Is that what happened with you?"

Quinn scored high on his first test and ended up number two overall. He cleared the selection process without any hassle. However, Quinn figured Koza needed to stay motivated right now, so he said, "Yeah, that's what happened."

Koza grinned. "Oh, man. That's great. Just great." He bounded down several steps and entered the next parking level. "It should be over here."

The car they were looking for was a blue Ford Escape. On the camera, it had been parked next to a red pickup and a white SUV. Now, the second level of the parking garage was empty except for the woman's car—it sat alone.

When Quinn and Koza approached the car, they headed toward opposite ends. The guard went toward the front.

Quinn stared at the Washington State license plate on the back of the car. Then his eyes traveled up to the stickers on the rear windshield. "The hell?" he mumbled

"No front plate," Koza called, but Quinn didn't answer.

The security guard moved to the driver's door. "Did you hear what I said?"

"Yeah."

Koza peered into the car. "Looks super clean inside. She must've been a neat person."

Loud footsteps approached, and Quinn glanced in their direction.

Police Chief Liam Dillon strode toward Quinn and Koza. He wore the department's blue rain jacket and a pair of faded jeans. His usually bald head was covered with a baseball hat that prominently displayed the letters SPD.

In the chief's wake was Lieutenant George Brand, commander of the Major Crimes unit. He also wore the department's raincoat, but he had on a pair of slacks. His newspaper boy hat was soaked, and water droplets covered his round glasses.

Brand appeared flustered. Quinn figured the weather caused the man stress as he always seemed pleased to be working around those of higher rank.

"One of the techs said you were down here," Chief Dillon said. "What are we looking at?"

The lieutenant pulled a small cloth from his pocket, then removed his glasses. He set to wiping the lenses as he studied the Ford Escape.

"This is the dead woman's car," Quinn said.

Dillon cocked his head. "It's a rental."

"A rental?" Brand parroted.

Quinn pointed at the stickers in the window. The black and green logo revealed the rental agency the car belonged to.

"You think she was a traveling salesperson or something?" Koza asked as he moved closer to the chief.

"Who are you?" Brand asked. Without his glasses on, he appeared cockeyed.

The security guard puffed his chest with pride. "I found the car."

"Well, thank you, but we can take it from here."

Koza's gaze went expectantly to Quinn.

"I'm sorry," the detective said. "Why don't you head back to the office? I'll come and talk with you in a few minutes."

Disappointment washed across the guard's face. "I get it." He shuffled toward the stairs.

Chief Dillon motioned toward the car. "Did you call this in?"

"Not yet," Quinn said.

"Do it over the phone. I don't want the press to get a whiff of this. Whatever it is, I already don't like the smell." The chief pushed his hat back on his head. "Got any leads?"

"No."

"We might have caught a break," the chief said, "courtesy of the county."

"How's that?"

Chief Dillon eyed the lieutenant.

Brand slipped his glasses back on and put the cleaning cloth into his pocket. "A deputy contacted the previous owner of the Chrysler 300. According to this witness, she sold the vehicle to Jaxson Reader. Ever heard of him?"

Quinn shook his head.

"SIU confirmed he's a member of the Dead Boys."

"So Jaxson Reader bought a car and gave it to the shooters from California?"

"That's what it's looking like."

"Why would he do that?" Quinn furrowed his brow. "You think there's a coup within the Dead Boys?"

Chief Dillon resettled his hat. "We might be getting a little ahead of ourselves. The shooters are confirmed members of the Vice Row Kings, a California gang."

"Do they have affiliation with the California Dead Boys?"

The chief shrugged. "SIU is looking into that."

"And the missing Durango?" Quinn asked. "Any leads on that?"

"The county is helping us contact the former owner," Brand said.

"SIU isn't getting anywhere with the Dead Boys," Dillon said. "None of them seem interested that their leader got ambushed tonight."

"You'd think they'd want blood," Quinn said.

The chief smirked. "You'd think." He waved a hand. "There should be blood in our streets, but everything is silent on the gang front."

"What is CTF saying?"

As much as Quinn disliked Jim Morgan and the

Criminal Task Force, tonight's events seemed like something right up their alley.

"Morgan is in Hawaii, and his team worked a twenty-four yesterday on that meth ring takedown. They're sitting this one out. Besides, this is primarily a gang issue, so SIU is more than capable of pulling the weight." The chief patted the lieutenant's shoulder. "Let's get back up top and check in with the press. If we don't give them something to run with, they'll make it up themselves." To Quinn, he said, "Call in the car—quietly. See if the rental company will play nice."

Quinn removed the cell phone from his pocket as the two men walked away and called dispatch.

Chapter 15

James Morgan reclined in his chair and put his feet on the railing. He enjoyed the night's warmth on his naked body while listening to the ocean's rolling waves. Occasionally, the strains of some stupid song drifted up from the club below and ruined the moment.

Morgan was on the seventeenth floor of his Honolulu hotel. His room overlooked the Pacific Ocean, but there wasn't much to see at this hour except for some blinking lights on the horizon. Perhaps it was a tanker of some sort or a naval ship.

He lifted an imaginary cocktail and toasted the Navy. "To the squids, you paste-eating window-lickers. I always appreciated the rides."

When he was in the Marines, Morgan hated being on the ships. It wasn't the water that bothered him or the cramped confines. It was the blackness of night while at sea. The utter hopelessness of it made him feel small.

We're all temporary, then we die.

Morgan cringed, and he rested the back of his head against his chair. He still felt tipsy after the alcohol he'd had earlier. Morgan wasn't much of a drinker anymore. He liked beer but mostly stayed away from the harder stuff. He'd gotten friendly with too many Mai Tais today.

He knew why he started drinking the fruity concoctions this afternoon. She was lying on the bed in his room. Her name was Sandy.

Morgan frowned. No, that wasn't right.

It was Olivia something or other, but she wanted to be called Sandy because they were day-drinking on the beach. He clicked his teeth together. Or did it have to do with some movie from the seventies? That one with Olivia Newton-John, where she sang in leather hot pants.

What was the name of it?

Morgan snapped his fingers while he thought. He had seen the pictures of Newton-John, but he never saw the movie. His father and grandfather would have called him a fag for watching a musical even though it had been a huge hit and the kids in the choir did a stage production of it. Goddamn parental role models, they weren't.

Grease! That was it. How could he have forgotten? Olivia Newton-John was a heartbreaker in those shiny black pants. Damn. It shouldn't have taken that long to remember the movie.

It shouldn't have been that hard to remember the woman's name in his bed. Whatever it was, Sandy or Olivia, she was a recently divorced mother who came to Honolulu to celebrate her independence.

For Morgan's part, he had purchased the cheapest ticket to Hawaii he could find in hopes of forgetting a week-long suspension the department had just handed him.

The sliding glass door opened, and the woman stumbled onto the deck. She was naked, and her hair was a mess, but she smiled with the lopsided contentment of a woman who also had consumed too many fruity drinks. He was sure her name was Olivia. She handed him his cell phone. "You're buzzing."

Morgan grinned. "Yes, I am."

"No, this." She wriggled the device.

He checked the phone's display before taking it. He swiped his thumb across the screen. Before he could respond to the caller, Olivia asked, "You coming back to bed?"

Morgan closed one eye to steady his vision and

considered her. "Inna minute."

"I'm still horny."

"Still?"

"Don't say that like it's bad." Her brow corrugated, and her wonky smile faded. She swooned in a half-circle before laughing. "I'm ready for seconds."

Morgan pointed at the phone. "I'm on a call."

"What do I care? They don't know me." Olivia turned and bumped into the glass door. "Whoopsy." She laughed without embarrassment, then stepped inside. She closed the sliding door behind her.

Morgan lifted the cell phone to his ear. "You there?"

"I catch you in the middle of something?" Tremaine Brown asked.

"Between shifts." Morgan rested his head on the back of the chair and closed his eyes. The world tilted. "What's happening?"

"Somebody tried to kill me tonight."

Morgan opened his eyes, but he didn't lift his head. The world slowed its spinning. "Who?"

Tremaine tsked. "No idea. Some brothers caught me outside NorthTown and followed me across town. Shot the shit out of my car. I think I might have got one of them."

Suspicion flooded Morgan's brain and worked its way past the alcohol. He tried to do the math on the time zones but quickly gave up. "What were you doing at NorthTown?"

"Seeing a movie."

"What movie?"

"You got a problem, Morgan?"

He tried to play it cool, so Tremaine wouldn't know he didn't believe the story. "Just wondering. Maybe I'll go see one tomorrow."

"You don't give a shit what I saw."

"You go by yourself?"

"The fuck?"

"Or you go with someone from the crew?"

"If I went with one of my soldiers, I wouldn't have been jumped, now would I? You all right?"

Morgan forced a chuckle. It sounded unnatural since it wasn't something he typically did. "I've been drinking. So you went alone?"

"Are you serious?" Tremaine tsked again. "I went with a girl, and I'm not telling you her name so you can add it to that damn file of yours." As an afterthought, he said, "Not that it would make much difference now."

"Why not?"

"She's dead."

Morgan sat upright. The sudden motion made him feel sick, and he fought back a wave of nausea. He remembered not too long ago when Tremaine's girlfriend had been killed during a drive-by shooting. The guy had terrible luck with women. Or more accurately, they had terrible luck with him.

"Have you gone to the cops?"

"That's why I'm calling you."

Morgan leaned further forward and rested his head in a hand. The world spun on several axes, like he was riding a carnival tilt-a-whirl. He looked up to stop the spinning. "I'm out of town."

"Where you at?"

"Hawaii."

"The hell you doing there?"

"Serving a suspension."

"They sent you to Hawaii?" Tremaine's voice rose with anger. "You cops are so corrupt. Even your punishment is cushy."

Morgan's face warmed. "Hey, asshole. I sent myself here. If you're gonna kick me in the balls, let's end this call. I got better things to do."

"I heard. What's her name?"

The call was silent for a moment, and Morgan tried to listen to the waves crashing on the beach. The ship lights on the horizon winked at him. A portion of Jimmy Buffett's "Margaritaville" drifted up from the club below.

Tremaine cleared his throat. "Why'd they suspend you?"

Morgan slowly leaned back and rested his head on the chair. The world calmed. "Remember that stunt I pulled with the get-out-of-jail-free cards?"

"No."

"That's why. I'm serving a week's penance for being more creative than the administration."

"You can't help me, is what you're saying."

Morgan stood and rested his lower back against the deck rail. He caught the reflection of his naked self in the sliding glass door. He made a disgusted face and turned back toward the ocean. He leaned his elbows on the railing and thrust his hips back toward the large windows. It was a comfortable position to stand in. Unfortunately, before Morgan could continue the conversation, he realized he was flashing Olivia his entire ass—crack and all.

He reluctantly returned to his chair. It probably wasn't any more of a flattering position, but at least he didn't have to see his reflection. "I'm out of the game for another week."

"What am I supposed to do?"

"Call nine-one-one."

Tremaine's laugh was without mirth. "Like I'm gonna do that. You know how they are. Any other cop is gonna think I'm dirty before they even hear what I gotta say."

Morgan knew he was right. Tremaine wasn't an angel—far from it. The guy had more than his share of moments when he helped Morgan. It always came at a cost, but that's the relationship Morgan built with the man. It wasn't built on trust; it was built on trade.

"Where are you now?" Morgan asked.

"Someplace safe."

Morgan didn't take offense that the guy didn't disclose his location. Had he done so, Morgan would have considered Tremaine going soft. Or perhaps the man was telling a lie. Morgan preferred Tremaine evading the question.

Tremaine continued. "I got a guy working on my problem, so it's not like I need you anyway."

Morgan wasn't jealous, but if Tremaine had another contact within the department, he wanted to know about it. There were specific rules to working with someone like Tremaine, and not everyone followed them like Morgan. "What guy?" he asked.

"Don't worry about it."

"Does he have a badge?"

"What if he does?"

Morgan stiffened. "Listen—"

"I should let you get back to whoever you were doing."

"Cute."

The call ended. Morgan lowered the phone and stared at it. Several thoughts rolled around in his head. First, who was stupid enough to take a shot at Tremaine Brown, the leader of the Dead Boys? Second, was someone else in the Spokane Police Department working with Tremaine? Or was it some County mope?

Morgan could defend his actions. He never stepped too far across the line, but what if another officer started taking money in exchange for favors? Morgan needed to investigate that when he returned stateside.

The sliding glass door opened, and Olivia stepped out.

She was still naked. She stood with her feet shoulder-width apart and her hands on her hips. "Are you done?"

"Almost."

Morgan searched his phone for another contact.

"I'm gonna start without you."

"Feel free."

Her eyes narrowed, and her jaw jutted out. "Don't you like me?"

"I like you fine, but I've got a work issue. Go back inside."

"Want me to order some drinks?"

Morgan found the contact he was looking for. He absently waved Olivia away as he lifted the phone to his ear. She stared at him.

"What?" Morgan said.

"I'm going back to my room."

"Whatever. Just do it quietly."

The phone call was answered after the third ring. "Hello," Nayla Senai answered groggily.

"It's Morgan."

Olivia huffed once, then slammed the sliding glass door shut.

"What time is it?" Nayla asked.

"Ten-ish."

"No, it's not. It's after one. Ugh. You're in Hawaii. Are you drunk?"

Morgan stood and faced the dark horizon. He was no longer worried about flashing his backside to Olivia. The relationship had run its course. "There was a shooting tonight."

"In Hawaii?"

"Spokane."

"Who?"

"Someone tried to take out Tremaine Brown."

"Did they try to call us in?" Her voice sounded clearer.

"No one called me. Dispatch should know you're not on the rotation."

"It wasn't dispatch," Morgan said. "Tremaine called."

"What'd he want?"

"Information. The guy's fishing. Something's going on, and he wasn't being truthful."

"Do you want CTF involved?"

"Only if you're called out," Morgan said. "Otherwise, stay far away. Right now, it reeks. If Tremaine is calling for help, it means he's out of options. Call the rest of the team and give them the same message. Right now, as far as we're concerned, Tremaine Brown is persona non grata. We're trading no information with the guy or his crew until I get back and can look into this."

"Got it."

Morgan ended the call and returned to the room.

Olivia stood at the end of the bed. She had her sundress on, and she was trying to pat her hair back into place. "Don't even try."

"I'm not."

She turned toward him. Confusion crossed her face. "Wasn't it good?"

Morgan tossed his phone onto a nearby chair. "It was fine."

"Why are you treating me like this?"

It was the push and pull—the game Morgan played with all women if they allowed it. He didn't respond to her. Instead, he turned his palms upward.

Olivia moved closer. "I thought we were connecting. Like maybe we had something special." She pouted now. "You don't really want me to leave, do you?"

Morgan wanted to smile, but he held it in check. "It's up to you."

Her eyes narrowed, and she reached out. Her hand touched him in a very familiar place. "Then I'm staying."

Her voice changed to a throaty moan. "Because I already ordered us another round of Mai Tais, and I know how you like those."

Chapter 16
0127 hours PST

Andrew Parker drove along Third Avenue. The rain continued, and the wiper blades of his Impala were losing the battle of keeping the windshield clear. A small portion of rubber from the right blade had separated and dragged lazily back and forth.

It irritated Parker as he liked everything neat and tidy—an unintended personality quirk from his time in the Army. He wanted to pull to the side of the road and yank the bit of rubber away, but he was concerned he might harm the window if he exposed a portion of metal. So he suffered with the irritating bit trailing behind the main arm.

His gaze drifted to Interstate 90, which ran parallel to Third Avenue. A white pickup with a large canopy sat at the Altamont Street off-ramp. Its yellow flashing lights flicked back and forth. A man was at the rear of the truck, and its two doors were open. It seemed as if he were assembling a sawhorse. Perhaps it was to redirect traffic to the next exit. At least, that's what Parker presumed.

He proceeded eastbound and passed a uniformed officer standing at a patrol car. The officer wore a raincoat and baseball hat. Although he looked miserable in the elements, he motioned for the Impala to proceed along its path.

Parker waved at the uniformed officer as he passed.

Up ahead, a large RV sat in the vacant lot on the southwest corner of the Third and Altamont intersection. The vehicle was older and in desperate need of upgrading, but the department used it as its command center in situations like this.

Parker pulled around the RV and parked. The engine stopped, and the wiper blades halted in the middle of the window. The little piece of rubber trailed the right blade.

Several press vehicles lined up along Altamont Avenue. In average weather, a gaggle of reporters would have waited outside with their cameras ready to catch a shot of something worthy of excessive repeating on the morning, midday, and evening news. Maybe something positive was coming from the downpour.

A Washington State Patrol evidence van was there, but none of the techs were in the underpass. Instead, several of them gathered near the rear of the vehicle.

A tow truck backed up to the Chevy Monte Carlo. The large vehicle's emergency lights whirred and lit up the small neighborhood in intermittent washes of yellow. It made sense to tow this vehicle as quickly as possible. With the broken rear window, the water could contaminate any evidence. Best to get it to the storage garage and let it dry out.

They could take their time towing the Chrysler 300 since it was under the overpass and out of the thunderstorm.

Parker slid out of his car and pulled the hood of his jacket up. The rain pummeled him until he walked into the tunnel.

Jessie Johnson met him at the tunnel's edge. "How'd it go?"

"Fine. Found a couple of plane tickets. Not much more, but we should have the techs run over there and process it, just in case. I've got the desk clerk watching it."

"Not a uniform?"

"Find me one and we'll assign him. Right now, it's a low priority and I don't think it's going to amount to much. But if it goes sideways, I'll take the rip." Parker eyed the white evidence truck. "What's with the staties?"

"They showed up right after you left. The chief called for additional help."

Parker recalled his earlier thoughts about inviting vampires into the house. It was too late now—the bloodsuckers were in. "How'd it go?"

"Smooth. They were in and out."

"Already?" Parker hurried toward the Chrysler.

"Where you going?"

"To get eyes on it."

"What for?"

Parker dropped the hood from his head. "Just because."

All the doors to the Chrysler were still open. He leaned into the driver's seat and discovered both bodies were gone. "Where are Foreman and Anderson?"

"The medical examiner's boys took them. Like I said, it all went smooth."

"Shit."

It wasn't important for Parker to be at the crime scene for the removal of the bodies. Johnson could note that for their report and document all the important details as it pertained to the chain of custody. The two of them would work together to assemble everything from the crime scene into a single narrative so the prosecution could serve it up to a jury in nice, easy-to-swallow bites.

What bothered Parker was he left the crime scene to check on a hotel room. Had he thought another evidence team would soon arrive, Parker would not have left. He and Johnson were partners, but he wouldn't have stuck the man with the responsibility of running the crime scene alone.

"I'm sorry handing you the turd on this."

Johnson smirked. "Whatever."

"I'm serious."

"Dude, it's fine."

Parker straightened and looked over the Chrysler's roof. He was about to tell Johnson about Delaney's phone call but kept quiet. Right now, Captain Gary Ackerman stalked toward them, and he appeared miffed.

The man was dressed in a yellow windbreaker, blue jeans, and running shoes. Silver hair peeked out from underneath a Seattle Mariners baseball cap. For the normally stylish captain, it was a peak into after-hours normalcy. Parker had seen it before, but it never failed to surprise him.

"Did your excursion away pay any dividends?" Ackerman asked.

Parker nodded. "I found where our two out-of-towners were staying."

Ackerman smirked. "You should have sent a patrol officer to do that and not hang your partner out to dry."

"Something happen while I was gone?"

"Besides the evidence team and M.E.'s boys?" The captain thumbed over his shoulder. "The command post arrived."

"Ah," Parker said knowingly. He was in the Army before joining the police department, so he understood the need for men like Ackerman to feel in control. There were things Parker liked about both organizations; the brass's need for absolute control wasn't one of them.

"Where's the chief?" Parker asked. It was a less-than-subtle dig to remind Ackerman that he wasn't in control of shit.

Ackerman's eyes narrowed. "Why?"

Parker eyed the RV. "I'm wondering why the command post is here. Why not set it up at NorthTown, where the whole mess kicked off?"

The captain stared at him.

Parker raised an apologetic hand. "Probably above my pay grade."

"You got that right." Ackerman pointed at both detectives. "Get your ducks in a row so you can brief the chief when he gets here. He wants up-to-date intel as soon as he arrives."

Parker looked at his partner, but Johnson seemed content to let him do all the talking. Parker asked, "Has SIU had any more luck contacting the Dead Boys?"

Ackerman frowned. "What did I just tell you?"

"Right. Get our ducks in a row. We'll make the call and get those answers."

"And find out where dispatch is with locating the owner of the Dodge Durango."

Parker wanted to push back and say Ackerman should be helping, but he didn't. First, the man was a captain, and that was like rolling a boulder uphill. Second, he didn't know what else Ackerman might already be working on. Lastly, he knew he could only push so far before getting himself in real trouble.

"Yes, sir," Parker said. "We'll get on that."

Johnson watched him with suspicion.

Even Ackerman seemed surprised by Parker's acquiescence. "You jerking my chain, Parker?"

"No, sir. Why?"

The captain frowned. "Just get that info, then see me in the van." He walked off.

Johnson started to say something, but Parker shook his head. He waited until Ackerman was out of hearing, then turned to his partner. "What?"

"You ate that shit sandwich without complaint."

"Not much I could do about it. Ackerman would rub my nose in it before still making me eat it. Better to swallow it whole and move on."

Parker walked back to the tunnel's edge and watched

the falling rain. The sky hadn't lit up in some time. Had the lightning finally slowed? Parker listened for thunder, but that felt slightly foolish. It was like waiting for his daughters to do something naughty. They only acted that way when he wasn't listening. It seemed to be a rule of parenting.

Johnson appeared at his side. "What's the plan?"

"The chief is coming."

His partner wriggled his fingers. "Don't make it sound so ominous."

Parker rolled his eyes. "We need to be prepared for him when he arrives. You call dispatch and ask for an update. I'll touch base with SIU."

Johnson pulled his cell phone from his pocket. "On it."

Parker shook his head. Whether they liked it or not, it was time to assemble their ducks.

Chapter 17

"Keenan Mack!" Rachelle Walsh shouted. She pointed excitedly at a bright red Chevy Suburban as it drove eastbound through the intersection of Washington Street and Riverside Avenue.

Kurt Botzon turned right at the corner, accelerated to the Chevrolet, and activated his vehicle's emergency lights. Wiper blades flicked the rain away from the windshield.

The Suburban started toward the curb but almost immediately jerked back into its lane as if the driver had second thoughts.

"He's gonna run for it," Botzon said.

Rachelle waved her hand. "But he's not driving any faster. Maybe he's coming up with a plan."

Botzon checked his rearview mirror and the side mirrors. "Call it in."

She grabbed the microphone from its clip on the dashboard. "Sam-38," she said, using Botzon's call sign. They were logged into dispatch under his identifier. "A stop."

"*Sam thirty-eight*," a female dispatcher responded. "*Go ahead.*"

"A Chevy Suburban eastbound on Riverside, approaching Bernard." Rachelle phonetically read the license plate. "The driver is Keenan Mack. A known associate of the Dead Boys."

"*Copy.*"

Rachelle keyed the microphone once more. "He's not stopping. We're headed toward Browne Street."

"*Sam forty-one,*" Jay Peterson called. "*We're in the area. We'll back them.*"

After the earlier stop of Fast Freddie Gilmore, Botzon had taken Jay Peterson and Hugh Swezey to the department so they could get another SIU vehicle. He wasn't sure what type of car they were driving now, but it made more sense to divide the team's efforts if they wanted to contact as many Dead Boys as possible tonight.

Botzon and Rachelle had struck out at a couple of known residences. Seeing Keenan Mack driving through downtown was lucky, just like finding Freddie Gilmore had been earlier. Were all the Dead Boys out and about this morning? Botzon was about to ask Rachelle that question when the Suburban activated its right turn signal before stopping for the traffic signal at Browne Street.

"Look at him," Rachelle said, "not breaking any traffic laws."

"Except for failing to stop for us."

She laughed. "Keenan's driving like my grandma. He's killing me."

Botzon activated a short burst of the Denali's siren. It was a loud screech. However, it appeared as if Keenan Mack hadn't noticed it. He craned his neck to check for oncoming traffic.

"That son of a bitch," Rachelle said. "He knows we're back here."

"He'll try to argue he was afraid we were someone other than cops. You watch."

She held up the microphone. "I can request a marked unit."

"Not yet."

The Suburban turned onto Browne Street.

Botzon fully activated the siren and ran the still-red traffic light. The Denali accelerated northbound onto

Browne Street until it was parallel with the Suburban. Rachelle rolled down her window. She yanked her badge off her belt and held it out the window.

Keenen Mack saw her and frowned. It would be hard to claim he didn't know they were cops since they'd had multiple contacts in the past.

The Suburban abruptly slowed and pulled into the gas station at Third Avenue. The Denali followed it closely.

Botzon slammed the Denali's gear into Park. "Think he'll run?"

"Not a chance."

Botzon hopped out of the Denali and approached the driver's side of the Suburban. The rain pelted his head and water rolled down the bridge of his nose. Rachelle walked up to the passenger's side.

Keenan Mack stuck both hands out the driver's window. "Yo, Botzon. I didn't know it was you back there."

"Gimme a break, Keenan." Botzon grabbed one of Mack's wrists as he neared the driver's door. "Step out of the car."

"But it's raining."

Botzon twisted the man's arm. "And I'm standing in it. Come join me."

"Relax! Jesus, relax." With his free hand, Mack opened the door. "Don't go all Rambo on me just because I can't swim."

Once Mack set both feet on the ground, Botzon released his grip on the man's wrist. "Touch the car."

Keenan Mack stood slightly over six feet tall. He was a thin man who wore a Los Angeles Lakers jersey, black jeans, and black tennis shoes. Two gold necklaces dangled around his neck. He shut the driver's door behind him. "Can we go over near the pumps and get outta this shit?"

"No."

"But you're gonna ruin my swag." Mack looked up into the falling rain, and it splashed on his face. "I don't have no jacket or nothing."

"How's that my fault? You should have dressed better." Botzon felt hypocritical for uttering the words. His longish hair was matted to his head, and his wet pants stuck to his thighs. The lightweight rain jacket might have kept his torso dry, but it failed to keep him warm. "Hands on the car."

Mack scowled, and his hands moved while he talked. "Yo, I'm seriously sorry, man. I thought maybe you guys were trying to pull a scam back there. You know, pretend cops and such. That shit happens all the time."

"No, it doesn't." Botzon latched onto Mack's upper arms and spun the man around. He then shoved him in the back. Mack caught himself before he collided with the truck.

"Easy, motherfucker! I'm not resisting."

"You got any weapons?" Botzon asked.

Mack clicked his tongue against the back of his teeth. "Do I look stupid?"

"Is that a rhetorical question?"

"The fuck is that?"

Botzon's hands walked over Mack's body as he searched for a gun, a knife, or anything else that might do him or Rachelle harm.

She walked around the front of the Suburban. "Hey, Keenan. Two times in one night."

"Say what?"

"You drove by when we were talking with Fast Freddie."

"That wasn't me."

She smirked. "I never forget a pretty face."

Mack grinned. "Ah, you think I'm beautiful."

"What's going on with Tremaine?" Botzon asked.

"How would I know?"

"He was ambushed tonight."

Mack's face pinched, and he looked over his shoulder at Botzon. "I didn't hear nothing about that."

Botzon spun him around. "Let me get this straight. The leader of the Dead Boys gets shot at, then goes missing, and the best you got is you didn't hear nothing?"

Mack shrugged, and he tried to affect a look of innocence. "I don't know what to tell you."

Botzon's eyes narrowed. "Fast Freddie didn't tell you about what we asked him?"

Mack's expression morphed into one of confusion. He bent his head and studied his shoes. "Well, sure, he said something about you guys talking, but it didn't make any sense. I just figured that was Freddie being Freddie. You know how he is."

"And none of you thought to track down Tremaine to make sure he was okay?"

Mack pulled the back of his jersey up over his head. This exposed his midsection and revealed the tattoos on his lower stomach. Members of SIU had photographed them previously. Skin ink was like a calling card. Witnesses might not remember a face, but they could recall a gun tattoo sticking out of a suspect's pants—just like the one Mack had. "C'mon, Botzon. This is some bullshit. Can't we do this over there? Like near the pumps?"

"No," Botzon said. "I like the rain. Answer the question."

Mack shrugged, but it was an effect mostly lost due to the pulled-up jersey. "Tremaine can do what he wants. He's a grown-ass man. He doesn't have to check in with me or anyone else. Maybe he's got himself some side pussy." Keenan eyed Rachelle. His smile was lewd, bordering on creepy. "You know how it is, Walsh."

She shook her head. "No, I don't."

"I can show you."

"What about Jaxson?" Botzon asked.

With his head buried in his shirt, Mack looked like a gopher checking for danger. "Who?"

Rachelle smirked. "Your cousin, genius. Jaxson Reader. Tremaine's lieutenant. You know I do this for a living, don't you?"

"Oh, *Jaxson*." Mack rolled his eyes. "Right. What about him now?"

"Where's he at?" Botzon asked.

"How should I know?"

"Give him a call."

"I don't have my phone."

Rachelle pointed into the Suburban. "It's right there on the console. I can see it."

Mack slumped. "I don't have it with me right *now*."

"Want me to reach through the window and grab it?"

"No," Mack said forcefully. He turned to Botzon. "Why do you want to talk with Jaxson?"

"His name came up."

"How so?"

Botzon didn't respond to Mack's question. Instead, he moved to the driver's door and peered inside.

"What're you looking for?" Mack asked.

"Can we search your vehicle?

"No."

Botzon looked back to Mack. "Why not?"

"Because I did nothing wrong. Why are you always in my ass, man? You like the smell or something?"

"If you did nothing wrong, why not let us take a peek?"

Mack smirked. "Don't try that Jedi mind bullshit on me. I'm not some buster who's going to fall for your shit,

Botzon. I got a job. I keep my nose clean, and right now, you're harassing me. This is some civil rights shit."

"Where are you working?"

"At the Super Clean."

Botzon eyed Rachelle.

"The car wash," she said. "The one up north. It's confirmed."

"Still on parole?" Botzon asked Mack.

"What's that got to do with anything?"

"I was thinking we could call your parole officer. You know. Wake his ass up. Drag him down here and let him search your vehicle. I'm sure he'd be happy to be called out on a Friday night."

Mack waved his arms. "Goddamn it, Botzon. I didn't do nothing."

"Hanging out with known felons is a violation of your parole."

"You see me hanging out with anybody?" Mack frantically motioned to his vehicle with both arms. "I'm alone."

"Speaking of which," Botzon said. "What are you doing out right now?"

"I couldn't sleep."

"So you got in your rig and went for a drive?"

"There ain't no law against that." Mack hunched when some thunder rolled in the distance. "*Damn.* Can we get out of this rain?"

"This is nature. Commune with it. What can you tell me about the Vice Row Kings?"

Mack cocked his head. "Who?"

"You heard me," Botzon said. "The Vice Row Kings."

"Never heard about them. Who are they?"

Botzon couldn't tell if Mack was lying. "Give us something about Tremaine or Jaxson and we'll be on our way."

Mack smacked his hands together as he said each word, "This is some fucking bullshit."

Botzon laughed. "That's what I'm thinking. You Dead Boys keep telling me you don't know anything about Tremaine. Now you're playing dumb about Jaxson, too. Something smells bad."

"Like bullshit," Rachelle said.

Keenan shuffled his feet. "I don't know what to tell you."

"Here's what's going to happen," Botzon said. "We're going to keep banging on the Dead Boys until we get the truth. Sooner or later, one of you is gonna talk. Someone always does."

"We didn't do nothing."

Botzon sniffed the air. "You smell that?"

"Yeah," Rachelle said. "Bullshit."

The two SIU officers walked back toward their vehicle.

"We didn't do nothing!" Keenan Mack yelled.

Chapter 18
0140 hours PST

Quinn Delaney rested his elbows on the pony wall and watched the rain fall. He had returned to the second floor of the NorthTown Mall parking garage so he wouldn't get wet. It was a nice place to take a break and think.

Twenty minutes ago, a dispatcher had called to inform him that the rental car company wouldn't provide their customers' details without a warrant. He didn't have much time to lament that information as the medical examiner's team arrived to collect the dead woman's body.

Quinn watched as two men unrolled a black body bag underneath the canopy. They lifted the still unknown woman into it, zipped it closed and lifted her onto a gurney. They rushed the body to a nearby hearse and shoved the gurney inside. Its legs and wheels collapsed beneath itself. Quinn was always impressed with the efficiency of the medical examiner's team, but they moved with the precision of a NASCAR pit crew this morning. No one wanted to be in the weather making small talk.

With the body gone, it was as if the murder had almost never happened. All that remained were the canopy, the white plastic sheet, and the dual lines of yellow CAUTION—DO NOT CROSS tape. Most of the initial blood traces had been washed away by the rain. Only a minor amount remained where her body had lain. Once the canopy was broken down, Quinn imagined the trace amounts would be whisked down the drain.

After the body was removed, Quinn had no reason to

remain on the upper deck. He returned to the lower level to get out of the storm. He now waited for the arrival of a tow truck to collect the rental vehicle.

Quinn watched a Toyota race northbound on Lidgerwood below. The driver likely had no idea a contingent of cops still lingered in the parking garage above, although most were preparing to leave the scene. Usually, a few patrol officers would hang around a crime scene like this to chat and compare notes. It was a form of decompression. Tonight's weather pushed them all back to the warmth and dryness of their cars.

Chief Dillon and Lieutenant Brand had left long ago for the Altamont crime scene. Quinn heard Captain Ackerman was down there with the command post. He had no qualms with any of the brass—even Brand, his fussbudget lieutenant, but he preferred to do his job without them around. Quinn imagined most people preferred to toil without a supervisor peering over their shoulders.

Once the tow truck arrived, he would seize the rental vehicle and place it in the city's evidence warehouse. That way, Quinn could take his time writing the search warrant. If they didn't tow the vehicle right now, it would be a horrible loss if someone showed up from the rental company and recovered the vehicle. Quinn didn't know if they had a GPS tracker on the car. Maybe the dispatcher's call to find out who rented the car would trigger someone to come looking for it.

Quinn straightened. If the Ford Escape indeed had a GPS tracker, was that used to locate the woman and Tremaine? Could someone at the car company have been involved in the murder? Quinn pulled his notebook out of his pocket. He didn't want to forget that question. It was unlikely it happened that way, but he'd learned long ago to eliminate all possibilities, including the unlikely ones.

When he finished jotting his note, he tucked his book away and then checked his watch. He wondered what was taking the tow truck so long.

"Excuse me."

Quinn turned to see an early-fifties man in a brown rain jacket and blue jeans. He wore brown hiking shoes. The man's salt and pepper hair was short and combed to the side. He didn't look tired, but rather weary, as if he'd been up for some time. The man's jacket bulged at the right hip.

"Yes?" Quinn said. He bladed his body and placed his hand on his gun.

"Marshal Criddle." The man pulled a wallet from his back pocket and flipped it open to reveal a circular badge and an ID card. Even in the low light, Quinn read the words *United States Marshal*. "From the Spokane office. One of the security guards said I could find you down here."

Quinn introduced himself, and the two men shook hands.

"What can I do for you?" Quinn asked. He wondered why the man wasn't wearing one of the department's blue raincoats that signified he was with the marshals. Perhaps he'd been camping somewhere? Or maybe he kept the blue jacket at the office, and he came directly from home. There were probably plenty of explanations for the wardrobe choices. The man wore a Seattle Seahawks baseball hat, just like Quinn.

"There was a woman murdered here tonight," Criddle said. "Have you identified her?"

"She wasn't carrying any identification, but we've determined that's her rental car." Quinn motioned toward the nearby Ford. "Her attackers stole the briefcase she was carrying. Her purse is in the car which we haven't been able to get into. Maybe she put her wallet and keys in the briefcase. We don't know. But we've got her prints, and our evidence team will run them as soon as they get back to the station. Might be a bit, though. It's a busy night."

Marshal Criddle pursed his lips and looked to the nearby vehicle. His face pinched in concentration. "They took her briefcase?"

"That's right."

"A witness saw this happen?"

"It's on video."

Criddle's attention returned to Quinn. "You've seen this?"

"That's right."

"Have you identified her attackers?"

"They wore masks."

Criddle shook his head in frustration. "Too good to be true, huh?"

"We know she met with Tremaine Brown, a member of a local gang known as the Dead Boys."

The marshal's expression flattened. "I heard."

Quinn cocked his head.

"How do you know it's Tremaine?" the marshal asked.

For some reason, the way the marshal worded the question bothered Quinn. It seemed too familiar. "He's known to our department. Our Special Investigations Unit and Criminal Task Force have had repeated contacts with him."

"It sounded like the county and the state were working with you on this matter?"

Quinn took a half-step back. "Excuse me?"

"I heard it on the radio."

"What's going on here?"

Marshal Criddle lowered his eyes and rubbed a finger under his nose. For a moment, he seemed lost in thought.

When he looked up, he said, "What I'm about to tell you is privileged information. With all that's happening right now, it may no longer be private. I don't know. This night might have changed everything."

The guy was speaking in riddles. "What are you saying?"

"The genie is out of the bottle, and the cat's out of the bag." Criddle spread his hands apart. "Hell, let's add the horse is out of the barn, too."

Quinn wasn't following anything Criddle said.

The marshal walked to the short garage wall and rested his back against it. He inhaled deeply and considered Quinn. "A couple hours ago, I was contacted about a missing assistant U.S. Attorney. She failed to check in as scheduled." The marshal motioned to the upper deck. "I believe the murdered woman was Emily Pratt."

Quinn removed his notebook from his pocket. When he finished writing, Quinn looked to the rental car, then back to the marshal. "She's not local?"

"Central District of California."

Quinn raised an eyebrow. "As in Los Angeles?"

"That's right."

"What's she doing up here? Meeting a known gang member in the NorthTown food court?"

Criddle lifted his chin and stretched his neck. "Those are good questions and ones I started asking after her people lost contact with her. The purpose of her visit was to meet Tremaine Brown. When she missed her check in, her team got worried. That's when I began monitoring the police radio."

"You kept hearing the Dead Boys referenced?"

"It doesn't take a rocket scientist to know something went down. From what I've pieced together, the Spokane Police Department has two homicide scenes, and you've called in help from the county and the state patrol."

Quinn waited for the marshal to continue.

"Therefore, we're unable to contain this."

"We as in the marshals?"

"And the United States Attorney's Office."

Quinn furrowed his brow. "I'm still not following any of this. What can't you contain? What was Emily Platt doing with Tremaine Brown?"

The marshal motioned toward the rental car. "She was part of a team starting a RICO case against the Los Angeles Dead Boys—the Originals. Supposedly, they found a willing informant after he was caught with an underage girl and a couple bricks of cocaine."

Quinn cocked his head. Tremaine? he wondered. It didn't sound like the man he'd heard stories about. Besides, if that happened in Southern California, he would still be locked up there. No, someone else was arrested, and the feds were squeezing them for information.

Criddle turned and rested his elbows on the pony wall. "What a night for all this to go down." Lightning flashed across the sky, followed by a burst of thunder. "What do you know about Dontari Brown?"

Quinn moved next to Criddle. "That name sounds familiar maybe because I've heard Tremaine so much tonight. Brothers?"

Criddle nodded. "Dontari is the younger of the two. Did you know he was banished from Spokane?"

Quinn shook his head.

"It sounds like he wasn't forthcoming with my counterparts on why that happened." Criddle held an open palm under the rain and let the water accumulate. "Frankly, all that matters is Tremaine protected him by sending him away. He wasn't allowed to come back to Spokane for fear of a rival's retribution or something.

You ask me, it all sounds very Shakespearean."

Quinn had no idea if the Dontari story was true. His interaction with the gang world was limited to its aftermath. If anyone knew the factual basis of Dontari's claim, it would be members of SIU or CTF. He made a mental note to check what the marshal said against their intel.

Criddle continued. "Dontari headed south to hang with the Original Dead Boys. Word is he found himself quickly over his head. From the stories being told, the Originals don't play the game the same as the crew up here. They're more ruthless—like dog-eat-dog corporate stuff. Lots of internal drama with guys stepping on each other to climb the ranks. Everyone watches their backs while looking for opportunities to take down their rivals. It keeps the soldiers in line. Unfortunately, Dontari couldn't get out of his own way. The guy kept stepping on his dick which offended a lot of people."

"Why'd they keep him around?"

"I guess this guy Tremaine was a good earner or something. Kept the peace up here a long time. Brokered some major deals. Even did something with the Wasted Souls a decade or so ago, although that might be total bullshit. The Souls are a freakshow, you ask me."

Quinn looked up from his notebook. "You sure know a lot for a guy who just started making calls two hours ago."

Criddle wiped his hands together. "People are talking for two reasons. First, they want me to hold this whole RICO business together with duct tape and baling wire. What they don't realize is it's beyond my control now. I've got to rely upon the kindness of SPD. Second, it's time to cover some very exposed asses. I think Emily came up here on some promises others might not have been able to get away with."

"What do you mean?"

"This might be sour grapes from some, especially now that she's dead, but there was talk she was aggressive in pursuing career growth. She batted her eyes and shook her moneymaker whenever it got her what she wanted. Then she bit like a great white shark."

Quinn rolled his hand for the marshal to hurry along his story. "Back to Dontari. What happened to him?"

"He went down to LA. The guy wasn't there but for a minute and started getting popped on low-level stuff. Traffic infractions, a bar fight, that sort of thing. Nothing that couldn't be easily handled. Then he went and really jammed himself up by boning an underage girl in his car. The kid said it was consensual, but it's statutory rape, no matter how it's sliced. After his arrest, the local cops found two bricks of cocaine in the trunk. Dontari likely would have been dumped into the prison system if Emily Pratt hadn't found his case and offered him a deal."

"As an informant?"

Criddle smiled. "Call him a rat. It's okay."

"Those are state crimes. Not federal. How did Emily find him?"

"No idea. Maybe the file landed on her desk. Maybe a little bird whispered in her ear that a Dead Boy was about to go down. I don't know. She put two and two together and offered him a deal. From what I heard tonight, they weren't getting anywhere with their RICO case until Dontari landed in her lap."

Quinn's gaze flicked to the rental car. "So why did Emily come up here?"

"To secure the same deal with Tremaine."

"No way she'd hop a flight to do that. She'd have someone in the local office do it."

"Hand to God." Criddle raised his hand as if taking an oath. "The Central District folks said Tremaine only trusted her."

Quinn furrowed his brow. "Why? It doesn't make sense. Her coming to him. Tremaine ratting anyone out. How would he even know her? None of it lines up."

Criddle shrugged a single shoulder. "Listen. All I know is what I was told. Dontari took a fall, and an AUSA showed up with a deal. You think Tremaine's going to let him take that walk alone? No, he's going to throw in with his brother so he can get baby brother immunity on the statutory rape and felony possession. Emily came up here to lock the whole thing down. End of story."

Quinn still wasn't buying it. "But she came up alone? Don't they need a team to do it—back up or support personnel?"

"I told you. Emily played it loose, and she got her way. She checked in with the local US Attorney's office as a courtesy. They advised her to contact our office, which she didn't. Had she, I'm sure we would have had a set of eyes on her. We were completely in the dark on this matter until the call my supervisor received. Tomorrow morning, Emily had a meeting scheduled at the downtown office with Tremaine and his lawyer. Supposedly, that was to be the official time to sign his informant paperwork, so maybe the meeting tonight was an informal get-together. You know, a show and tell before the royal screwing. Who knows? That's probably why they did it in such a public place."

"Who's Tremaine's lawyer?"

Criddle shrugged. "That I don't know. I wish I did. Emily probably had it in her notes."

Quinn would have liked to have confirmed the meeting tomorrow morning with the attorney. "What do you know about the Vice Row Kings?"

"Who are they?" Criddle asked.

"A California gang. Two of their members tried to kill Tremaine tonight. It didn't go well for them."

"That's the suspects shot dead down at Altamont?"

The marshal had been paying attention to the radio. "Are you here to take over our investigation?"

Criddle opened his palms. "This snafu has the potential to become a political mess, so it should stay with you."

Quinn cocked his head. Something in the way Criddle spoke made Quinn quickly replay their conversation. He'd missed something—something important. "The briefcase. Why'd they take it?"

"That's a good question."

"They wanted to know what she was offering him."

Criddle shrugged. "They had to guess it was immunity."

"Then they'd want to know what he was telling the U.S. Attorney."

"It's unlikely he would have told her that before his grant of immunity."

"Maybe they thought he had," Quinn said. "The Dead Boys only had to think he told her something, and she became a target. Maybe they were really after her and not after Tremaine." A new idea occurred to Quinn. "How did the Dead Boys know Tremaine was meeting with an AUSA out of California?"

"Now, you're thinking."

"That means there's an informant for the Dead Boys in the Central District Office."

Criddle touched the side of his nose.

"Which is the real reason you want us running point."

"Your department is contained," the marshal said. "We trust your investigative integrity."

Quinn lifted his eyebrows. "What about Dontari?"

"We pulled him from his cell. He's been in a safe

house for the past few days. For security reasons, the local field office will relocate him now."

A heavy sounding engine whined as it came up the ramp to the second level. A tow truck slowly turned toward them.

"Taking her car into evidence?" Criddle asked.

Quinn nodded. "We'll write a warrant on it later."

"Finish up with the tow operator, then meet me in the security office. I want to see what the guards have recorded."

Quinn frowned as he watched Marshal Criddle head toward the walkway. It seemed everything with this case kept getting more complicated.

He pulled his cell phone from his pocket and dialed Lieutenant Brand.

Chapter 19

Traffic barriers blocked the off-ramp at the Altamont exit. This forced John Cutler to continue eastbound on Interstate 90 to the Thor/Freya off-ramp. It was a slight inconvenience, but he'd been in Spokane for more than fifteen years now. He knew his way around town.

Cutler drove eastbound on Second Avenue—a one-way. He passed Camp Faith—a shantytown illegally set up on Department of Transportation land—before looping under the interstate at Perry Street, where he connected with Third Avenue—a westbound one-way. He headed back toward Altamont Street.

It didn't take long to see the flashing lights of a stopped patrol car up ahead. A uniformed patrol officer climbed out of the unit. One hand shielded his eyes from the headlights of Cutler's pickup while the other impatiently waved a flashlight as a signal to proceed northbound onto Lee Street.

Cutler turned his GMC Sierra slightly before stopping. He rolled down his window, and rain fell inside the cab. "What happened?" he hollered.

The cop stooped against the elements. He had on a raincoat and a baseball cap. He lowered the hand from his eyes and now pointed the flashlight directly into Cutler's face. The officer would argue it was for his safety, but Cutler considered it a power play—the cop was being a dick.

"Move along," he said.

Cutler turned his head slightly and closed his left eye, the one closest to the flashlight. "Was it a collision?"

Cutler knew it wasn't, but he hoped to engage the officer in some discussion.

The cop stepped closer but kept the light trained on Cutler's face. "You hard of hearing, asshole? I said, move it."

"Yeah, yeah. I'm going."

Cutler accelerated up Lee Street. It was too much to hope to find a friendly cop, especially on a shitty night like this. He drove up to Fourth Avenue and cruised east for a block. He parked in front of an old Craftsman-style home and climbed out. He reached behind his seat for an umbrella.

In his younger years, he would never carry one. Cutler would have considered it uncool. He'd put too much stock in what others thought of him. Regarding the new truck he bought a few years ago, he probably still did. As much as Cutler wanted to believe he was a man evolving, he still dragged his knuckles every now and then.

He walked up Altamont Street. A cluster of reporters gathered on the sidewalk ahead. Several of them held larger umbrellas than his. He didn't feel so uncool now. Cutler moved among them and surveyed the scene.

An older RV sat in a vacant lot on the southwest corner. He might have thought it the residence of some itinerant due to the proximity of the homeless camp about a mile away. However, there were lights on in the van, and several people moved about within it. One of them was a uniformed officer. Seattle PD also used an RV as a command post while he was a member of their department, but it was maintained in better condition—an obvious benefit of a better budget and more pride.

Tremaine had said he left his Monte Carlo in this intersection, but it was no longer there. Underneath the overpass, a Chrysler 300 remained.

Yellow crime scene tape still marked an inner and

outer perimeter. Two men in plain clothes stood in the underpass and chatted. Their expressions were severe as they pointed in various directions. Cutler made them as detectives.

Two patrol officers at the opposite edge of the tunnel talked amongst themselves. They laughed and didn't seem overly concerned by the moment they were in.

Cutler's gaze returned to the detectives. If they still had the scene locked down, why had they removed Tremaine's car so quickly? Or was it truly fast? Had Tremaine's arrival at his house skewed his view of the timeline?

He worked it backward. He first considered the time it took for Tremaine to get to his place. The distance was likely four miles. Cutler wasn't positive, and he admonished himself for not checking the odometer before heading over. If it was four miles, how long would it take for Tremaine to cover that distance on foot? An hour and a half if Tremaine walked. He surely ran some of the way, so maybe an hour. Yet he had to be careful not to be seen, so there must have been some time spent hiding or taking a less than direct route.

To be conservative, Cutler remained at ninety minutes.

Was that enough time for the detectives to respond and fully process a scene? Most definitely not. So why did they move the Monte Carlo?

A burst of thunder called Cutler's attention to the weather, and he listened to the pitter-patter of rain falling on his umbrella. He nodded with satisfaction.

Yeah, he thought. A window or two was likely broken in the Chevy; therefore, rain was reaching the interior. Better to pull that vehicle to somewhere dry and protect whatever evidence they anticipated to find.

Cutler listened to the reporters, hoping to gain some insight, but it mainly was whining about the weather and the lack of openness from the SPD command.

"This rain is horse shit," a woman to his right said. "I passed on working in Fresno for this?"

"You're the one who wanted quality of life," a man replied with a satisfied chuckle.

A man on Cutler's left said, "When are they going to give us an update?"

Another woman commented, "Ackerman said he'd get back to us soon, but I saw the chief arrive. Maybe they'll really have something for us now."

Cutler perked up when he heard the name Ackerman. For years, he'd been acquaintances with Gary Ackerman, but they'd had a falling out shortly after the man was promoted to lieutenant. It had been some time since they talked. Maybe Ackerman would be willing to chat tonight, to let bygones be bygones. He was a captain now; Cutler had read that in the newspaper. Perhaps the promotion had brought a different perspective on their quarrel.

The side door of the RV opened, and light spilled onto the vacant parking lot.

"Here they come," the first woman said. "What do you want to bet the chief tells us to hang in there?"

Chief of Police Liam Dillon approached the small group of reporters. Cutler had seen his picture many times in the newspaper. In his wake were two men. The first was a tall, rotund man with wire-rimmed glasses and a newsboy hat. Raindrops spotted his spectacles, and Cutler wondered how the man could even see.

The second man with the chief was Gary Ackerman. He was dressed for the weather, and his face showed the wear of the night's events. He looked older than Cutler remembered, but that's what a few years would do to any man.

Chief Dillon cleared his throat and began to speak, but

Cutler didn't hear the words. His eyes had locked with Ackerman's. The captain's face hardened, and he jerked his head away from the assembled reporters.

Cutler stepped back from the crowd and walked toward Ackerman. The captain motioned for him to follow. The two men walked over to the RV.

Cutler felt sort of stupid holding the umbrella now. He wasn't getting wet, but he seemed like a wimp next to the captain, who didn't let the rain bother him.

"The hell are you doing here?" Ackerman asked. He kept his voice low but didn't make an effort to hide his anger.

"I came to see what was going on."

The captain shook his head once. "What's it look like?" He turned toward the underpass, but the RV blocked their view. Ackerman quickly turned back. "It's a homicide investigation."

"Who was killed?"

Ackerman's face pinched. "Who the hell do you think you are? You think you can waltz up here and start asking questions?"

"That's not what I think. Listen, Gary—"

"It's *Captain*."

"Whatever happened between us—"

"You know what happened. Don't try any of that Cutler bullshit on me, pal."

"I'm not."

"Maybe not now, but you fed it to me plenty before." Ackerman started to say something else, but he stopped. He looked toward the assembled press and the police chief. His head snapped back to Cutler. "Wait. What *are* you doing here?"

"I said—"

"I know what you said, but how did you know what happened down here?"

"I was driving by and saw the lights."

Ackerman cocked his head. "The lights?"

"That's right." Cutler pointed in the direction of the officer he had encountered earlier.

"And you just had to get out like some sort of mouth-breathing looky-loo."

"What can I say?" Cutler spun the umbrella. "Not my finest moment."

"You've had a few of those. Nice umbrella, by the way. Did it come with a purse?"

Cutler forced a smile. "Good one."

Ackerman didn't reply. Instead, his eyes narrowed in suspicion. "You got a client?"

"No."

"Why don't I believe that?"

"Seriously. I was just driving by and saw the lights." Cutler hated lying to Ackerman. It's one of the things that led to their falling out. "You're clearly upset. Why don't I just take off?"

Cutler stepped back. It was a tentative move. He expected Ackerman might reach out and grab him. When the captain didn't, Cutler turned around and walked southbound on Altamont. He fought the desire to look over his shoulder.

The sound of raindrops falling on the umbrella didn't drown out his concerns.

Chapter 20
2:03 a.m. PST

Tremaine Brown pulled open the desk drawers as he listened to the phone ring. He had his cell phone set to speaker so he could work with both hands. The call went to voice mail, and Tremaine hung up. When he didn't find what he was looking for, he moved to the neighboring room.

He was about to stop calling the members of his crew. All the unanswered calls were irritating him. Not because they weren't picking up but because he was concerned for the safety of his guys, and he hated that emotion. It made him feel vulnerable.

The room Tremaine had entered was the one he changed his clothes in earlier. Considering it now, it appeared set up for guests. It wasn't anything fancy—just a twin-sized bed, a dresser, and a wingback chair. The pictures on the wall were photographs of a girl through the years. He remembered Cutler mentioning he had a daughter, but he couldn't recall her name. The pictures were probably of her.

There was no avoiding the truth now. Something happened to Tremaine's crew. For the ambush to coincide with their lack of communication was the only logical explanation at this point.

But from who? The Giants?

There had been peace with them for some time. Before that, both sides indiscriminately spilled blood, which went against the Dead Boys' philosophy—to blend in. The Boys didn't flash colors like other sects, and they rarely used nicknames. The Giants wore blue baseball hats from the New York football team of the same name. As far as the Dead Boys were concerned, identifying yourself in that manner was like wearing a name tag for the cops—it was stupid.

In the words of N.W.A, "Fuck tha Police." Why give the cops any help? The Originals had it right—do business under the radar. There were plenty of opportunities to bang heads with the cops. No need to advertise. Make them earn their pay.

Tremaine shook his head. He was going down a rabbit trail. His thoughts returned to the Giants.

When they started losing more men in the war—both in the streets of Spokane and Seattle, their hierarchy called for a truce, and the Dead Boys agreed. The agreement might have been shaky west of the Cascades, but that ceasefire still held in the 509. Tremaine adhered to the teachings of the Originals.

He pulled the dresser drawers open and found blankets, extra towels, and sweaters. He closed them and let his contemplations return to who might have been behind the attacks.

Maybe it was the Dog Town Titans.

Tremaine immediately scoffed at that idea. That group of pissants wasn't doing anything more than dealing dope out of Hillyard. Maybe they could have mounted the hit on him, but they couldn't have taken down his whole crew. No way. They didn't have enough men, reliable firepower, and they definitely didn't have the tactical knowledge to make it happen.

No, this was someone bigger than them.

Tremaine opened the closet. Winter coats hung on the rack. Several boxes lined the shelf above it. He opened them all and found nothing but old pictures. They didn't interest him. On the floor were more boxes. Those were filled with paperwork. Cutler was a goddamned bore.

He closed the closet doors. Tremaine put his hands on his hips and surveyed the room once more.

The Wasted Souls had the manpower to pull everything off, but the shooters at the mall were black. Even with their masks on, Tremaine could tell what color they were because their hands were exposed. The biker club was the palest group he knew. Shortly after he got with the Dead Boys, Tremaine helped establish a working relationship with the Souls. It helped cement his rise within the gang. That opportunity made the Boys money for several years. Like anything else, it eventually went away. He shook his head. Those were memories he didn't need to recall now. He needed to stay focused. The reason it ended with the Souls had no bearing on tonight.

Tremaine bent and looked under the bed. Nothing.

He straightened and headed toward the back of the house. He passed through the kitchen, entered a short hallway, and was at a second bedroom and the bathroom. The home was tiny. Cutler had to be in his fifties now, and this was all the man had achieved in his life?

Tremaine was about to tear Cutler down further until he realized he was wearing the man's shirt and pants. His own sweatsuit and shoes were tumbling dry right now in Cutler's basement. And the man was out in the rainstorm helping him find answers.

Still, the house was as small as a box of cigarettes. The guy should have done better with his life.

He entered the bedroom, which wasn't decorated any nicer than the guest room. A three-drawer dresser was on the west wall. A nightstand and an unmade full-sized bed were the only other pieces of furniture in the room. Another picture of the girl Tremaine suspected was Cutler's daughter was on the dresser. She smiled as she hugged a German Shepherd.

Cutler had lived in this house for at least fifteen years,

and his bedroom barely looked better than a prison cell. The guy had major issues.

Tremaine opened the dresser drawers and searched them. There was only clothing in each.

A spontaneous thought occurred to Tremaine, and he went with it. He pulled out his phone and made a call. His stomach knotted as he listened to it ring. He didn't want to report this problem to L.A., but they would find out sooner or later. He hoped he could handle it, then let them know about its resolution. That's how he'd had always done it in the past. They liked him because of his leadership skills.

After the fifth ring, the phone was answered by a digital voice. *"The voicemail for this subscriber has not been set up yet. If you would like—"*

Tremaine hung up, but he didn't worry. He was happy his call wasn't answered. Now, he could say he tried to reach out if the bosses ever asked why he didn't let them know what had happened. He had plausible deniability. He discovered that term in a book once. At the time, it seemed those words were only used in the white world, but he found everyone used the concept. He used it all the time with cops and women. Now he found himself thinking about them in regard to the Originals.

He opened the closet doors. Old shoe boxes lined the upper shelf. Tremaine pulled one down. It was heavy and filled with compact discs. He cocked his head at the musical acts. Some of the names included Snoop Dogg, Doctor Dre, and Parliament. There was nothing close to rock and roll, which would surely seem more fitting for a man of Cutler's complexion.

Tremaine closed the box and grabbed the next. It contained names like Nate Dogg, James Brown, and The Isley Brothers. The third box held acts like Keith Sweat, Too Short, and Sir Mix-a-Lot.

Tremaine put the boxes back as he found them. He would wonder about Cutler's choice of music another day. He checked the floor and discovered only shoes. He closed the closet doors and stepped back.

His phone rang. It was L.A.

Tremaine answered it as casually as possible. "Hey."

"What up, man?" Quentin Wagner said. He was one of the lieutenants for the Originals. This was Tremaine's primary contact. He never spoke with anyone else on the phone. He dealt with the entire organization but only in person. That was the rule with them—compartmentalization. It wasn't as bad as the CIA or the old KGB, but it was close. Discussions were always on a need-to-know basis when on a phone. It got looser when they were in person.

Tremaine had visited Los Angeles at least twice each year for the past decade. They never called it his performance review, but he knew that's what it was. He learned that term from a book, too.

"Some shit went down tonight," Tremaine said.

"Yeah? How's that?"

"Somebody came at me." Even though they all used burner phones, they needed to be careful with their conversations. Everyone had seen *The Wire* and knew the police might be listening. The cops were sneaky that way.

There was a pause on the other line, and Tremaine cupped a hand over his other ear to hear better.

"You okay?" Quentin asked.

"I'm fine."

"Uh-huh." There was a pause before he added, "That's lucky, I guess."

"Tell me about it."

"Anyone else hurt?'

Tremaine said, "A citizen."

"Someone you know?"

"No," Tremaine lied. "Just some bitch standing nearby."

Several more beats passed before Quentin asked, "Who's responsible?"

"I'm working that out."

"Cool." Yet another long pause before he uttered a second, "Cool."

Tremaine sat on the edge of Cutler's bed. He struggled to hear what was happening in the call's background. Was someone there with Quentin? He usually didn't sound as distracted as this.

"How you doing?" Tremaine asked.

"Why you asking?"

Tremaine waved his free hand. "No reason."

"We're fine. Don't worry about us."

Tremaine pulled himself in tighter, and he fought to hear anything in the call's background. Quentin seemed odd, as if he were picking his words more carefully than usual. He was always concerned about being overheard, but this seemed to border on paranoia. Tremaine thought carefully about the words he'd said. He was always cautious with his words when on the phone. That had been ingrained into him since he started running with the Dead Boys.

"You still in control?" Quentin asked.

"Sure."

"What I'm saying is, do we have anything to be worried about?"

"I'm good. I'll take care of the problem."

"Cool." Another pause. "Cool."

Tremaine bent over and strained to listen. He could hear Quentin's breathing, but he couldn't pick up anything else.

Quentin cleared his throat. "Yo, man."

"Huh?"

"Have you heard from your brother?"

Tremaine straightened. "What about him?"

"They pulled him from gen pop."

"What for?"

"We don't know."

"Is he in solitary?"

"No." Quentin's voice hardened. "Here's the deal—he's not inside anymore."

Tremaine stood, but he didn't say anything.

"You know anything about that?"

"How would I know?"

"He's your brother."

"I haven't heard from him."

"So you don't know where they took him?"

"I just said."

"He didn't call you?"

"No."

Several beats passed until Quentin said, "Where you at right now, motherfucker?"

Tremaine hung up. He tossed the phone on the bed. "Shit."

He resumed his search, although now he did so with his thoughts clouded with worry for his brother. Tremaine bent and searched under the bed. He found more boxes, but nothing was inside them except trinkets and shoddy items he assumed were family heirlooms.

The phone rang again, but it was Cutler this time.

Tremaine didn't feel the least bit weird answering the man's call while searching his bedroom. He stood, swiped his thumb over the screen, and placed the phone on speaker mode. He set the phone back on the bed. "Hey."

"Get out of the house." Cutler sounded panicked.

Tremaine moved toward the nightstand. "Why?"

"The cops are headed that way."

"How do you know?" Tremaine's fingers hovered at the pull ring of the single drawer.

"I ran into a captain I used to know."

Tremaine pulled open the drawer and smiled. "It went bad?"

"He's gonna put two and two together and know I'm helping you. It's the only reason that will make sense for me to be at that crime scene. Get out of the house and call me back when you're clear."

Tremaine lifted a Colt 1911 automatic out of the drawer. "No problem. I'll leave right now."

Chapter 21
0210 hours PST

Deputy Aubree Shull parked near an overgrown maple tree. Several of the branches scraped against the top of her car. It was dark along this run of Maringo Drive as there weren't many streetlights.

The homes abutting this road did a nice job illuminating themselves, though. All had their porch lights on, and several lined their walkways with little solar lights. The small bulbs fought to shine after many hours of darkness.

The rain continued, but Shull wasn't complaining as it slowed the number of calls her shift typically received. The city might be dealing with a mess following a shooting and a couple of the county's detectives were stuck cleaning up a murder/suicide in the small city of Fairfield, but for deputies like Shull, the night was mostly calm.

She had the rain to thank for it.

She checked out at her location via her Mobile Data Computer. Its bright glow illuminated her face. Usually, she would do this before pulling onto the street of her target house, but this wasn't an active incident. Besides, it was two in the morning, and she was about to wake some citizens.

In her book, Shull divided her county into three categories—citizens, drama queens, and shit birds. The latter were those with extensive criminal records who Shull and her counterparts were consistently arresting for one reason or another.

Shit birds wouldn't do the right thing if they were paid

for it. It went against their code.

Drama queens could be of either gender, but they rarely got arrested. They often found themselves in relationships with shit birds because they were drawn to turmoil. They called 911 whenever something didn't go their way. Drama queens needed to be at the center of a spectacle.

Citizens were those folks who lived their lives with only the rarest of law enforcement contact. Often those contacts were due to a brush with a shit bird or a drama queen.

Shull knew Geoffrey and Eleanor Metkin were citizens because she ran their names through the system while driving from the small town of Riverside. She had some time and wanted to know who she was about to meet. They had reported correctly to the Department of Licensing that they sold their Dodge Durango a week ago. She assumed they were husband and wife since they shared a residence and had once owned the vehicle together.

Geoffrey's DOL report showed him to be 72 with no history of traffic infractions. Eleanor was 71 with one reported collision—no ticket was issued. An NCIC check of their names came up empty. Therefore, she deemed them citizens.

Shull climbed out of her car and quietly closed her door. Even though it was a low-risk contact, patrol habits were maintained. Best practices and all.

She walked eastbound along Maringo Drive—there were no sidewalks in this part of the valley. Only the most recent residential developments had them. It gave the county a wild west feel. It was one of the reasons she liked being a deputy as opposed to a city cop. She had grown up watching westerns with her grandfather—the man who raised her.

The home was brick with white trim. In the driveway sat a new dark-colored Dodge Ram. As she walked up the front sidewalk, Shull kept her head down and let the rain pour off the brim of her baseball hat.

Shull stood to the right of the front door, away from the danger of the fatal funnel—that area where an unsuspecting gunshot could take a deputy down. She rang the bell and rested her hand on her firearm.

She attempted to listen for the tell-tale sounds of approaching footsteps, but rain slapped the aluminum gutter above her, and a nearby wind chime loudly clanged. Shull waited for what she figured was a reasonable amount of time and rang the doorbell again.

"Who's there?" a man hollered from behind the door. Since she wasn't standing in front of the door, he couldn't see her through the peephole.

"Mr. Metkin? I'm Deputy Shull with the County Sheriff's Office. I need to speak with you."

"I can't see you."

"Open the door, sir. I'd like to ask you some questions about a car you sold."

"It's two in the morning. Why can't I see you?"

Shull wasn't about to step into the fatal funnel. Not until she knew Geoffrey Metkin wasn't holding a gun. "I'm standing to the side of the door, sir. Officer safety reasons. Please open up so I can see you."

It was quiet for several beats, and Shull listened intently. The weather frustrated her. The damn chimes continued to clank, and the rain beat against the gutter. A burst of thunder rolled off in the distance.

"What happened to my car?" Metkin hollered.

"It was involved in a murder, sir."

A lock turned, and the door opened. Geoffrey Metkin stood in the doorway. He had thinning silver hair, a leathery face, and a pot belly. He wore a white T-shirt and blue shorts that fell to his knees. Geoffrey gripped a snub-nosed revolver in his right hand. "Whose murder?"

Shull yanked her Smith and Wesson from its holster and leveled it at the homeowner. "Sir, put down your weapon."

Metkin's eyes widened, and he looked down at his gun as if he were surprised to be holding it. "Oh my."

"Put it down."

"Yes, certainly. I'm sorry." He bent and carefully placed it on the floor next to his bare feet. When he stood, he lifted his hands into the air. "I forgot I had it."

"Step away from the gun."

Geoffrey Metkin shuffled backward. "Who was murdered?"

"May I come in?"

"Of course."

Shull opened the door with her free hand and stepped forward. When she was inside the house, she used her foot to slide Geoffrey's gun behind her. "Where is your wife?"

"In bed. We heard the bell, and I came to investigate. That's why I brought the—" He motioned toward the revolver with his foot.

Eleanor Metkin hobbled into the room. She wore a long T-shirt nightie with Tweety Bird on its front. Her yellow slippers also had Tweety Bird emblems on them. When she saw Deputy Shull's gun, she self-consciously covered herself. "What's going on?"

Shull holstered her weapon.

Geoffrey turned to his wife with his hands still in the air. "This officer said our old car was used in a murder."

Eleanor's eyes and mouth widened. "A murder?"

"That's what she said." He faced Shull. "Isn't that right?"

"Yes, sir. And you can relax now."

Geoffrey jerked his arms down. His awe vanished and was replaced by humiliation.

Eleanor took an awkward step forward. "Are we in some sort of trouble?"

Shull shook her head. "No, ma'am, but we need to know who you sold the car to."

Geoffrey's face hardened into a scowl. "We filed the Report of Sale."

"Yes, sir, but the buyer didn't register the vehicle. It's a two-part process."

"How's that our fault?" Geoffrey crossed his arms, and his face reddened. "We did our part."

"I understand," Shull said.

"Do you? Because we followed the rules only to get woken up and embarrassed because some blacks can't be responsible enough to follow through."

Shull ignored the racist sentiment. Her job wasn't to correct anyone's beliefs or how they used their language. It was to get the truth. "The Department of Licensing," she said, "particularly its records section, won't be open until Monday."

Geoffrey angrily said, "That's not our problem."

Eleanor gently set her hand on his shoulder. He glanced at his wife. She shook her head—it was a gentle rebuke, a woman's reminder to her husband he had gone too far. Embarrassment flashed over Geoffrey's face, and he looked at the floor.

"A woman was murdered," Shull said. "Two other men are dead, and another man is on the run. City detectives are piecing it together right now."

"That's terrible," Eleanor said. "We kept a copy of the sale. I'm almost positive about it. I think I know where it is." She hurried off without waiting.

Shull and Geoffrey Metkin stood quietly in the entryway. She shifted her feet, and her leather duty belt creaked.

After a moment, Geoffrey apologetically smiled. "So."

"Sir?"

"How is it being a lady cop?"

"It's fine."

"Uh-huh." Geoffrey nodded several times. "Gotta be tough dealing with angry codgers like me."

She raised an eyebrow. "It has its days."

"Sorry about that comment before—about the blacks. I don't normally say that stuff. It's just, I'm tired and—" He shrugged. "That's no excuse. You shouldn't have to listen to me popping off like an old steam kettle."

Eleanor came back into the room. She proudly waved a single sheet of paper. "I found it."

Shull took the document and read it. The buyer was listed as Jaxson Reader. She pulled out her notebook and copied the relevant information. When she was done, she handed the paper back to Eleanor. "Thank you, ma'am."

Geoffrey Metkin put his arm around his wife. "That fella didn't seem so bad when he bought it from us."

"He was real nice," Eleanor agreed. "A very polite young man."

"It'd be a shame if he did what you said he did." Geoffrey nodded. "I sort of liked the kid."

Eleanor nodded. "Me, too."

Shull lifted her notebook in a display of gratitude. "Thank you both, and I'm sorry for interrupting your sleep." She opened the door. "I hope you can get back to bed."

Chapter 22

Kurt Botzon stood to the left of the door and knocked with the flat of his fist. He'd already tried the doorbell and gotten no result. Rachelle Walsh took the other side of the door. Her attention was on the neighborhood.

They were in a part of town officially known as West Central. Over time, the citizens of Spokane had given this area the derogatory name of Felony Flats. Kurt liked the latter better. It was more honest—like truth in advertising. The city would never go for changing it, though. Luring new citizens to the Lilac City would be problematic if they knew they were moving into neighborhoods with derogatory names like Felony Flats, Vinegar Flats, Dog Town, or Little Africa.

Botzon shivered as the temperature dropped further. Rain fell onto the small porch with the help of the blowing wind. He wasn't going to complain about it to Rachelle but damned if he didn't feel stupid for not dressing warmer tonight.

He banged harder this time. "She's not home."

"You trying to wake up the whole neighborhood? Give her time. She's old."

Botzon frowned. So far tonight, they had been to the last known residences of seven Dead Boys and struck out at each one. It was two in the morning. He had no expectations any of them were the type to get a good night's sleep, but surely one of them would have been home by now. Maybe even hooking up with someone. It *was* Friday night, after all.

Hell, if he wasn't working, Botzon might be doing the

exact same thing—if he still had a girlfriend.

The lock turned, and the door pulled back slightly. An eyeball appeared in the opening. "Yes?"

"Mrs. Moore?" Botzon asked.

"Yes?"

"Is your grandson home?"

"Who are you?"

"Corporal Botzon, Spokane Police." He motioned toward Rachelle. "Officer Walsh."

"What do you want?"

"We'd like to speak to Tariq. We're trying to find his friend."

Maxine Moore pulled the door open further. She was a small woman with ashy skin. Her hair was unkempt, and she squinted as if she had trouble seeing. She wore a pale blue robe that fell to her knees. It was tightly tied around her thin waist. Her feet were bare, and her toes were painted red.

"Do you know what time it is?" Maxine asked.

"Yes, ma'am. We apologize for waking you."

Maxine frowned as she studied Botzon. After a moment, she analyzed Rachelle with the same squinting intensity. "I don't know if he's home. I went to sleep after my shows."

"May we come in and check?" Rachelle asked.

"No."

"Please, ma'am," Botzon said. "Tremaine Brown— Do you know him? A woman he was with tonight was murdered, and he's missing now. We know he didn't hurt her. We're only trying to locate him."

Maxine studied both officers again before standing on her tiptoes to look beyond them. "I can't see too well, especially in this weather. Is there a car in my driveway?"

Botzon shook his head. "No, ma'am. No car."

"Then Tariq's not home. He sleeps in the basement, so

I wouldn't hear if he came in."

"But could we check?" Rachelle asked. "Just to make sure."

Maxine frowned again. "I already said no, but I'll go look." She closed the door and spun the lock.

"Shit," Rachelle said. "I'll take the back."

She jumped off the porch and bunched her shoulders when she entered the rain. She muttered something as she pulled down her baseball cap. Botzon was sure it was an expletive, but he didn't bother to ask her to repeat it. Rachelle disappeared around the corner of the house.

Lightning danced across the sky to the east. A few seconds later, a blast of thunder rumbled through the night.

Botzon's phone rang. It was Parker. He swiped his thumb across the screen. "Botzon," he said.

"County just found the last known owner of the Dodge Durango."

"Yeah?" Botzon listened for movement inside the home.

"Jaxson Reader."

He stiffened. "Reader bought both cars used in the ambush of Tremaine Brown. So he's taking over the gang."

"If you say so," Parker said. "You're the expert."

"We'll work on confirming that. You ever get anything back on the Vice Row Kings?"

"Rachelle left messages for a couple of SoCal contacts. She hasn't heard back but it's Friday night. If you weren't working, would you check your voicemails?"

"Not a chance."

"Thought so." Botzon glanced up and down the street. "We're still banging on the Dead Boys. We'll let you know if we hear anything."

"Copy that," Parker said. He hung up.

Botzon slid his phone into his pocket. He wiped his mouth with the back of his hand. If Jaxson Reader wanted to stage a coup, he couldn't do it alone. Is that why he brought in outside shooters? How did he connect with a group like the Vice Row Kings?

Also, were all Dead Boys in on the overthrow? Were they all looking to take out Tremaine? If true, then it wasn't a coup. It was something else entirely.

The lock turned, and the door opened again. This time Maxine opened it fully. She wore glasses now and did not squint. "He's not home."

Botzon pulled a business card from inside his jacket. "When he returns—"

"Where'd your friend go?"

"She stepped off the porch."

Maxine smirked. "You thought maybe I was going to tell Tariq to run or something?"

"No, ma'am."

"Mm-hmm." She snapped the business card from Botzon's fingers. "I wouldn't do that. That goes against the teachings of the church."

Rachelle came around the corner of the house.

"Oh, there she is." Maxine's head bobbed. "Don't bother stepping on my porch, young lady. You're not staying either."

Rachelle's foot hovered above the step. "Ma'am?"

Maxine's eyes shifted to Botzon. "Go on and get, the both of you. You got what you wanted."

Botzon turned his palms upward. "We're serious, ma'am. Something strange is going on tonight, and we want to make sure Tremaine is okay."

"I'll let my grandson know." She stepped back and closed the door. Once again, Maxine secured the lock.

Botzon stepped off the porch and hurried for the

Denali. He hopped into the driver's seat and started the rig. Warm air blew from the vents.

Rachelle jumped into the passenger seat and took off her hat. She ran her fingers through her hair. "You want to explain that? You sounded weird back there." She mimed his voice. *"We want to make sure Tremaine is okay."*

"Parker called. Jaxson bought the Durango, too."

Rachelle cocked her head. "Both vehicles?"

He nodded. "Riddle me this, Batgirl. Every Dead Boy is out and about right now and none of them seem worried their leader was ambushed tonight. Why?"

"Jaxson is making a power grab. It's a coup."

"It's not a coup if everyone is involved."

"Then what is it?"

Botzon slipped the SUV into gear and pressed the accelerator. "It's a mutiny."

Chapter 23
0220 hours PST

Andrew Parker stood under the awning of Clarks Cleaners, which was located on the southwest corner of Hamilton and Mission. The gaudy building provided shelter from the rain but didn't offer any protection from the cold or wind. Parker shoved his balled fists into his pants pockets and stiffened his arms.

Officer Laurie Sandaker pointed across the street. "According to witnesses, the whole incident started when a Durango rammed the Monte Carlo and shoved it into the intersection. Multiple collisions happened after that. One car even burst into flames. It was a goddamned mess."

This was one of the busiest intersections in Spokane. Even though there were eight lanes—twelve if Parker counted the turn lanes—there was barely any traffic at this time.

A flash of lightning lit up the sky.

"So," Jessie Johnson said, "the Durango and the Chrysler chased the Monte Carlo to here, and this is where Tremaine finally gets jammed up with traffic. Damn lucky if you ask me."

Sandaker shrugged. "I don't know about that."

She wore the black jumpsuit most patrol officers wore in the cooler weather. Her baseball cap hid most of her short, blond hair. Sandaker was one of the more fit officers in the department as she competed in triathlons. Parker liked her for that. He knew Johnson did as well. Fat cops bothered Parker just like fat soldiers did. They had no business wearing a uniform if they couldn't chase a suspect or hold their own in a fight.

Sandaker continued. "From what we've pieced together, the Chevy ran southbound on Lidgerwood until Empire. That's mostly residential neighborhoods, so he probably blew some stop signs, but traffic would have been almost non-existent. The only way we even knew the chase was happening was because of shots fired reports. Then witnesses reported racing cars eastbound along Empire until they reached Nevada." She pushed her hand out like she was riding a surfboard. "That's smooth sailing until the road turns into Hamilton, and they got pinched here. They must have timed the lights wrong or something."

"What happened at the intersection of North Foothills?" Johnson asked.

Parker raised an eyebrow at his partner's question. He'd forgotten there was a traffic light there.

"Tremaine must have caught it green," Sandaker said. "That's who you're figuring drove the Monte Carlo, right? Anyway, there were no collisions at North Foothills. There were reports of gunfire, though, coming from both the Durango and the 300."

"Any from the Monte?" Parker asked.

She shook her head. "Only the trailing cars."

Parker grunted, "Huh."

"Unfortunately, with the time delay of the phone calls followed by dispatch's broadcasting the location of the chase, they were already gone by the time units arrived. Add to that the calls about an active shooter at NorthTown, and the whole situation was a giant clusterfuck. Hard to tell until later which direction the chase even went."

"What's done is done," Johnson said. "We're working on assembling the timeline. We only want to know what you saw when you arrived."

Before Sandaker could respond, Parker's phone rang. He pulled it from his pocket and saw it was Quinn Delaney. Two times in one night. He stepped away from Johnson and Sandaker and answered. "Hey."

"Got a minute?"

"Fire away."

"The feds are here."

Parker wasn't sure he heard Quinn correctly due to the traffic on Hamilton, so he covered his open ear with his other hand. "Say again."

"The U.S. marshals," Quinn said louder. "They're here."

"What for?"

"Get this. The victim was an assistant U.S. Attorney out of Los Angeles."

Parker spun and eyed his partner. Johnson caught the motion and cocked his head. Parker held up a finger telling him to wait.

"What was she doing there?" Parker asked.

"Meeting with Tremaine Brown."

Several moments passed as Parker worked to put the pieces together.

"You still there?" Quinn asked.

"What's an AUSA out of California want with a Spokane gang member?"

"Tremaine's brother turned state's witness against the ODBs. They're building a RICO case against the gang, and we believe the feds offered Tremaine a deal."

A loud semi drove southbound on Hamilton, its engine roaring as it went by. Parker hunched and moved closer to the building. "What deal?"

"The marshal I spoke with didn't know the specifics, but he thinks that's what the woman had in her briefcase."

"The one they stole." Parker straightened. "Wait. Was

she the target all along?"

"Maybe. The marshal doesn't know. He thinks the Originals might have a mole in the AUSA's office."

"Are they taking over our investigation?"

"No," Quinn said. "According to the marshal, the cat's out of the bag. It's our baby now."

"The old game of pass the turd."

"That's one way of saying it." Quinn chuckled once. "Listen, the marshal is reviewing the incident video now."

"How can I help?"

"There's nothing for you to do. I just wanted you to be aware. I updated Lieutenant Brand, but who knows what the brass will do? The marshals and the U.S. Attorney's office want to keep it confidential, so Chief Dillon might compartmentalize it. I figured you and Johnson needed to know. My money is on the mole being the reason this whole night is happening. Anyway, I better get back. Stay in touch."

"Hold on."

"Yeah?"

"Anything on the Vice Row Kings?"

"Nothing," Quinn said. "The marshal was a clueless as I was."

They ended the call. For a moment, Parker stared at his phone. He didn't ponder the information about Tremaine, the AUSA, or the marshals. Instead, he thought about Quinn. Before he joined Major Crimes, he had heard Quinn and his partner referred to as the Glory Hounds. He often thought of them in that manner as he went about his daily business.

Yet the man reached out to Parker and Johnson to ensure they were kept up to speed. Parker wondered if the roles were reversed, would he have done the same? He slipped his phone into his pocket and walked to Johnson and Sandaker.

"Who was that?" Johnson asked.

"Delaney." Parker patted his partner's shoulder. "I'll tell you about it later."

Johnson furrowed his brow.

"So, are we good here?" Sandaker thumbed over her shoulder. "The calls are stacking up and I need to get back out there."

"Shouldn't you be off by now?" Parker asked.

"They've held over power shift until you guys wrap up everything."

Johnson grimaced. "Sorry."

She waved him off. "It's cool. From what I hear, Delaney's still at NorthTown doing his Glory Hound act."

Johnson laughed, but Parker didn't join in.

"Besides," Sandaker said, "I've gotta finish my reports, and the overtime will come in handy for the holidays."

"We're good here," Parker said. "Thanks for the breakdown."

He headed for his car and left Johnson and Sandaker to finish their goodbyes.

His thoughts now were jumbled, and not all of them were on the case.

Chapter 24
0224 hours PST

Officer Hugh Swezey pulled to the curb along Spofford Avenue and parked. He grabbed his portable radio and exited the dented Ford Mustang—a vehicle seized by the department years ago pursuant to a felony drug arrest. Even though the storm's noise covered his actions, Swezey gently closed the driver's door. Patrol habits, he thought. Swezey and Jay Peterson had picked up the rust-colored sports car—the Rusty Trombone in department slang—after Kurt Botzon had dropped them off at the station.

Peterson was approaching the back of the house now. They drove through the alley first and his partner got out behind a dilapidated garage.

Swezey walked toward the last house on the block. He paused underneath the heavy branches of a tree on a neighboring property. At the far end of the block was a small parking lot. Across the street was the West Central Community Center. In the soft glow of streetlights, the rain seemed to fall at an angle. Water dripped from Swezey's baseball cap as he walked.

"Sam forty-two to forty-one," Jay Peterson called.

Swezey lifted the radio to his lips. "Sam-41. Go ahead."

"I've got eyes on the back."

"Copy. I'll make contact now."

Swezey left the cover of the tree and approached the target house, cutting through the lawn as he went. He climbed a few steps and took a position on the right side of the small porch. The screen was missing from the aluminum door. A porch light illuminated him. He reached up to unscrew the light bulb but noticed a sign underneath it—*John Cutler Investigations*. Swezey twisted the bulb, and the small landing went dark.

He reached through the aluminum frame to bang on the front door with a balled-up fist. He waited a few seconds and hammered the door a second time.

"Forty-two to forty-one."

Swezey keyed his radio. "Go ahead."

"I'm being watched," Peterson said.

Swezey leaned back and checked the windows. None of the curtains had moved. He transmitted again. "From which room?"

They dropped all pretense of radio etiquette. *"There's a car at the end of the alley on Belt Street,"* Peterson said. *"Looks like an older Ford Bronco."*

"You're sure someone is in it?"

"Hundred percent. They lit up a cigarette. I keep seeing the ember."

A dispatcher cut in. *"Sam forty-one and forty-two, would you like an additional unit?"*

Swezey hopped off the stairs and ran toward his car. "Forty-one, affirmative. Forty-two, stay where you are. I'm coming to you."

The radio chattered in his hand as Swezey ran. It only took a few seconds for him to return to his vehicle. Hugh Swezey yanked open the door and hopped inside. No interior light illuminated. The Mustang had been modified by Fleet Services to operate as an undercover vehicle. Its engine fired up, and Swezey dropped it into Reverse. He didn't turn on the headlights as he was concerned doing so might illuminate the community center.

Swezey continued in reverse until he passed Cannon Street. He slammed the brakes, slipped the car into Drive, and accelerated. The wheels spun on the wet asphalt. Swezey briefly eased off the gas until the tires caught then he applied more pressure. The car rocketed up Cannon.

He passed the alley. If the subject in the Bronco noticed him from the opposite end of the block, there was nothing that could be done. At least he was mobile now.

Swezey spun the wheel at Augusta Avenue and slowed. He didn't want the whine of the sportscar's engine to alert the driver of the Bronco to his impending arrival. The wiper blades flicked the rain from the windshield.

He turned south on Belt Street. Up ahead and perpendicular to the alley was a Ford Bronco. The brake lights were bright red; the driver was resting his foot on the pedal.

Swezey's vehicle crept forward. He grabbed the microphone from the under-dash radio and called dispatch. "Sam-41, a stop." He didn't wait for an operator to acknowledge him. "A mid-eighties Ford Bronco" before phonetically reading plates. Then he flicked on the emergency lights located behind the Mustang's grill. He flicked on the high beams since there was no spotlight to illuminate the driver.

Blue and red lights splashed over the Bronco, the neighboring community center, and the nearby homes.

Inside the Bronco, it appeared the driver was on a cell phone. He looked over his right shoulder, then calmly turned forward. He waved his hand as he spoke, but it wasn't frantic. Instead, it seemed emphatic, as if he were trying to communicate an important point.

Swezey switched the radio to bullhorn, grabbed the microphone, and stepped out into the rain. He remained behind the driver's door for protection. From the corner of his eye, he noticed Jay Peterson jogging toward the back of his car.

"Driver," Swezey said into the microphone. It was amplified through the bullhorn hidden under the Mustang's hood. "Turn off your engine."

The sportscar's passenger door opened, and Peterson stepped behind it.

Swezey couldn't hear if the Bronco's engine had quieted or not. The rainstorm was too loud. Overhead, lightning flashed through the night sky.

"He's still on the phone," Peterson said.

Swezey pressed the microphone's transmit button. "Driver, get off the phone."

The man in the Bronco stuck his left hand out the window and dropped a set of keys. However, it appeared he was still talking on the phone.

"Driver—"

"Gimme a minute!" the man yelled.

Swezey turned and looked around. Maybe the driver was calling for help. He eyed Peterson. "I don't like this. Watch our backs and call for additional units."

Peterson turned to face the north. When he spoke, his voice also came through the car's radio, "Sam forty-two, start additional units. We've got an uncooperative subject."

The dispatcher responded. "*Additional units to back. Be advised the vehicle is registered to Denzelle Wright. He has a Failure to Appear warrant on a misdemeanor assault.*"

Peterson glanced at Swezey. "Denzelle?"

"Denzelle," Swezey said through the speaker. "Show us your hands!"

Inside the Ford Bronco, it looked as if the driver had ended his call.

"*Sam thirty-eight,*" the patrol radio chirped. "*The subject is a member of the Dead Boys. Cancel the other units. We're headed their way. Only a couple minutes out.*"

Denzelle stuck his head out of the window and looked back. "Aw, c'mon, man! Gimme a fuckin' break."

"Show us your hands!"

The driver shoved his arms out of the window. "Let's get this over with," he shouted. "I got places to be!"

Chapter 25
2:28 a.m. PST

The third floor of the NorthTown parking garage was empty. John Cutler remained in his pickup and slowly drove around. This is where Tremaine said the whole thing started tonight. Cutler couldn't be sure at which walkway the shooting occurred —there were several.

He drove by them all, yet there was no evidence of a homicide—no cops, no press, and no cluster of witnesses. Usually, when everyone cleared a crime scene, there was detritus left behind. That flotsam and jetsam created by medics, firemen, and cops—latex gloves, bandages, packaging, or pieces of yellow tape. He'd seen plenty of crime scene garbage during his short time with Seattle P.D., however, the third floor of the parking garage was immaculate tonight.

Cutler suspected why. The mall had an image to maintain. It wouldn't want a shooting to mar its family-friendly identity. A janitor or other staff member would likely have cleaned it up.

He stopped his truck near a walkway and pondered his next move.

A small, white pickup with whirling yellow lights approached him. Sonic Security was written on the side of the vehicle. It looped behind Cutler's truck and stopped. A spotlight turned and pointed into the rear window.

Cutler cocked his head and watched his side mirror.

A young man approached. He touched the back of the truck like a police officer might do to the trunk of a car. The security guard stopped at the support rail behind

Cutler's head. He tapped on the window and motioned for Cutler to roll it down.

Cutler did so, and rain fell into the cab.

"Evening, sir. I'm Officer Koza. Mind telling me what you're doing here tonight?"

"I'm a private investigator." Cutler handed the guard a business card. "I'm working a case."

Koza held the card with both hands, one of them protecting it from the rain. His brow furrowed as he studied it. "Like a real private investigator?"

"As real as they come."

His face brightened. "How'd you get involved in that?"

"I used to be a cop. Then I fell into this."

Koza's eyes widened. "No shit?"

"Mind if I ask you some questions?"

"No, sir. What do you need?"

The guy didn't seem bothered to be standing in the storm, but Cutler figured his questions might take a while. "Want to get out of the rain? I've got an umbrella. Or maybe we can go over there under the awning?"

Koza looked up toward the walkway. "Yeah, sure. Let's go over there." He stepped back and let Cutler out of his truck.

The two men walked toward the overhang.

"There was a shooting tonight," Cutler said.

"Right over there." Koza pointed about a hundred feet away from where they were. "That's the case you're working?"

"Confidentially?"

Koza leaned in expectantly.

"But you gotta keep the secret."

"You bet." The guard crossed his heart with the business card. It was the type of gesture a kid might do.

The rain pelted the awning and created a frenetic

rhythm.

Cutler said, "My client was the man here earlier. The one who escaped the shooting."

"Get out!"

"He asked me to figure out what happened, to help prove his innocence."

Koza whistled. "Like that movie, *The Fugitive*."

"Just like that." It had been some time since Cutler had seen the film, but he didn't see any harm in agreeing with the guard.

"Why don't the cops think he's innocent? He didn't shoot that girl. We have the video."

"There was another shooting across town. He might have killed a man."

Koza whistled again. "Geez, that guy can't catch a break. What can I do to help?"

"He said he met his girlfriend at the food court. When they came out, a couple of guys shot at them. Is that right?"

Koza's face pinched. "Basically, yeah."

"What didn't he tell me?"

"I'm surprised he said she was his girlfriend. They sure didn't act that way. I mean, no offense to your client and all, but that lady was out of his league."

"Pretty?"

"More like classy. Like a million-dollar businesswoman." Koza whistled. "She had a briefcase and everything. And he looked like a—" Koza cut himself off. "Well, he's your client. You saw how he was dressed."

Cutler nodded.

"They didn't act lovey-dovey to each other either."

"How did they act?"

"Like it was a business meeting. She showed him some documents. Like super official." He stiffened and held out his hand to mime a handshake. "There were zero romantic vibes between the two of them. No hand holding or kissing. Zip." Koza snapped his fingers. "Oh, and the guys who shot her stole her briefcase. Well, one of them did. The other guy chased your client."

Cutler crossed his arms. "Why do you think they did that?"

"Stole the briefcase? I don't know, but I'll tell you this much; that U.S. marshal seemed more concerned about that than the woman getting killed. At least, I thought so. Maybe there were nuclear codes in there or something."

"A marshal was here?"

Koza grinned. "I know, right? Totally cool. Although, I didn't get to see his badge." He shrugged. "One of the other guys did. He said it was impressive. Still, it's super cool we got to work with a fed. You just missed him. He left like ten minutes ago. Maybe fifteen. The homicide detective, too."

"What did the briefcase look like?"

"Like a briefcase." The security guard held his hands a couple of feet apart. "I don't know how else to describe it." Koza shrugged. "The marshal and the detective checked out our footage of the attack. The only person who could be in there with them was Norah since she's the best operator of the system. She told me they sort of talked in code the whole time. The detective didn't do that when it was just us. He was cooler than the marshal, less uptight. The marshal wanted a copy of all the security footage for the night. Supposedly he's going to run facial recognition software on everybody or something. That's crazy, huh?"

Cutler nodded.

"At least that's what Norah said. I wonder what they'll find when they run my face through it." He smiled. "Anyway, what happened with your client? I'm supposing he's okay?"

"He's good. We're trying to get to the bottom of this is all."

Koza considered Cutler's business card again. "You took the test, right? The one to be a cop."

"That's right."

"Can I ask you for some advice?"

Cutler tapped the card in Koza's hands. "Call me this afternoon, and I'll give you any advice you want. Right now, I'm under a time crunch."

Koza held up the card. "Thank you, man. I appreciate it."

The two men left the protection of the awning and headed back toward their respective trucks.

Cutler climbed into his GMC and pulled out his phone. He found Tremaine's number and dialed.

Koza honked twice as he drove away. The whirling yellow lights quieted.

"Hey," Tremaine answered. It sounded noisy wherever he was.

"I take it you left the house?"

"I did. Thanks for the heads up."

Cutler rested an arm on the steering wheel. "What's really going on, Tremaine?"

"I don't understand the question."

"That wasn't your girlfriend who was killed."

"Sure, it was."

"I spoke with a NorthTown security guard. He described her as a high-class businesswoman."

"I've dated classy broads," Tremaine said. "I bet you have, too. Some of them get off slumming with guys like us."

Cutler rubbed his temples with his free hand. "She had a briefcase. She showed you some documents. What was that about?"

Tremaine clucked. "She's got a job, man, so she was showing off. You know how bitches can be."

"What's her name? What's she do?"

"Don't worry about it."

Cutler leaned back in his seat. "You got me mixed up in something, and you're not being straight."

"Relax. You're not mixed up in anything."

"The marshals were here and they've got copies of the security footage."

Tremaine was silent.

"Why are the feds investigating this shooting?"

"I don't know."

"If you don't tell me what you're involved in, I can't help."

"We're good, Cutler." A couple of beats passed before he added, "I appreciate what you've done for me, man. I mean it, but you don't need to do anymore."

The call ended.

Cutler dropped the phone onto the seat and watched raindrops run down the window. He should drop the whole matter and go home, but that felt like failing, and he hated that. He turned on the wiper blades and cleared the window.

Then Cutler dropped the truck into gear and accelerated toward the exit.

Chapter 26
0231 hours PST

Before Kurt Botzon could slip the gearshift into Park, Rachelle Walsh had already jumped out of the passenger seat. Her door slammed, and she trotted toward the Ford Bronco. Hugh Swezey and Jay Peterson stood with the now handcuffed Denzelle Wright.

Botzon left the microphone seated in the dashboard holder as he waited for the chatter to stop on the patrol radio. A couple of officers were out on a Domestic Violence call and had just taken a husband into custody. When there was a break in the radio traffic, he pressed the transmit button and said, "Sam-38. On scene."

He clicked off the engine, which killed the radio before a dispatcher could respond. The wiper blades stopped in mid-swipe. Droplets splashed against the windshield.

Botzon steeled himself for another blast of rain, then slipped out of the GMC Denali. His pants were soaked, and the SUV's heater had failed to dry them. His rain jacket did an adequate job of keeping any wetness from reaching his shirt, but it ultimately failed to keep him warm.

The whole night had soured his disposition, and he felt like taking it out on someone. Denzelle "Droop" Wright might fit that bill.

"Aw, fuck." Droop's face contorted. "The whole team's here."

"Don't be a bitch," Rachelle said. "When we heard your name, we had to come say hey."

Droop clicked his tongue against the back of his teeth

and faced Swezey. "You see the shit I gotta put up with her?"

He wore a Las Vegas Raiders jacket that was opened to reveal a white tank top underneath. His faded blue jeans were too baggy, and they sagged below his waist and exposed the plaid boxers he wore. It was likely Droop held his pants up from the rear with his cuffed hands. The jeans were too long and puddled around his Timberland boots. The man was one of the few Dead Boys to carry a nickname. His moniker was courtesy of a droopy left eyelid earned in a prison knife attack.

"What was he doing?" Botzon asked.

"Watching us." Swezey thumbed toward his partner.

Peterson lifted his chin in acknowledgment to Botzon. The two officers stood on opposite sides of Droop. They both lowered their heads slightly against the rain. Water dripped from the brims of their baseball hats. It was the same stance Botzon and Walsh used.

Swezey continued. "We were attempting contact on that house." He motioned toward the home at the end of the block, next to the community center's extended parking lot.

"Who lives there?" Botzon asked.

"Some private detective named Cutler. We got a call from dispatch that supposedly came direct from Ackerman. He thought Tremaine Brown might be there. It was kept off the air."

Botzon and Rachelle exchanged glances.

"Why'd they call you and not us?" Botzon asked. He was the corporal after all and a request from the captain should have gone through him.

"You were out on a contact or something."

"Why'd the captain think Tremaine was at this detective's house?" Rachelle asked.

"Supposedly, this detective came round one of the

crime scenes," Swezey said. "That's all dispatch had. Sort of crazy we found Denzelle here."

"This is some bullshit," Droop said.

Botzon smirked. "You know how many Dead Boys have told me that tonight?"

"Doesn't mean it's not true."

Lightning zigzagged across the sky. It seemed as if the rain came down harder then. It was probably Botzon's sour mood that made it feel that way. Water cascaded down the sides of his head. Seeing everyone else dressed appropriately made him angry at his shortsightedness.

Rachelle leaned into Droop. "What was your plan? Were you looking to ambush Swezey and Peterson? Maybe score some points with the crew?"

"No way." Droop shook his head. "You know me, Ray. I would never do something like that. I saw some dudes sneaking up on that house, and I wondered what was going on. That's all." He looked to Botzon now. "Come on, bro. You know I wouldn't do no harm to you guys."

"Subsequent to his arrest," Swezey said, "we found a loaded .38 underneath the driver's floormat."

Rachelle cocked her head. "Jesus, Droop. You're carrying? That's a felony and a parole violation. Sure looks to me like you were setting an ambush."

"If that was true, why was I sitting in my truck doing nothing? Huh? I gave up without a fight."

Peterson pointed into the alley. "You saw me down there. Maybe you were waiting for me to walk back and take a pot shot."

"Yeah," Rachelle said, "that'd be the perfect time for a pop and run."

Droop flopped against his vehicle. "Don't you bitches gotta read me my rights or something?"

A thought occurred to Botzon, and he turned to the

house on the corner. Then he looked up Belt Street to where the Mustang sat. "Did you see the Bronco when you arrived?"

Peterson said, "No."

Swezey shook his head. "I'm sure it wasn't there."

Botzon faced Droop. "How did you know Tremaine was supposed to be here?"

The Dead Boy's face tightened. "Lawyer."

He straightened and slapped his hands. "Shit."

Rachelle cocked her head. "What?"

None of them could ask any more guilt-seeking questions since Droop wanted a lawyer—even without advising him of his rights. What Botzon did now had to be done carefully. He eyed Rachelle. "We've been banging on the Dead Boys all night."

"So?"

"They're out looking for Tremaine, too."

"Okay."

"Maybe they're following us now in hopes of finding him through our efforts."

When Botzon looked at Droop, the man turned away. "Lawyer," he muttered.

Botzon eyed Peterson. "Call dispatch. Alert everyone for possible tails. The Dead Boys could have flipped the script on us. They want to find Tremaine as much as we do. I want to know why."

Peterson nodded. He stepped back from the group and lifted his radio to his lips.

"There's something else," Swezey said. "This guy was on the phone with someone when we contacted him. He stayed on for a while. We grabbed the phone pursuant to his arrest and searched it."

Droop looked at the officer. "You can't do that!"

"His last call was to J.R. Looks like all his contacts are in here by initials only."

The Dead Boy used his shoulders to push off the Bronco. "You sumbitch, I'll bust you—"

Botzon shoved him back against the vehicle. "Can it, Droop." He pointed at the man. "You got yourself into this situation."

Droop scowled. "I want my lawyer. You can't look at my phone."

"Mean mug me all you want. You'll get your lawyer soon enough. Chill out."

Rachelle moved closer to Botzon. "J.R. Jaxson Reader, maybe?"

"You got no proof I called anybody," Droop interrupted.

"Your phone says you did," Botzon said. "I bet the camera in the Mustang does, too."

It was a bluff; there wasn't a camera in the undercover car.

Droop's lip curled. "Doesn't mean shit." He turned away.

"Think that all you want, Droop." Botzon grinned. As long as he stayed away from guilt-seeking questions, he could stand here with the Dead Boy a little longer. He turned to Swezey. "There's a mutiny happening tonight."

Swezey crossed his arms. "Do tell."

"The Dead Boys are overthrowing their leader."

Droop tsked but didn't look their way. "You don't know nothing."

"Here's the rub," Botzon said. "These geniuses didn't consider a mutiny requires a conspiracy."

Rachelle lowered her head and fought back a smile. "Well, well, well. This just got bad for ol' Droop."

Swezey's eyes widened. "Oh shit, it did."

Droop furrowed his brow. "What are you guys talking about?"

Botzon faced the Dead Boy. "For a conspiracy to

work, everyone's gotta keep the secret. Everyone's gotta pull in the same direction. Understand? If it all breaks bad, everyone carries the same weight."

"So?"

"Tremaine was attacked tonight up at the mall."

The Dead Boy shrugged. "I don't know nothing about that."

Botzon waved off the comment. "A woman was killed. Maybe you knew. Maybe you didn't."

Droop said, "I didn't."

"I wasn't asking." Botzon looked at Rachelle. "Did I ask if he knew?"

She shook her head. "You didn't ask."

He turned to Swezey. "You hear me ask a question?"

Swezey thought about it for a moment. "No. No questions."

Botzon nodded. "Just clarifying." He turned back to Droop. "So the shooters got into a Chrysler 300 and a Dodge Durango. Interesting bit about the shooters—they're from California."

Droop swallowed with some difficultly. "Hey, bro, I don't know nothing about nothing."

"That's cool. I wasn't asking. We know they're members of the Vice Row Kings." He lifted a hand. "Don't bother denying you've never heard of them because I'm not asking if you have. I'm just stating facts. They were running with the Kings."

The Dead Boy looked away.

"But here's something you probably want to know. Something you should take into consideration when you talk with your lawyer. Jaxson Reader bought the 300 and the Durango. We got him linked to the ambush of Tremaine and a woman's murder."

Droop's gaze returned to Botzon.

"If there is a conspiracy to get rid of Tremaine, which

I think there is, that means anyone who helped goes down for the woman's murder."

Droop shook his head. "Listen to me, man. I wasn't a part—"

Botzon held up his hand. "Stop. You wanted a lawyer. I'm not asking questions. I'm just laying out the facts we know. You take your chances with the prosecutor, now. You know as well as we do he's got no history with you. To him, you're just a number. A stat on his log sheet." He looked at Swezey. "Call for a unit to transport him to jail."

Kurt Botzon headed toward the Denali. He was tired of the rain and wanted to get warm. Rachelle walked alongside him.

"Botzon!" Droop shout. "Hey, bro. Gimme a second."

"Too late," Botzon yelled over his shoulder. "You had your chance."

"Yo!" Droop hollered. "What if I tell you where Jaxson is?"

Chapter 27
2:33 a.m. PST

Tremaine Brown wordlessly paid the driver before climbing out of the taxi at the corner of Washington Street and Second Avenue. The Well lurked on the southwest corner—its neon signs now dark. A signal to downtown's drunkards that respite still remained a few hours away.

Tremaine wasn't where he wanted to be—that was still a block or so away—but getting out early was something he learned from observing the cops. They never drove to the front of their target. They always approached from the side. The cops got eyes on a target before attacking it. It was a good strategy and one he started using.

He pulled a Seattle Sounders baseball hat down on his head. Tremaine had purchased it from the convenience store at Maple and Maxwell. It was only a few blocks from Cutler's house. He had fled there after getting the phone call. Tremaine took enough time to grab his shoes from the dryer and snag Cutler's leather coat. Then he split out the back and ran down the alley.

Tremaine had called a cab from the convenience store. The clerk didn't even bother to worry about him while stocking the candy isle. The Middle Eastern man had undoubtedly seen stranger things than a guy in an oversized leather coat waiting for a ride.

When a police car drove westbound on Mission, Tremaine faded into the rear of the store. He wanted to avoid being discovered inside a Stop and Rob and arrested for the shooting at Altamont. He still wasn't sure if he hit anyone, let alone killed them, but the cops would certainly try to say he had been in possession of a gun. The more he thought about that, the more confident he was of it. If that were the case, the cops would surely arrest him for it. They wouldn't go easy on him just because someone tried to kill him. Most cops he'd known played the game as if every arrest was personal. He breathed a sigh of relief when a taxi finally pulled into the convenience store's parking lot.

Now, Tremaine strode southbound on Washington Street. His hands were shoved into the coat pockets, and his head bowed against the driving rain. He turned onto Third Avenue and walked toward the Baker Apartments.

They were low-rent units. Maybe they were something nicer to live in when they were built, but Tremaine doubted it. With apartment buildings like the Hope converted to condos and the Clairmont burning down years ago, it pushed the displaced poor to places like the Baker. It didn't take a real estate genius to know these folks didn't improve a place after moving in—they beat it to holy hell.

As a Dead Boy, Sidney Booker should be living in someplace better than the Baker, but this was considered his exile. The gang would have booted him out if the guy wasn't a legacy. His older brother, Micah, had taken a rap to protect Tremaine and several others and then was murdered while inside Walla Walla.

Micah had died for the sins of the Dead Boys, Tremaine thought, just like Christ had done for the world's sinners. He knew the story of the Son of God since his mother had preached it to him for so many years. Even though Tremaine didn't believe in the bible, it felt sort of blasphemous to compare Micah to Jesus. However, it was the most appropriate reference Tremaine could come up with whenever he thought of his former friend.

Sidney Booker was the long-term beneficiary of his brother's sacrifice. He was a terrible earner and a worse soldier—both sins in the world of the Dead Boys. Tremaine had been very close to Micah and promised the man that he would look out for his younger brother. The two men had similar troubles with Sidney and Dontari.

A homeless man pissed in the entryway of the Baker Apartments. The bum leaned his head against the wall. He swayed as if all his energy was consumed in keeping himself upright.

Tremaine pushed open the door and entered the hallway. The first level smelled musty. He bypassed the elevator and climbed the stairs. There were five levels in the building, and Sidney lived on the third.

This stop was a gamble, but Tremaine was looking for an oblique way to attack his problem. His mentor had taught him the meaning of that years ago by showing him a trick shot on a pool table. He pointed out several angles with his cue.

"Some problems require you hit them head-on," his mentor had said. "Others require you come at them from the side. Both are predictable lines of attack—front, back, left, and right. Understand? You need to learn to attack from new angles—to come in from the oblique. When you do that, your enemies are less likely to see you coming."

Tremaine had liked the word since he'd never met anyone who used it in conversation. For that matter, he didn't either. Tremaine never went to college, but he had hoped to do so. He was smart, read a lot, and was a gifted baseball player in school. When his brother joined the Dead Boys, Tremaine did as well in order to protect him. That's when he discovered a natural gift for the game. It came from a combination of intelligence, bravery, and leadership. He quickly rose through the ranks.

None of his trusted lieutenants or soldiers had answered or returned his calls tonight. He could have gone to one of their homes, but that seemed like coming at the problem head-on. After talking with Quentin, he thought he knew what all the trouble was about tonight. He just had to confirm it, and then he could figure out how to respond.

Oblique, he thought.

Tremaine entered the third-floor hallway. The lights were low, and his footsteps echoed on the hardwood. About a third down the corridor, he stopped at apartment 312. There was no peephole in the door.

He removed the gun from the back of his pants and hid it along the side of his leg. He didn't need some looky-loo sticking their head out of a unit and seeing him holding a weapon. Tremaine knocked with his left hand. The sound reverberated down the hall.

"What?" a groggy male voice called from inside the apartment.

Tremaine knocked again.

"Whozzit?"

"It's me," Tremaine whispered.

"Who?"

"Open up."

"Hold on."

Footsteps padded across the apartment. A bolt slid back before a lock turned. The knob spun, and the door opened.

Sidney Booker stood there in a pair of boxer shorts. He rubbed a fist into his left eye. "This better be good."

Tremaine shoved him. Sidney stumbled backward, tangled his feet, and fell into a heap. Tremaine stepped into the room and closed the door behind him.

"Hey, man," Sidney said.

"Stay down." Tremaine flicked on the light.

Sidney lifted a hand to shield his eyes. "What'd I do?"

The studio apartment stank like a man's unwashed funk. The kitchen was messy as if Sidney hadn't cleaned up after himself in days. Cereal boxes and a nearly empty milk container were on the counter. A pyramid of beer cans was on the stove.

A bong sat on the end table near the ugly couch where Sidney had been sleeping. The blankets gathered at the far end. On the wall was an eclectic mix of movie posters—*Baby Driver*, *Aquaman*, and *The Raid*. There were also several pin-ups of naked blond women—all had fake tits and deep tans.

It was a wannabe frat boy's apartment, and Tremaine hated it whenever he was forced to be there.

Sidney's attention snapped to the gun in Tremaine's hand. "What's going on?"

"I'm here for the truth, Bumbles."

Tagging Sidney with this nickname was a show of disrespect.

Sidney's face tightened. "The truth is all I ever give you, man." Tremaine leveled the gun at him, and the man flinched. Sidney lifted both hands as if they would somehow stop a bullet. "All right, all right! What did I do?"

Tremaine motioned with the gun. "Sit up. Put your back against the couch. Shove your hands in your pits."

Sidney scooted across the floor until he was near the ratty old sofa with its flower-print covering. He crossed his arms and stuck his hands under his armpits.

"What's going on tonight?" Tremaine asked.

"How do you mean?"

He pointed the gun at Sidney.

The man turned his face away and closed his eyes. "I wasn't doing nothing. You woke me."

"With the crew, Bumbles. What's going on with me?"

Sidney opened his eyes and faced Tremaine again. "How would I know? Nobody tells me nothing."

Tremaine frowned. "You think I'm stupid? Denzelle and Tariq still let you hang out with them. You think I don't know?"

Sidney briefly looked away. When his attention returned, his face hardened as if he were challenging Tremaine. "Maybe friends are more important than the crew."

"That's why you're an idiot."

"You think you're so smart." Sidney smirked. "Always talking down to me. Talking down to everybody, but you don't know nothing."

"All right, Bumbles. School me."

"I hate that name."

Tremaine lifted the gun once more. "Start talking."

Sidney shook his head. "You won't shoot me. It'll make too much noise and wake the neighbors."

The shot boomed in the small apartment.

An explosion of stuffing erupted from the couch cushion next to Sidney's head. He jerked away and stared at the hole. "Jesus!"

"Tell me again what I won't do."

Sidney returned to his seated position. He crossed his arms over his bare chest and stuck his hands back into his armpits. "Those guys wouldn't tell me what they were doing."

"They told you enough."

A moment passed, and Tremaine heard the ticking of a clock somewhere. He wanted to turn and search for it, but it didn't matter. Keeping Sidney worried about a bullet between the eyes was the most important thing in the world.

Sidney swallowed with some difficulty. "Don't shoot

me when I tell you."

"Spill."

"Denzelle said you were a rat."

Tremaine lowered the gun.

Sidney lowered his chin. "I know, right? That's what they said—just like that. Tremaine's a rat. Dontari, too. But I couldn't believe any of it."

"Where did Denzelle get that from?"

"He said Jaxson heard it straight from the Originals."

Tremaine clicked his teeth while he thought.

Sidney chuckled nervously. "When I heard that, I called bullshit. I was like, there's no way. Not Tremaine."

Everything made sense now. The shooting at the mall. The freeze-out by the crew. That's why everyone was in on it. The Originals had reached out to Jaxson to set the plan in motion. He was the most likely to take over the Spokane territory if something happened to Tremaine.

It pissed Tremaine off that he hadn't seen it sooner, but he was running for his life earlier. Survival was the most essential goal. He didn't have time to work out the whys and wherefores of the attack.

"Did Denzelle say anything more?"

Sidney shrugged. "Nah, man, that's it. Isn't that enough?"

"What about Jaxson?"

"What about him?" Sidney waved a dismissive hand. "He never comes around. We were never close. You know how it is. I only see my friends."

Tremaine nodded. Jaxson would have followed the rules about Sidney's exile—he never liked the man from the beginning. He was never Micah Booker's friend either. If Jaxson ever gained control of the Dead Boys, Sidney's days were likely numbered since he was a liability.

Right now, he was an estranged pet. The Dead Boys

kept him fed and housed because of his brother's sacrifice. That's what made this moment difficult for Tremaine. Micah's selfless act saved Tremaine and several others from prison, but he lost his life because of it. Tremaine and the Dead Boys owed Micah for that, and the only way to repay that debt was to take care of Sidney.

Tremaine knew what it was like to have an idiot brother.

He scratched his chin with the barrel of the gun. "If I walk out of here, will you call Denzelle and tell him we talked?"

Sidney laughed uneasily. "No way, man. I'll keep this myself."

"Because if you tell him anything, Denzelle will call the Originals. They'll know I know what's going on."

"What is going on?" Sidney's expression hardened. "It's not true, is it? You and Dontari aren't working with the feds?"

Tremaine leveled the gun.

Sidney's eyes softened and he smiled. His right hand slid from his arm pit and rested over his heart. "I'll take what we talked about to my grave, man. You got nothing to worry about. I swear on my life."

It was a lie. All of it. And Tremaine knew it.

A flare of regret passed through him. Legacy or no, there was no other way to handle this moment.

"I'm sorry, Bumbles."

"For what?"

"This."

Tremaine shot Sidney.

Chapter 28

Kurt Botzon and Rachelle Walsh raced toward a Rosauers parking lot. Their GMC Denali came off the Maple Street Bridge and swung onto Second Street, bringing them into the neighborhood called Browne's Addition.

They had left Hugh Swezey and Jay Peterson in the West Central neighborhood with Denzelle Wright. Patrol officers had yet to arrive at their location to transport the man on his outstanding warrant, but he'd given the SIU team actionable intelligence on Jaxson Reader's location.

For Botzon's entire life, the Brown's Addition neighborhood contained was the city's most eclectic mixture of Spokane's haves and have-nots. This was probably due to its proximity to downtown. Mansions lined the cliff overlooking the river. Once-exquisite estates were chopped up and turned into multi-unit, low-rent apartments. A cluster of trendy restaurants attracted visitors from other neighborhoods. In the center of it all lay a beautiful park that Botzon never visited except as a patrol officer to arrest homeless men on charges of lewd conduct.

Up ahead was the grocery store that Denzelle had told them about. The Second Avenue side of the parking lot was lined with large trees. The foliage along the Sunset Boulevard stretch was spread further apart, allowing them to see waiting vehicles.

Botzon swung left. He didn't slow as he raced along the boulevard. They caught brief flashes of cars in the lot. It was almost three now, so only the night crew was working.

A gray Cadillac Escalade sat with its nose pointed toward downtown. Its running lights were on, and its wiper blades swept rain from the windshield. The parking lot lights reflected off the top of the vehicle. A figure sat behind the steering wheel.

Botzon was about to point it out when Rachelle excitedly said, "There he is." She jerked her thumb toward the passenger window. "Like Droop said."

To curry some favor with Botzon, Denzelle Wright had stated Jaxson Reader was calling the shots from the Rosauers parking lot. He admitted the Dead Boys were looking for Tremaine but wouldn't explain why.

"Call it in," Botzon said.

She snagged the microphone from its clip. "Sam-38."

"*Sam thirty-eight*," a female dispatcher responded.

Botzon didn't focus on the communication with the radio operator. Instead, he slammed the brakes, and the Denali skidded to a stop.

A homeless woman with two shopping carts full of items blocked the entryway into the parking lot. She wore a black trash bag and didn't seem bothered by the raging storm nor the sound of the sliding SUV. The woman picked through the first cart as if there wasn't a care in the world.

Botzon glanced over his shoulder, but it was too hard to see the waiting Cadillac due to the angle of the trees lining Sunset Boulevard. Anxiety rose within him. He didn't want to honk his horn at the homeless woman and possibly alert Reader, but he couldn't drive around the two shopping carts. Trees were placed on both sides of this entry point.

"Whoever designed this landscaping was a moron," Botzon yelled.

The woman still hadn't looked in his direction.

Instead, she lifted a dirty teddy bear from the cart.

"There's another!" Rachelle pointed further west.

Botzon cranked the wheel and accelerated. The Denali jumped the curb before springing back into the street. They raced toward a second entrance located nearer the grocery store. The SUV bounced as it entered the parking lot.

The two vehicles were now at opposite points of the property. Botzon reached for the emergency lights but refrained from activating them. He wanted to wait until the last possible moment to turn them on.

The Denali had covered a third of the distance when the Escalade's brake lights winked off, and it rocketed forward. It cut through the landscaping and bounced onto Sunset Boulevard.

"Sam-38," Rachelle called. "A pursuit."

"*Channel is restricted,*" the dispatcher responded. "*Sam thirty-eight, go ahead.*"

The Denali jounced through the landscaping and narrowly missed colliding with a tree. The SUV rocketed into the street, its rear end swinging wildly on the west asphalt.

Rachelle's response came in stops and starts as she was thrown about her seat like a woman on the back of a bucking bronco. "Thirty-eight—we're in pursuit—Cadillac Escalade." She phonetically read the plate. When the Denali righted itself, she got the rest of it out. "We're eastbound on Second, just passing Maple."

There wasn't much traffic on the streets at that time of the morning, but they were running the wrong way down a one-way street. A car headed in their direction pulled to the side of the road.

Rachelle continued. "Sam-38, we suspect the driver is Jaxson Reader, who is involved in tonight's homicide."

"*Copy.*"

When the dispatcher didn't call for additional units to back them, Botzon knew why. Patrol officers were jumping onto the call via their Mobile Data Computers. The SIU team didn't have an MDC in the Denali, so their communication was done only through the radio.

The Escalade's brakes brightened a moment before it swung left onto Cedar Street. The SUV failed to manage the turn cleanly; it sideswiped a parked car, then corrected its trajectory.

Rachelle lifted the microphone. "The suspect is northbound on Cedar now. Hit a parked car at Second and—"

Botzon cranked the wheel and turned the Denali. Rachelle bounced off the window.

"Christ!" she yelled.

He stomped the gas, and the engine roared.

"Say again your last, Sam thirty-eight."

The two vehicles raced under the train overpass. The Escalade didn't bother to stop at First Avenue. Botzon slowed slightly to check for cross traffic before accelerating again.

"Passing First Avenue," Rachelle announced into the microphone. "On Cedar."

"Copy," the dispatcher responded. *"Captain is monitoring the call. Advise speed and road conditions."*

Rachelle leaned over to check the speedometer. "Fifty miles per hour. No traffic. Roads are wet."

Up ahead at Sprague Avenue, the road turned into a T. A patrol car appeared from the east with its emergency lights spinning. It turned and blocked the street. Now, Jaxson couldn't turn right and race downtown.

The Escalade slammed its brakes and jerked left to where the sharp turn abutted a drop-off to the Pleasant Valley community below. If the SUV successfully navigated the maneuver, Jaxson Reader could run north across the Maple Street Bridge or return to Browne's Addition. Unfortunately, Reader executed the maneuver too late for the vehicle's speed and the road's condition.

Botzon jammed his brakes and gripped his steering wheel. "No!"

The Escalade's front right tire caught the sidewalk curb and folded underneath the vehicle. The SUV's momentum pushed it forward and sheared off a fire hydrant. In a blink of an eye, the vehicle was across the sidewalk.

It disappeared over the cliff's edge as water erupted from the hydrant.

Chapter 29
0249 hours PST

Quinn Delaney stood just inside the command vehicle door and watched Chief Dillon, Captain Ackerman, and Lieutenant Brand. The three men sat around a small table in the middle of which was a single portable radio. They were quiet as a couple of SIU officers pursued a suspect believed to be involved in the night's events.

The captain was also on his cell phone with a radio dispatcher. He had just asked for an update on speed and road conditions.

"*Sam thirty-eight,*" Rachelle Walsh called. "*Cedar and Sprague. Another collision. Suspect vehicle is off the cliff.*"

Dillon smacked the table. "Goddamn it!"

Brand jumped, but Ackerman simply turned away and resumed his telephone conversation with the dispatcher.

Walsh continued. "*Start fire and medics. Advise a supervisor. Also.*"

"*Go ahead, Sam thirty-eight,*" the dispatcher said.

"*We've got a sheared fire hydrant out here. Start the water department.*"

The chief slid out from behind the table and stood. He bent and looked through the window. "Are we done here?"

Brand looked up at him. "Sir?"

"Are we needed here any further, or can we move this heap over to the calamity SIU just created?"

"No, sir," Brand said. "I mean, yes, sir. We can move it."

"Then let's get going." The chief straightened. "I'll let

the press know what's happened. They're going to love us for the ratings boost." His attention swung to Delaney. "Right. The feds. Thank you for that piece of good news, Delaney."

Quinn opened his hands. "They're letting us run with it."

"Beware of Greeks bearing gifts."

Lieutenant Brand started to slide out of his seat, but he paused. He was a stickler for the chain of command, so the chief talking directly to Quinn would likely create some consternation in the man.

Dillon rubbed his forehead. He looked as tired as Quinn felt. "How'd this marshal seem?"

"Like a guy doing his job."

"You get the feeling he was trying to lay something off on us?"

"I believe what he said. If this situation could have been contained, they would have done just that, but it's out of control."

"*Sam thirty-eight*," the dispatcher called. "*The water department has been notified.*"

The chief waved at the radio. "Your point has been made."

"What's that?" Ackerman said into his cell phone. He covered his open ear with his hand. "Say again." He turned away from everyone.

Dillon watched the captain for a moment, then faced Quinn. "This guy who went off the cliff."

"Sir?"

"How's he fit into the investigation?"

"If it's Jaxson Reader, like they say, he's the guy who bought both cars used in the shooting."

Chief Dillon's frown deepened. "Then let's hope he's not dead. That'd be the cherry on top of this shit sundae."

Lieutenant Brand grimaced.

Ackerman lowered his phone. "Chief? We got another body."

"Is it a full moon and someone forgot to tell me?"

The captain continued. "Dispatch sent an officer on a disturbance call at the Baker Apartments. They've just confirmed one dead."

"Why do I feel there's a punchline coming?"

"Name of Sidney Booker. He's in the system as a known member of the Dead Boys. Looks like he took a round to the chest. Maybe that blood we've been expecting is finally getting spilled."

"About time." Chief Dillon bent and looked out the window again. "Where are Parker and Johnson?"

"They just left for the station," Brand said. "They're starting the warrants for the vehicles and the hotel."

The chief eyed Ackerman, then Brand. "How do you guys want to handle this Baker situation?"

The lieutenant said, "I'll call in Nash and Higgins. We could use the full team tonight."

Quinn raised a hand. "I'll take it. I'm out here anyway, and it's probably connected."

"You're tired," Brand said, "and you've already got one."

"We're all tired, Lieutenant, and what're we going to do if something happens not connected to this event? You should save Nash and Higgins in case that happens."

The lieutenant seemed taken aback by Quinn's recommendation. His gaze flicked to the chief, then the captain.

"It's a good suggestion," Ackerman said, "but it's your call, George. Either way works."

Quinn tapped his chest. "I've got it."

Brand pointed at Quinn. "Sold."

The captain returned his attention to his phone call.

Chief Dillon moved closer to Quinn. "So I get this

right, your marshal said they were building a RICO case on the ODBs?"

Quinn nodded. There was something odd in the chief's look. "Does that seem odd?"

"Sure, it does. He told *you* but didn't bother to tell any of us." Dillon motioned toward Ackerman and Brand. "Doesn't that bother you?"

"I guess." Notifying a detective rather than the administration reeked of unprofessionalism if nothing else.

"It *should* bother you. The reason he did it is deniability. The higher up the food chain this goes, the less ability there is to walk away from it."

Quinn didn't understand what the chief was saying. Criddle couldn't walk away from it; he knew about it, so he was involved.

Dillon must have sensed Quinn's confusion. "Right now, the upper echelon of the marshal service can deny any of this is happening. The U.S. Attorney's office can deny it, too. We've got no proof of anything. Just some marshal who talked to a detective at a crime scene. A mall parking garage. He's Deep Throat, for Christ's sake. If this mess goes bad, who's any the wiser?"

Ackerman ended his call and handed Quinn a slip of paper. On it was the address for the Baker Apartments, a unit number, and the name Sidney Booker.

Quinn looked up to find Chief Dillon still waiting for an answer to his question. "No one is the wiser" was the best he could muster.

The chief didn't bother looking at Brand or Ackerman before continuing. "No one will be held accountable, and that bothers me. We're running around cleaning up a mess started in California, brought to our city courtesy of an Assistant U.S. Attorney, and no one has the courtesy to stop by and tell us why."

Quinn remained still. He wanted to leave and begin his investigation. This felt like he was in the middle of some administrative quagmire. It was beyond his pay grade. He liked solving crimes. He had no interest in political maneuvering or its outcomes.

His gaze dropped to the scrap of paper he held.

"Are we ready to move, George?" the chief asked.

Brand struggled to get out from behind the table. "I'm on it."

"I thought we'd be moving by now."

"In a minute, sir." The lieutenant squeezed by Quinn on his way out the door.

"Detective," Dillon said.

"Sir?"

"Keep us updated on what you find at the Baker. I've got a sneaking suspicion not much is what it seems tonight."

Quinn nodded. He opened the RV's door and stepped outside. For once this evening, he was happy to be back out in the dark.

Chapter 30
0309 hours PST

A group of firefighters gathered around the crumpled Cadillac Escalade. It was lodged upside-down against a cluster of trees. All its windows were busted or missing. The men and women who descended the hill did so without the aid of rappel lines; it wasn't too steep to traverse by foot.

The firefighters could have walked down the set of stairs off to the west and then cut over when they reached the same level as the upside-down rig, but Kurt Botzon figured that wouldn't have been as cool as running down the hillside.

He and Rachelle Walsh stood on the sidewalk and observed the commotion. Behind them, several patrol cars blocked the nearby streets—the officers were responsible for redirecting civilian traffic.

Two fire trucks idled alongside the Sprague Avenue curb. The sound of their engines combined with the storm to create a constant hum—a mixture of man and nature—that made hearing the activity below difficult.

Flood lamps were set up along the sidewalk to illuminate the hillside. Cascading rain angled through the rays of light.

A towline was brought down by one of the firefighters, who tugged on it to create additional slack. The winch at the front of one of the fire trucks unwound further.

It appeared a firefighter said something to Jaxson Reader, the driver of the Escalade. Then the man looked up the hillside and hollered, "Cancel the board."

Three more patrol cars pulled on scene. Botzon knew it was abnormal to have this many available units at this time of the morning, but the power shift teams had been held over. These officers wanted to witness the debacle.

"How much trouble are we in?" Rachelle asked.

Botzon shoved his hands into his pockets. The administration would find a way to make this collision about them. He didn't want to voice that negative opinion right now, so he shrugged. "What'd we do?"

"Are you serious?" Rachelle faced him. Water ran off the edges of her hat.

He sort of hated her now for wearing that hat. Either they both should have one, or they should suffer the same fate together. He blinked against the falling rain, and water flowed down his forehead.

She pointed over the hillside. "The pursuit ended with Jaxson down there. We're not even a marked unit. They're going to crucify us for that." She waved her other arm along Sprague Avenue. "And we've got a goddamned circus here."

He shook his head. "It's not that bad. It's maybe twenty feet down there."

"More like thirty!" She sounded hysterical now.

Botzon smiled. His former girlfriend would have told him the hysterical thought was sexist.

"The fuck are you smiling at?"

"Nothing."

"You think this is funny?"

"No." He didn't think any of it was funny. Especially not Jaxson Reader sitting in an upside-down Escalade. The administration would surely question SIU's lack of forethought in pursuing a vehicle through rain-slicked streets. He could hear it now.

"Maybe we should take a trip."

He looked at her. "Excuse me?"

"You and me. When they suspend us, I mean. Let's take a trip. Like Morgan did."

"They're not going to suspend us."

"It doesn't have to be anything dirty. We could go someplace warm just as friends."

Botzon didn't think he could handle taking a trip with her as a friend. The department's rumor mill definitely couldn't handle it.

"I'd be on my best behavior," she said. "Cross my heart." Rachelle made an X between her breasts.

He rolled his eyes. She was crazy. Botzon's ex-girlfriend would tell him that was a sexist comment too, but he felt he could back up the claim with Rachelle. Her invitation to take a trip was insane for too many reasons to count. Maybe it was the stress of the moment that caused the suggestion.

She turned to observe new activity along Sprague Avenue. "Oh, this is bad. Real bad."

Botzon didn't bother looking; whatever she saw, he didn't want to know.

He was still trying to formulate his response for when the chief arrived. Word was the mobile command post was enroute. As far as Botzon was concerned, the SIU team caught Jaxson Reader, which meant something following tonight's events.

The guy was the lynch pin for this investigation. Jaxson connected the California shooters to Tremaine Brown. Jaxson could answer the questions of why everything had happened tonight and who put the shooting into motion. The man was clearly okay since one of the firefighters had told him to stay in the vehicle. Botzon hoped Jaxson could be interviewed and not tucked away in some cushy hospital room.

Botzon squinted against the rain as the firemen moved back from the Escalade's driver's door.

"The press is here," Rachelle said.

"Good. Let them get wet like the rest of us."

One of the firefighters yanked on the driver's door, and it popped open. Two other firemen reached inside.

"Oh, great." Rachelle smacked his arm. "And the battle van just showed up. I guess we're ground zero now."

Botzon still refused to look away from the upside-down SUV. He would deny the arrival of the brass for as long as he could.

"I'm gonna let you do the talking, Corporal Botzon," Rachelle said. "That's why you get paid the big bucks."

The firefighters helped Jaxson Reader emerge from the Escalade. He appeared shaky at first. The man draped his arms around the shoulders of the firefighters until he got his legs underneath him. They exchanged some words. The firefighters nodded, their helmets bobbing as they did so.

Jaxson looked up the hillside. He lifted a hand to shield his eyes from the flood lamps.

"No," Botzon muttered.

"What?" Rachelle said.

He sprinted toward the stairs off to the west.

"Where you going?" she called.

Jaxson shoved a firefighter out of the way. He ran around the front of the Escalade and loped toward the bottom of the hill.

"Stop!" Botzon yelled. He leaped the stairs two at a time. When he reached a landing, he bounded it in a single step before launching down the stairs again, doubling them up as he went.

Behind him, Rachelle yelled, "Sam-38, foot pursuit!"

Off to Botzon's right, Jaxson slipped on the hillside and fell to his butt. He immediately hopped back to his feet and ran into the trees. Some of the light from the floodlamps trickled through the thicket, but the man had become a shadow.

Botzon reached the bottom of the stairs and frantically searched for Jaxson Reader, shining his own flashlight at the foliage. Rain slashed through the white glare wherever he directed it.

They were in Peaceful Valley, the community that sat directly below downtown and along the river.

Footsteps trampled down the stairs. Rachelle continued to update dispatch on their location. Botzon should call his own pursuit, but with her so close behind, he could focus on catching Jaxson.

He spotted the man a quarter block ahead. Botzon leaned forward and ran. "Stop! Police!"

Jaxson didn't heed the warning, though, and continued to run in the middle of the street. The man had not trained, though, and it was clear he was already gassed. He loudly sucked for air, and his strides were stumbling and erratic. Yet he didn't stop.

"Northbound on Cedar," Rachelle yelled, "approaching Clark! Get a car down here!"

Botzon got near enough that he could have tackled Jaxson, but he shoved the man in the back instead. Jaxson's arms windmilled, and he stutter-stepped as he tried to regain his balance. It was like watching a kid on roller skates for the first time. Eventually, Jaxson fell to the street.

That's when Botzon pounced on him.

Jaxson fought to escape by twisting and turning and elbowing Botzon in the head.

Had this been a year ago, Botzon would have slipped his arm around Jaxson's throat and put the man to sleep with a Lateral Vascular Neck Restraint. However, the Washington State legislature removed that tool from his metaphorical toolbox. So, Botzon was left with blunt force strikes. He kneed Jaxson in the side.

"You're under arrest," he yelled. "Stop resisting!"

Jaxson rolled over and punched him in the head.

Rachelle entered the fray then. She reached for Jaxson's arm, and he punched her in the stomach. She reached for the arm again.

Botzon kneed the man once more. "Stop resisting!"

Rachelle also kneed him, but on the other side. "Stop fighting!"

Jaxson punched Botzon in the chest.

Botzon pushed off the man and stood. "Clear!"

Rachelle rolled away.

Jaxson lay on his back, surprised the fight had ended suddenly.

Botzon yanked his gun from his holster. "Stop resisting, or I'm going to shoot you."

"Fuck you." Jaxson rolled over and prepared to run again.

Botzon kicked the man in the ankle.

"Yow!" Jaxson dropped onto his back and grabbed his leg. He rolled around as he held his ankle. "Abuse!"

Botzon holstered his gun and hopped back onto Jaxson. He grabbed an arm and twisted it behind the man's back. Jaxson flopped to his belly. Rachelle snatched the other arm, and the two ratcheted a pair of handcuffs around Jaxson's wrists.

"I want your names," Jaxson yelled. "I want your badge numbers!"

Botzon stood. "You're under arrest. You have a right to an attorney."

He shook his head. This wasn't how he wanted things to go. They might not get anything from the guy at this point. He walked away and spat.

The administration might have a legitimate reason to stick their foot up his ass now.

Chapter 31
3:11 a.m. PST

John Cutler parked in front of his house. When he turned the engine off, it seemed like the rain fell harder. He paused for a moment as it splattered against his windshield, then he bowed to rest his head against the steering wheel. It was only a short run to the front door, but Cutler was exhausted.

As a private investigator, he occasionally worked into the wee hours, but it was rare. If that type of activity was planned, he might nap to prepare his body and mind. The younger version of himself could operate a full twenty-four hours without sleep. At fifty-four, he could not pull it off without considerable discomfort.

After leaving NorthTown Mall, he drove aimlessly around for some time. He didn't want to give up on the Tremaine problem, but he couldn't figure out the next step. There was no one in the police department for him to talk with anymore.

Wasting gas while driving in ever-elongating circles while hoping to discover a next step didn't do anything but make Cutler feel like a failure. He'd had enough of that in his life and this profession. He certainly didn't need to feel that for an ungrateful bastard.

Tremaine had told him to drop it. If Cutler wasn't working the problem for Tremaine, who was he doing it for? Cutler knew the truth—he was doing it for himself. He didn't like feeling that Tremaine had played him somehow. Cutler still wasn't sure how the guy had done it, but it felt like Tremaine had gotten one over on him.

The story Tremaine told Cutler earlier in the night was

filled with half-truths. Cutler wanted to know where the lies stopped and the honesty started. Unfortunately, he might never get to know that.

Cutler pushed himself upright and poured himself out of the truck. He shuffled toward the front of the house with his head bowed and shoulders hunched. The storm distracted his sense of hearing, but the exhaustion certainly dulled his alertness. He failed to realize he wasn't alone until he reached the steps leading to his front door.

He spun and reached for the gun tucked into the back of his pants, but it was too late.

Two black males stood about six feet apart. Both had guns clutched in their fists. Neither was dressed for the weather, and rain splashed against their faces.

"Don't," the first man said. He was tall and wore a Buzz City jersey over a long-sleeved white T-shirt. Both pieces of clothing stuck to him. "Open up and get inside."

Cutler left his gun tucked in the back of his pants and raised his hands. His house keys dangled in the left. "I don't have anything of value."

Buzz eyed the other man and then jerked his head. It happened quickly, but Cutler was alert now and ready for what was about to come.

The second man transferred the gun to his left hand. He wore a white hooded sweatshirt with no logos. His black jeans were too long and bunched at his tan boots. Even though he was heavyset, the man was surprisingly quick.

Heavy stepped forward and reared back with his right hand. Cutler shifted his weight and brought his arms up to protect his face, so Heavy kicked him in the shin. This surprised Cutler, and he lowered his guard. Heavy punched him across the chin, which dropped Cutler to the ground.

"Just like that," Heavy said. He stood above Cutler like a conquering gladiator.

Cutler didn't lose consciousness, but he lay there on the edge of it. He felt helpless. There were no other emotions except that one, and he was being swallowed by it.

"Get his keys," Buzz said.

Heavy snatched them from Cutler's hand. He ascended the stairs to the front door and unlocked it. While the fat man did that, Buzz pulled the gun from Cutler's pants.

"Hey." Heavy tapped on the sign attached to the house. "You see this? This guy is a detective or something."

"We'll ask him about it inside. Open the door." Buzz kicked Cutler in the ribs. "Get up."

It took effort to stand. Cutler felt like throwing up. The fat one had caught him good. Cutler shuffled toward the stairs. They moved past Heavy and into the house.

"Grab a seat," Buzz said.

Cutler headed toward his chair, the one behind the desk.

"No." Buzz grabbed his shoulder and shoved him into one of the folding chairs that the customers sat in. "You sit there."

Cutler dropped heavily into a chair.

Heavy closed the door behind them. "This place is a shit hole. I'da figured a detective would have a nicer place, like they do in the movies."

Buzz pulled Cutler's desk chair back and sat. He opened the middle drawer, put Cutler's gun inside, and closed it. "Is he right? You a private detective or something?"

"License is on the wall."

"No shit?" Buzz turned to read the permit. "A real-life

private dick. Why they call you guys that, anyway?"

Cutler had looked it up shortly after becoming an investigator and knew a couple of theories about its etymology. However, now didn't seem the time to discuss it or to make a snarky joke, so he shrugged.

Buzz returned his attention to Cutler. "All right, man. I'm going to give you one guess as to why we're here. Get it wrong, and my fat friend is gonna take off your head."

Cutler looked over his shoulder, expecting to see Heavy waving a fist. Instead, the man leveled his gun at him. He faced Buzz and told the only truth he knew. "Tremaine."

"Winner, winner, chicken dinner." Buzz leaned back in the chair and set his feet up on the desk. "Why did the man come here?"

"He wanted some dry clothes."

"You two friends?"

"We haven't spoken to each other in years."

Buzz glanced at his partner. "But he came here?"

"He said he had nowhere else to go."

"Why's that?"

"Apparently, someone ambushed him tonight."

"And he came to you?"

Cutler turned his palms upward.

"I don't get it. How do you guys know each other?"

"It's hard to explain."

Buzz picked up his gun—a 9mm Smith & Wesson—and pointed it at Cutler. "Try."

Both men were too far away for Cutler to attack. He'd be shot before he got close. His best bet was to keep talking and come up with a way to separate them or to change their positional dynamics within the room. "Tremaine's mother had a friend," Cutler said. "That friend was my friend, too. This was years ago. He asked me to keep an eye out for Tremaine."

"Like a concerned uncle?"

"Something like that."

Buzz pursed his lips. "Okay, Uncle Detective, where's Tremaine now?"

Cutler shrugged. "I don't know."

"Do I really need to keep threatening you with this?" Buzz pointed the gun at Cutler again.

"He was here," Cutler said. "And now he's not."

"We know that," Buzz said. "The cops arrested our brother around the corner. He was watching them watch this house. We wanted to know if all that hullabaloo had anything to do with Tremaine, so we staked it out. Then you showed up." Buzz leaned forward. "So where did he go?"

Cutler shifted in the chair so he could see both men. "I don't know."

"How do you mean you don't know?" Buzz said. "He didn't tell you? Or are you playing dumb?"

"I thought he was still here." Cutler let a beat pass before adding, "In the house."

Buzz's eyes narrowed, and he looked sideways as if he were listening. Outside, the storm continued. In the distance, thunder rolled. He snapped his fingers and motioned for Heavy to come closer. Quietly, he said to the heavy-set man, "Search it."

Heavy hunkered and moved into the room off to the left.

Buzz twirled a finger—a signal to restart the conversation. "Tell me a story, Uncle Detective."

"About?"

"How a guy gets into the business of snooping through people's dirty laundry."

"I fell into it."

Buzz looked toward the kitchen. It was as if his

paranoia peaked with the idea that Tremaine was hiding somewhere in the house. His gun lay on the desk, and his hand covered it.

"How's a guy fall into this business?" Buzz asked.

"I was a cop before."

Buzz's face hardened, and he lifted the gun. "In Spokane?"

"Seattle."

Heavy returned to the room. He walked while in a crouch and continued through to the kitchen. Beyond that was Cutler's bedroom and the bathroom.

"And you quit?" Buzz asked.

"I was fired."

"For what?"

"Conduct unbecoming."

"Doing wrong shit, huh?" Buzz lowered the barrel of the gun. "How'd that happen?"

"A girl."

"You lost your job over some pussy?" Buzz set the gun on the desk, but his hand remained on the butt. He looked over his shoulder toward the kitchen. "You went from Seattle cop to Spokane dick? That's not a career path you hear about every day."

Cutler remained quiet. Heavy would return from the back of the house soon. There was only the basement left to search. Perhaps they would abandon the idea that Tremaine was still there. If that happened, then Cutler missed his window to make a move. He had already seen a couple of chances to grab the weapon. They weren't great opportunities, but they were better than the alternative.

If he didn't try to escape, he knew the outcome—they would shoot him. He had to do something soon.

Heavy returned to the kitchen with his gun still clutched in both hands. He shook his head.

Buzz eyed the door in the living room, then faced Cutler. "What's that?" he whispered.

Cutler hesitated. Right now, he needed to sell his response. He closed his eyes and looked away. "Basement," he said.

Heavy crossed the room and opened the door. He entered the narrow stairwell and stepped onto the first wooden step. It creaked.

Buzz looked over his shoulder. His hand rested over the gun on the desk. "Quiet," he whispered.

Cutler leaned forward slightly and brought his legs back so the weight shifted to the balls of his feet. His calf and thigh muscles engaged.

The stairs sighed again as Heavy took another step. Buzz twisted further in his chair to watch his partner descend into the darkness of the basement.

Outside, another crash of thunder punctuated the night.

Cutler jumped. His hands clasped the gun, and he rolled into Buzz's lap. Both men were in the chair now. Buzz brought his arm around Cutler's waist and fought to gain control of the gun.

"Jalen!" Buzz shouted.

There was a commotion on the narrow stairwell as if Heavy tumbled down the remaining steps.

Cutler kept his hands on the gun but elbowed Buzz in the head. He struck him again with the same elbow.

"Jalen!"

Cutler yanked the gun back and forth. A round exploded from the barrel. The slide racked and tore skin from Cutler's hand. He twisted the gun and felt Buzz's trigger finger break. The man screamed in pain.

"I'm coming," Jalen called from the basement. He sounded winded. "I'm coming!"

Buzz snaked his free arm around Cutler's chest and

tried to jerk away. Cutler planted his feet and drove himself into Buzz. The chair banged against the desk. Cutler threw his head backward. It crunched into Buzz's nose, and the man howled with pain.

Footsteps clambered up the stairwell.

Cutler yanked the gun free from Buzz's injured hand.

Jalen reached the top of the stairs. He held onto the door frame and leaned into the living room like he was in a Hollywood action film. The gun he held arced widely across the room. His eyes widened when he realized Cutler already had a bead on him.

Two shots hit Jalen in the upper chest, and the man flopped backward. The body tumbled down the stairwell.

Cutler tried to push off the chair, but Buzz latched onto him now. The man bit into his shoulder and Cutler grunted in pain. They wrestled for control. Their feet sought purchase on the ground, and the chair repeatedly bounced against the desk.

Cutler grabbed the gun with both hands—one over the barrel and one on the grip—and reached around his left side. It was a contact maneuver he had trained while on the department many years before. It minimized slippage and reduced the likelihood Buzz could take the gun from him.

The Smith & Wesson touched Buzz's midsection. Cutler squeezed the trigger. Buzz screamed and released his hold.

Cutler jumped from the chair. He racked the slide because the weapon had not cycled due to his hand holding the barrel. Cutler lifted the gun and covered Buzz.

The man slid from the chair and fell to the floor. He moaned as he held his side. "Get me to a hospital."

Cutler pulled his phone from his pocket and punched in two numbers. He hesitated to press in the final digit.

"What's this about?"

Buzz grunted, then screamed, "Hospital!"

"What's Tremaine got himself into?"

"Call the cops! I need a hospital!"

Cutler lowered the phone. "Tell me what's going on, or I'll let you bleed out."

Buzz glared at him but didn't speak.

"I'm serious," Cutler said.

Several seconds passed before Cutler lifted the phone and pressed the last digit. The call was answered after single ring.

"Nine-one-one. What is your emergency?"

Andrew Parker tossed a notebook onto the small table. "You want anything?"

Jaxson Reader picked at something on the white wall. It might have been a dried paint bubble or a piece of dirt that got rolled over. Whatever it was, Reader concentrated on it like it was the most important thing in his universe. His fingernail repeatedly pulled at it.

"You called your lawyer?" Parker asked.

Reader scratched his face with his other hand as he continued to work on the wall with that fingernail. "Left a message."

Parker dropped into his metal chair and studied the man across from him.

Reader's left eye was swollen shut, and his lip was cut. A bloody scrape ran from his forehead into his hairline. It was difficult to tell which injuries came from the rollover crash and which came from the struggle to get away from the SIU officers. The man's clothes were soaked from his time in the rain, and he dripped water onto the interview room's linoleum floor.

Parker flicked the video switch to start the in-wall camera. "They read your rights at the scene?"

"Uh-huh." Reader leaned closer to the wall. He studied it as if he were an archeologist unearthing a rare find. "But I ain't sayin' shit until my lawyer gets here."

"I get paid either way." He pointed up at the red light. "We're being recorded."

"The fuck for?"

"So you can't say I did something inappropriate."

Reader smirked. "You cops are a bunch of jumpy bitches."

The two men fell silent for a time. The only sounds in the interview were the ticking of the overhead clock, the hum of the heating unit, and the occasional drip of water to the floor. Eventually, Reader tired of the white wall, and he shifted in his seat. His gaze passed over Parker and continued toward the opposite end of the interview room.

Reader acted as if he had all the time in the world. Based on his record, he'd been in many interview rooms before, so this wasn't his first face-to-face with a detective. The man knew what to expect. All he had to do was drag things out until his attorney arrived.

There was no reason for Parker to rush the moment. Reader's request for representation meant Parker couldn't ask any guilt-seeking questions. Besides, hurrying through an interview led to sloppiness. There was too much at stake at this moment. Three people were dead, and Quinn Delaney was investigating another murder that might be tied into the night's events.

Usually, Parker's partner would join him in an interview of this magnitude. Since Reader wanted a lawyer, the two detectives agreed to split the duties. Parker would make a run at the Dead Boy while Johnson continued to finish the warrants. They would run them to the on-call judge, then search the impounded cars.

Leads on Tremaine Brown's whereabouts were still coming in. He was the suspected shooter in the Third and Altamont killings. Parker wanted to be available when units snagged him if there was any chance to interview him today.

Reader shifted in his chair, and its legs scraped on the floor. His left hand was cuffed to the bar running the length of the short wall. There was no way the man was making a break for the door.

Parker cocked his head. "You might have gotten away if you were smarter."

It was an aggressive statement. He would not have made it so early with another suspect, but this was a lieutenant in the Dead Boys. His feelings weren't going to be hurt; even if they were, the guy had already requested counsel. There wasn't much that could be lost with that assertion.

Reader's lip curled, yet he remained silent.

"We tied you to the NorthTown shooting through the cars you bought. You should have used a shill."

"A what?"

"A middleman. Someone to buy the cars instead of you."

"You mean a bitch."

"Tuh-may-toe, toe-mah-toe."

Reader shook his head. "Man, I don't know what you're talking about."

"The Dodge Durango and the Chrysler 300. Both sellers say it was you."

"Someone lied." Reader tapped the table with his free hand. "They must have used my name. What's that called? Identity theft. I didn't do the shit you're accusing me of."

Parker considered the denial. It was a possibility and one he would circle back to for no other reason than to close the loop. He or Johnson would take a photo array and ask the previous owners to identify the man who purchased their cars. He had no doubt it was indeed Reader who did the deals. The man was simply throwing up chaff.

"Maybe," Parker said with a dismissive wave.

"Maybe nothing." Reader slapped the table, then pointed. "Believe that."

"Doesn't negate the fact some hitters went after your boss."

Reader's eyes hardened, and his lips pressed together. His left hand gripped the railing, and his right held on to the table. He looked like a man holding on to the edge of the world.

"You okay?" Parker asked.

"Still waiting for my lawyer."

"Me, too."

"Then you can stop talking any time."

"Don't you want to know what we know?"

"Not really." Reader looked to the upper corner of the room like a petulant child. "You can shut the fuck up for all I care."

Parker crossed his arms. A moment ago, Reader grabbed the railing and the table when he mentioned the out-of-towners had ambushed Tremaine. It was a topic Parker should continue to poke around. He just needed to be careful how he did it.

"We talked to a lot of Dead Boys tonight," Parker said. "Not one of them showed any concern for the fact Tremaine was ambushed. That seems odd. Like, if someone went after the chief of police, I'd get pretty pissed about it."

Reader didn't look at Parker. His gaze remained firmly planted in the upper corner of the room.

"Because he's our leader, and that's what you do for the guy taking the heat."

"Right." Reader sniffed.

"Tremaine must have done something to piss you guys off."

Reader glanced at Parker, but he didn't say anything.

"Or maybe he pissed off the California contingent."

"Contingent?"

"Group. Maybe Tremaine pissed off the Originals and

they sent up some hitters from the Vice Row Kings to whack him."

Reader pushed his chair away from the table, then slid down until his head rested on its back. He stared up at the ceiling. "Got any food?"

"What do you want?"

"A burger. Maybe some fries." He lifted his head and looked down his nose. "Jack in the Box is still open." His eyebrows rose in a hopeful expression.

"I'll get you some chow if we talk, but I'm not rewarding you for shutting me down."

Reader returned his head to the back of the chair. "Never mind."

The door to the interview room opened, and Johnson stepped in. "We need to go."

Parker turned in his chair. "Why?"

"Patrol is out with a couple shooting victims. One of them is DOA."

"So? Let the brass call in the Old Dogs. We got our own situation."

Johnson tilted his head toward Reader. "They're Dead Boys."

Reader straightened in his chair. "Who?"

"No idea yet. They attacked a private investigator in his home. It didn't turn out well for them."

Parker eyed Reader. "Know who they are?"

Reader didn't answer. Instead, he slid back down into his chair and returned his gaze to the ceiling. His jaw tightened, and his eyes narrowed.

"If you're not going to talk, you can wait for your attorney over at jail. Get up."

Parker stood and waited as Reader languidly got to his feet. Both detectives worked to unhook the man from the metal railing, then cuffed his hands behind his back.

"Text me the address," Parker said to Johnson. "I'll

meet you there after I book him.”

Johnson stepped out of the way and let Parker and Reader pass.

“C’mon, princess,” Parker said. “Your fairy castle awaits.”

Chapter 33

Tremaine huddled in the darkened doorway of the downtown building. Not much traffic was on First Avenue. A few minutes ago, sirens ran south of his position. He had a good idea where the cops were headed.

After shooting Sidney, Tremaine left the Baker Apartments and walked northbound on Washington Street. He thought about stopping under the railway underpass to get out of the storm, but that would leave him exposed and in the open. He needed to get off the street.

This was a good hiding spot, though. To the north was a parking lot. On the other side was Sprague Avenue and its row of now-closed businesses—PM Jacoy's, Mootsy's, Lucky's and Chicken N Mo. Tremaine had spent money in each of them at one time or another. With their lights off, only Mootsy's yellow front door stood out.

He peeked out from his hiding place, and rain splashed against his head. No one was coming from either direction on the sidewalk. He leaned back into the shadow and removed his phone from the leather jacket. All Tremaine wanted to know was the time. He slipped the phone back into his pocket. An invisible weight dropped on his shoulders, and he suddenly felt tired.

Tremaine was out of options. None of the Dead Boys had taken his calls. Certainly, he had built an ally or two during his time as leader, but if the Originals had labeled him a rat, he would have been ostracized. Anyone talking with him would risk the marker, too. He didn't feel like running through his phone's contacts once more in hopes of finding someone who might not believe what they heard. Tremaine didn't have friends or family outside of the Dead Boys—the gang had been his entire life and now it was gone.

He crossed his arms and leaned a shoulder against the building. The fatigue ate at him. Maybe he should find somewhere to rest—to get a cup of coffee and something to eat. That would allow him to rally. He'd have to leave downtown to do that. There was a Perkins on Division that ran twenty-four hours. A plate of syrup-covered pancakes sounded good right about then.

Whoever was hunting him wasn't resting, nor were they dreaming about food. He believed that in his heart because if he were in their shoes, he'd press his advantage. They had Tremaine on the ropes.

Maybe he should try to call one of the girls again. They hadn't taken any of his calls, but he couldn't imagine any of them out hunting for him. They weren't soldiers; they were comfort and occasional accomplices. What would he expect to get from them? He already got most of the story from Sidney. Maybe one of the girls could color it in, but they wouldn't know for sure. They'd be too far removed.

His phone rang, and he jumped. The ringer sounded extremely loud at this time of the morning. Tremaine silenced the phone as he pulled it from his pocket. The screen identified the caller as DeWayne. The son-of-a-bitch was finally calling him back.

Tremaine answered it with an angry, "Yo."

"Hey, T. Where you at?"

"Like I'm gonna tell you, motherfucker."

There was a pause on the other end.

Tremaine leaned out of the doorway to check for anyone on the sidewalk. Had they figured out where he was hiding? No one was coming from either direction. He straightened and hid back in the shadows.

"Shits out of control," DeWayne said.

"Tell me about it. Where you at?"

"Driving around."

"Looking for me?"

Another pause. "I was, yeah, but not anymore."

Tremaine covered his open ear with his free hand. He thought he heard the thwip-thwip-thwip of wiper blades. So, DeWayne was telling the truth—he was driving around. Tremaine dropped the hand covering his ear. He didn't want to miss any nearby sounds.

"Why'd you call?" Tremaine asked.

"Because this shit is all wrong. Has been all night."

"Maybe you're trying to mess with my head. Convince me to step out so you can take a kill shot."

"If that's what you think, I can hang up and pretend we never talked."

Now, it was Tremaine's turn to pause. He lost his train of thought while watching the rain splatter into a puddle near the curb.

"T?" DeWayne asked.

Tremaine shook himself back into focus. "You alone?"

"I wouldn't be calling you if I wasn't."

He reached behind his back and touched the gun he'd stolen from Cutler. "Where you at?"

"Downtown."

Tremaine looked up and saw the yellow door on the other side of the parking lot. "Meet me at Mootsy's."

"It's closed."

"No shit. Stop in front of it."

"Right."

Tremaine didn't need to cover his ear to hear the revving of DeWayne's engine. "How long will it take you to get here?"

"Two minutes. Maybe three."

"See ya." Tremaine hung up.

Maybe DeWayne really reached out in good faith, but more likely it was a setup. There was no way to know for sure. If the order was to shoot Tremaine on sight—which was the assumption based on what occurred at the mall— he needed to approach DeWayne with extreme caution.

There wasn't much time now.

Sprague Avenue was a one-way which meant the DeWayne's vehicle would come in from the east. Tremaine couldn't cross the parking lot because DeWayne would have plenty of time to see him.

Tremaine tugged the gun from his waistband. He hopped out of the doorway and sprinted westward. His shoes slapped the concrete and caused little explosions of water with each step. He turned right on Stevens and sprinted an entire block toward Sprague Avenue.

Fear lanced through his chest when he crossed the street. He was exposed now, and he had just told DeWayne where to find him. He was heading in this direction and would arrive any moment.

Tremaine jumped onto the sidewalk but didn't slow. He bolted for another block until he reached Riverside, then he cut right. Riverside was a two-way street. Perhaps DeWayne was driving along this stretch of road to get to Mootsy's. Tremaine repeatedly looked over his shoulder. There were no headlights behind him, nor were there any ahead.

He slowed to a jog. Tremaine made it to the end of the block and turned right onto Washington. He was finally headed back toward his hiding position. Tremaine ducked in and out of doorways as he moved. When he made it to PM Jacoy's convenience store, he glanced around the corner to where Mootsy's was.

Twenty feet ahead sat an idling GMC Yukon. Its brake lights were lit, and light-colored exhaust drifted up from the tailpipe. Tremaine looked down Sprague Avenue for a trailing vehicle. Was someone waiting to pop out and shoot him when he approached DeWayne?

Tremaine stepped around the corner. He crouched and hurried toward the driver's side of the car. When he reached the door, he tapped the window with his knuckle.

DeWayne jumped in his seat, then rolled down the window. "Yo, man. Get in."

Tremaine pointed the gun at him.

"Hey, T." DeWayne leaned away from the weapon. "I called you, remember?"

"Gimme yours." Tremaine snapped his fingers.

"Yeah, sure."

"Be smart about it."

DeWayne reached between his legs and lifted a Glock, pinching it between his thumb and forefinger. He handed it to Tremaine by the barrel.

Tremaine tucked the new gun into his armpit. "Scoot over. I'm driving."

DeWayne slipped the Yukon into Park before climbing into the passenger seat. "This ain't necessary. I'm on your side."

"Yeah? Why'd you wait until now to call me?"

Tremaine opened the door and climbed in. He tucked the Glock into a side compartment before rolling up the window. The Yukon's interior was warm. Tremaine wanted some answers but staying downtown was just asking for problems. They needed to get rolling. He dropped the SUV into gear and pressed the accelerator.

"Hey, man," DeWayne said. "What are you wearing?"

"Don't worry about it."

"You look like an old white man."

Tremaine wanted to head to the South Hill and the

safety of his apartment, but he worried the cops might be waiting for him. If not the cops, definitely some of the other Dead Boys.

"Explain it to me," Tremaine said.

DeWayne leaned against the passenger door. "They said Dontari turned, and you turned with him, too."

"Who is they?"

"The Originals."

"And you believed it?"

DeWayne shrugged. "They said they had proof. They got a mole in the attorney general's office or something. They said you were going to take the whole gang down."

"They said, they said." Tremaine gripped the steering wheel. "You ever stop to ask who they are?"

DeWayne furrowed his brow. "Huh?"

The Yukon stopped at a red light.

Tremaine eyed the other man. "You think I turned?"

"That's what they said." DeWayne cringed. "You know what I mean."

"That wasn't my question. Do you think I turned rat?"

DeWayne hesitated to answer. "Not really but what could I do? Jaxson and the others were all pressing hard that you did. And you know the rules."

Tremaine did. When he was kid, the saying was *Snitches get Stiches*, but when he joined the Dead Boys it changed to *Snitches get Ditches*.

DeWayne continued. "Jaxson said the Originals had proof." He pointed out the window. "Light's green."

Tremaine spun the wheel, and the SUV turned left. "Who'd they bring up to do the job?"

"Four hard bastards from the Vice Row Kings."

"Outside help?" Tremaine eyed him. "What the fuck for?"

"In case shit went bad. They needed—"

Plausible deniability, Tremaine thought.

"An alibi," DeWayne said, "in case shit broke bad. The Originals did a job for them in return."

"You met them?"

DeWayne looked down and nodded. "Rashard, Spencer, Malcolm, and Christian."

"And Jaxson ran point on this operation?"

"What were we supposed to do?" DeWayne asked. "He was next in line. We followed his lead."

"Where they at?"

"Where who at?"

"Jaxson and the hitters."

DeWayne sniffed dismissively. "The whole thing is a mess now. You killed two out east—Rashard and Spencer."

Tremaine cast a sideways glance. "They were in the 300?"

"And now something is going on with Tariq and Jalen."

Tremaine frowned. Tariq and Jalen were soldiers in his crew. "What?"

DeWayne threw his hands in the air. "I don't know. They were supposed to be watching some house near the community center. Nobody heard from them in a while, so one of the girls drove by to check on them. She said there are cops everywhere now."

"The West Central Community Center?"

"That's the one."

Tremaine spun the steering wheel and headed north on Post Street. He was careful not to break the speed limit. He didn't need to call attention to himself. "Why were they watching that house?"

"Denzelle followed some of those SIU pricks there. He was on the phone with Jaxson when one of them stopped him. Jaxson wanted us to find out why that house was so important."

Tremaine smacked the steering wheel. It was Cutler's house. He was sure of it. Cutler had warned him to get out because the cops were on the way. "Why were you following the cops?"

"They have been kicking us like dogs all night. Jaxson figured it was because of you. He wanted us to start spying on them if they were looking for you as much as we were. Maybe we would get lucky."

"What would you have done if you found me?"

DeWayne shook his head. "Man, I wouldn't have done nothing. I'm just trying to survive out here."

Tremaine stopped asking questions then. He'd have to decide how to handle DeWayne later.

The wiper blades punctuated the silence with their constant *thwip-thwip-thwip*. It only took a few minutes for them to make Maxwell Avenue. The SUV hummed westbound and passed A.M. Cannon Park. As they rounded the curve where the avenue turns into Pettet Drive, the police activity in front of Cutler's house was visible.

"That's Tariq's car," DeWayne said. He pointed out the window. "That must be..." His words trailed off, but he didn't look away.

Tremaine wanted to get closer to confirm Cutler was okay, but it was too risky to do so. If Tariq and Jalen didn't make it out alive, that meant Cutler had overpowered them somehow. The old, crafty bastard still had some moves. Losing a couple of his men didn't make Tremaine happy, but they should never have gone to Cutler's home. He would never have sent them there.

The Originals were responsible for this. So was his lieutenant.

"Where's Jaxson?"

DeWayne eyed him. "The cops have him."

"How'd that happen?"

"A pursuit or something. One of the boys saw them towing his car off that cliff in Browne's Addition."

Tremaine left Pettet Drive and drove slowly through the neighborhood behind Cutler's house. His world had caved in on him tonight, and he wanted vengeance. His hands tightened around the steering wheel. He would never get revenge on Jaxson now that he was in custody, but he'd take the next best thing.

"The Kings in the Durango," he said.

"What about them?"

"Where are they?"

"In a hotel on Sunset Hill."

The Yukon jumped when Tremaine stomped the accelerator.

Chapter 34
0336 hours PST

The elevator jerked to a stop. When the doors opened, they revealed a difference in floor heights of nearly an inch. Quinn Delaney stepped into the dimly lit hallway of the Baker Apartments.

Regardless of the strange hour, most of the floor's residents stood just inside their apartments and watched the activity outside apartment 312. They wore various types of sleepwear, and most had baggy eyes and mussed hair. A couple appeared wide awake as if this hour in the morning was their normal waking time. Many nodded or said some form of "Good morning" to Quinn as he walked past them.

Officer Josh Hernandez leaned his back against the wall. He lifted his chin in greeting. "Must be homicide Friday."

"Technically, it's Saturday."

"Whatever. I'm still on the same shift."

Standing on both sides of the open door were SIU officers Hugh Swezey and Jay Peterson. Both were wet and appeared exhausted. They nodded but refrained from saying anything.

Quinn stepped closer to the doorway but did not enter the apartment. A black man wearing only plaid boxer shorts lay in the middle of the apartment. The coffee table was not aligned with the couch the way most people would place it. Two pairs of blue rubber gloves sat near the body—a set on each side.

He eyed Hernandez. "Fire was here?"

"I requested them upon revival. They have to confirm

he was dead since the powers that be don't trust us to do it."

Quinn eyed the rubbish around the body. "Would be nice if they learned to pick up after themselves."

Swezey lifted his chin. "They'd need a modification to their contract. Probably call it janitorial duties or something and get paid more for it."

Quinn pulled a pair of latex gloves and a set of booties from his pocket. "So this guy is connected to the Dead Boys?"

Swezey motioned into the apartment. "That's Sidney Booker. Went by the moniker of Bumbles."

"I didn't think the Dead Boys were big on nicknames."

"They aren't, but this guy was a fuck-up."

"And the Dead Boys kept him around? That was nice of them."

Swezey shook his head. "They owed his brother, Micah. About ten years back, before Jay and I got on the team, Micah took a fall over a drug rip of the Dog Town Titans. Whole deal went bad, and two men ended up in body bags. Someone was going to get hit with a double murder charge, and Micah took it to protect the Boys. As soon as he landed in Walla Walla, he was marked. The Titans bought a hit and got their pound of retribution. Taking care of Bumbles was the Boys paying tribute to Micah."

Quinn finished tugging on his booties. "So Sidney getting whacked means what?"

Peterson yawned. "Guy must have known something."

"But what?" Swezey asked. "Guy wasn't in the loop for shit." He faced Quinn. "From what we know, they kept Sidney around like a pet, but Tremaine didn't let him play in their reindeer games."

Quinn frowned as he pulled on the first latex glove.

"You guys go inside the apartment?"

Both Swezey and Peterson shook their heads. "We waited in case you had questions."

Quinn's gaze shifted to Hernandez. "Did you get the names of the firefighters who walked in?"

The officer patted his left breast pocket. "Got 'em right here. I'll include it in my report."

"You're on the log," Quinn said. He worked his hand into the second glove.

Hernandez smirked. "Two in one shift. I'm the prom queen."

"You need us for anything else?" Swezey asked.

"No," Quinn said.

"We're going to head over to the scene Parker and Johnson just picked up."

Quinn raised his eyebrows. "Any ideas what that one's about?"

"Who knows? Some private investigator shot a couple home invaders that turned out to be Dead Boys. Seems their whole world is falling apart tonight."

The SIU officers patted Quinn's back before they headed toward the elevator. The residents lining the hallway smiled and greeted them much the same way they had the detective.

Quinn turned his attention to the small apartment. Before entering, he examined the unit one more time.

There weren't any wet footprints on the hardwood. He would have hoped some transfer would have occurred, but they were on the third floor. Anyone coming to this unit would have walked to the elevator, stood in the box for the slow ride, then made their way down the long hallway. Or taken the stairs. Either way, that was plenty of opportunity for any rainwater to be knocked off their shoes.

Quinn didn't notice any blood or other evidence near

the doorway. He spoke over his shoulder to Hernandez, "I want you to witness my entry."

"All right."

"Which means write what you see and hear. Got it?"

"Not my first rodeo."

Quinn crossed the threshold and stopped. The apartment stunk of body odor.

His gaze drifted to the small kitchenette. Dirty bowls were stacked in the sink. Opened cereal boxes and a mostly empty jug of milk huddled together on the kitchen counter. Several cans of beer created a pyramid on the stove.

A ticking clock caught his attention, and he found it hanging above the doorway. He checked it against his watch and saw it was seven minutes late.

Movie posters hung on the walls—*Aquaman*, *Baby Driver*, and *The Raid*. Quinn had heard of *Aquaman* but hadn't seen any of the movies. There were also photographs of naked women that appeared to have been magazine centerfolds.

A red plastic bong sat on the coffee table. A lighter and plastic bag of marijuana sat nearby.

Quinn considered it all then—the cereal, the beer, the movie posters, the nude pictures, and finally, the bong. It was the apartment of a sexually frustrated teenager—not a twenty-something Dead Boy.

"Bumbles," Quinn muttered. Gang monikers were often odd, but not usually derogatory. Bumbles certainly sounded disparaging. He wished he would have asked the SIU officers about it before they left.

"What'd you say?" Hernandez asked.

"Nothing."

Quinn moved closer to the body and squatted.

Sidney Booker lay on his back after being shot in the chest. It was a significant wound, but there was no way to judge the caliber. That was only done in bad movies and cheesy TV shows. Sidney's eyes stared up at the ceiling. His arms were splayed out to the side as were his legs. It was a strange pose as if he flopped back and threw out his arms and legs simultaneously.

Quinn's attention shifted to some white cottony substance on the hardwood near Sidney's head. He stood and moved around the body to get a better look. That's when he noticed a hole in the couch cushion. It was hard to spot at first due to the flowery pattern on the fabric. He squatted again and touched the material next to the bullet hole.

Could the round have been from the exit wound in Sidney? Quinn wondered. Or was it something else?

He looked over his shoulder. "How many shots were reported?"

"Two," Hernandez said. "And the witnesses say they were pretty far apart."

Quinn moved to where he believed the shooter would have stood in front of Sidney Booker. He held his arm out in front of him and extended his thumb and forefinger into an imaginary gun.

What had the killer wanted?

Quinn considered the apartment again. It didn't seem the man had much for anyone to take.

Maybe this was a crime of passion. Perhaps Sidney got involved with another man's woman, and the jealous boyfriend had shown up to exact revenge.

The two shots the witnesses reported didn't make sense in that case. It appeared there was only one wound on the man. So, was the first shot a warning? If so, why?

If taken as a standalone homicide, the shot might not mean anything.

Yet an ambush at NorthTown Mall led to a pursuit through the city that ended in the killing of two out-of-state gang members. Now, Sidney Booker was murdered, and two Dead Boys were shot in the home of a private investigator.

That meant this single bullet in the couch wasn't likely a stray or a misfire. It was supposed to scare Sidney Booker into talking about something.

What could a guy like Bumbles know?

Quinn grunted once, then left the apartment. All he could do now was wait for the forensics team to arrive.

Chapter 35
0354 hours PST

Parker slammed the door of his Chevy Impala after climbing out of the driver's seat. It was early in the morning, and the residents along this strip of Spofford Avenue should likely be sleeping, but he was tired and growly. He jerked the raincoat hood over his head and trudged toward the house.

The downpour continued. Droplets splashed onto the plastic hood, creating a crazy rhythm in his ears. He passed several patrol cars as he headed toward the west end of the block.

On the south side of the street was A.M. Cannon Park. Parker cast a disinterested glance in its direction. Half of his vision was blocked by the hood. No one was in the park—the time of morning and the rain shower guaranteed that. It seemed the only vehicular traffic out now was the cops.

When he arrived at the target house, he ducked under a line of yellow CAUTION tape and motioned toward an officer holding a clipboard. No words were exchanged since the woman appeared as miserable as he felt. Parker continued toward the house and ascended a small flight of stairs. On the wall next to the door was a sign that read *John Cutler Investigations*. Even in the low light of a single bulb, the sign appeared weather-beaten and sun faded.

Parker stepped inside an aluminum screen door then reached for the doorknob. However, the front door opened. SIU Officers Jay Peterson and Hugh Swezey stood in the doorway. Both seemed surprised to see

Parker standing there.

Peterson grinned. "You're late to the party."

Parker moved to the edge of the small landing and motioned for him to go. "Move your ass."

Peterson's smile faded. "Always a pleasure, Parker." He hurried down the steps and into the rain.

Swezey followed his partner. "Better late than never, right?"

He watched the two men walk down the sidewalk. Parker wanted to holler something snarky but decided against it. He was tired and didn't have the motivation to get into it with the two SIU officers. He needed to conserve what little energy he had left for more important duties.

Parker stepped inside and closed the door behind him. He first noticed how small the front room felt with five adults standing there. It would have felt like a crammed subway car with the other SIU officers.

Also present were Jessie Johnson, Kurt Botzon, Rachelle Walsh, and a white male around fifty that he assumed to be the homeowner—John Cutler.

Parker immediately disliked the private investigator. The guy seemed arrogant with how he stood with his hands casually shoved into his pockets. He didn't even break his account of events to acknowledge Parker's entry. Instead, Cutler's gaze shifted and coolly took him in—judging Parker the same way cops did unknown suspects who entered their sphere of influence.

On the nearby metal desk was a disassembled Glock. Next to that was a large plastic bag containing a dismantled Smith & Wesson. The desk chair was pushed against the wall and had blood on it. There was a red stain on the carpet near the desk.

A door behind the desk led to a basement below. There was blood spatter on the stairwell wall.

Johnson stood with his notebook out and nodded as Cutler spoke. Walsh studied the detective as if she didn't want to miss a single detail. At least, Botzon acknowledged Parker's entry with a wink.

"We wrestled for the gun," Cutler said.

Johnson nodded. "That explains how Tariq got the broken finger."

Cutler grunted an affirmation. "About that time, the big fella came up the stairs and popped his head around the corner." He pointed at the doorway behind the desk. "It was an easy shot, maybe five feet away."

Botzon leaned to Parker. "Jalen Gregory is at the bottom of the stairs."

Parker shuffled around the group so he could look down the stairwell. A fat man lay near the bottom of the steps; his feet were above his head. Blood pooled on the concrete floor.

"How did Tariq get the bullet in his side?" Johnson asked.

"We were still in the chair," Cutler said, "and he was fighting to stop me from getting free. Since I couldn't create distance, I used a contact hold—" He mimed grabbing a gun by the grip and barrel. "—reached around to his side and fired."

Johnson raised his eyebrows. "Where'd you learn that technique?"

"In-service training."

Parker cocked his head. The others seemed to have the same reaction as he did. In-service training was the term police officers used for continuing education.

"You were a cop?" Johnson asked.

Cutler took a moment to respond as if he were weighing his answer. "Long time ago. In Seattle."

"How'd a Seattle cop get tangled up with Tremaine Brown?" Botzon asked.

"It's a long story."

Parker crossed his arms. "Make it short."

Cutler's eyes narrowed. "I had a friend who liked Tremaine's mother. Before my friend's death, he asked me to look out for Tremaine. Short enough?"

Parker pointed down the stairwell. "This was you looking out for him?"

"That was self-defense. Tremaine came asking for help. I told him to stay here while I checked on his situation."

Botzon snapped his fingers and looked at Rachelle. "That's why Ackerman sent Swezey and Peterson here."

She didn't turn in his direction. Instead, she focused intently on Cutler. "Where's Tremaine now?"

"How would I know?"

"Call him."

Cutler pulled out his phone. He searched for a number and dialed it. He tapped a button and switched the phone to speaker mode. Even though it rang loudly through the small room, everyone moved closer. After the third ring, the call was answered.

"Hey," Tremaine said.

Cutler looked up from the phone. "Hey to you."

"You okay?"

"Why do you ask?"

"I heard they sent some guys after you."

Cutler frowned. "You heard that?"

"A little birdie told me. So you're good?"

"I am. They're not. How are you doing?"

"I'm fine."

Rachelle mouthed, "Ask him where he is."

Cutler nodded. "The cops want to know where you're at."

Botzon and Rachelle threw their hands in the air.

The phone was silent for a bit. It sounded as if

Tremaine might be driving. There were road noises and the sound of wiper blades swishing across a windshield.

Eventually, Tremaine said, "Tell them it'll all be over soon."

The call ended.

"That was stupid," Rachelle said.

Cutler shrugged a single shoulder. "You said to ask where he was. I did."

"He's responsible for two deaths," Botzon said. He held up two fingers. "You should have played ball with us."

"The way he described what happened, it would be self-defense." Cutler thumbed toward the hallway door. "Same as what happened here."

"You're not a judge. You don't get to make that call."

"Maybe not, but I get the feeling you've already judged him."

Botzon stepped forward. "I should arrest you for interfering with an investigation."

"I was attacked," Cutler said. "Or are you thinking I ambushed two guys in my own house?"

"Enough." Parker waved a hand. "You two—" He motioned to Botzon and Walsh. "Out of our crime scene."

They started to protest, but Parker said, "You can wait for him outside. When Johnson is done, you can ask him more questions. Right now, we're investigating a homicide."

Botzon glared at Parker as Walsh exited. He slammed the door on his way out.

Parker inhaled deeply to calm himself. He then forced a professional smile. "All right, Mr. Cutler. Let's start from the beginning. What time did Tremaine show up at your house tonight?"

Chapter 36
3:57 a.m. PST

"That's the place," DeWayne said as he pointed up ahead.

"You're fucking kidding," Tremaine said.

He flicked on the Yukon's brights. The headlights shone on the rapidly approaching pylon sign. A large looping, yellow arrow pointed toward a set of clustered bungalows on the opposite side of the highway. A font reminiscent of the 1950s announced that *You found THE HIDE-A-WAY! Spokane's best kept secret.* Most of the sign's paint was faded or chipped.

The black and white reader board near its base advertised *Air-Condition/HBO/Clean Sheets.* An orange neon sign announced that they currently had a vacancy available.

The two men were westbound on the Sunset Highway, or what the state called US 2. On their left was a motor lodge, a concept way past its prime. Tremaine had never stayed at this one, but he was familiar with them because of his mother. His family stopped at places like this when they traveled while he was a boy. His mother preferred motor lodges as her parents had stayed in them when she was little.

The bungalows were laid out in a small campus setting. Overgrown trees were interspersed among the buildings giving it a dark, haunted feel. Vehicles were in front of most of the cabins. This place likely had a fair amount of activity before the freeway came through and stole all the traffic.

DeWayne turned toward Tremaine. "What's wrong?"

"The Hide-a-Way?"

The wiper blades swiped rain away from the windshield. DeWayne bent to check out the pylon sign. "Jaxson thought it best to have the two teams in separate locations." He grunted a positive-sounding affirmation. "The Originals thought it was a good idea, too."

Tremaine cast a sideways glance. "They did, huh?"

DeWayne leaned slightly to observe the motel as they drove past. "Uh-huh," he said absently. His gaze tracked with The Hide-a-Way. When his eyes landed back on Tremaine, his eyebrows rose, and he straightened in his seat. "But that's what Jaxson said. I don't know."

"You and Jaxson are tighter than I remember."

"No, man. Not really. Jaxson didn't say that shit to me. Denzelle told me. I was never in the need to know. I'm low-level."

They continued westbound.

DeWayne glanced over his shoulder. "You're not stopping?"

"What else did Jaxson say?"

"How would I know?" DeWayne waved a hand. "I swear. I'm not in the loop. Denzelle was the one who told me everything."

"Who reached out to who?"

"What do you mean?"

"Did Jaxson start this process, or did the Originals reach out to him?"

DeWayne furrowed his brow. "He never said. But it's got to be them, right? If they think you're a—" DeWayne didn't say the word.

A strip of asphalt that connected the eastbound lanes was ahead. A sign announcing *No U-Turns—Emergency Vehicles Only* quickly approached on the left. Tremaine checked his rearview mirror, slowed, and made the illegal maneuver.

"Before all this went down," Tremaine said, "why didn't you warn me?"

DeWayne looked at him and swallowed. "They said you were a rat." His voice was small.

"They said."

"Yeah, that's what they said."

Tremaine slowed and entered the parking lot of The Hide-a-Way. The GMC Yukon pulled around to the back. A single cabin had its lights on. A Dodge Durango sat in front of it. He stopped the vehicle and turned it off. "Get out."

"What are we going to do?"

Tremaine grabbed his gun. "We're going to talk with the hired guns."

"Why do I need to go?"

"Because I said so."

DeWayne seemed confused, but he nodded, nonetheless. "All right. Yeah. Okay."

"You run, and I'll shoot you."

"Where the fuck would I run to?"

"You say anything I don't like, and I'll shoot you. Understand?"

"I get it."

"Right now, I've got nothing to lose."

Tremaine slipped out of the truck. He kept the gun pointed at DeWayne as the man left his seat. The two met at the front of the vehicle.

The rain continued to fall. DeWayne hunched his shoulders against the downpour, but Tremaine ignored the inconvenience. He had more immediate concerns. He waved the gun. "Knock."

DeWayne stood in front of the door labeled #7. He lightly rapped on it with his knuckles.

Tremaine pressed against the side of the bungalow.

"Whozzit?" a voice called from inside.

"DeWayne Taylor."

"Who?"

"Jaxson sent me." DeWayne flashed a thumbs-up signal to Tremaine.

A lock unlatched, and the knob turned.

Tremaine moved then. He stepped behind DeWayne and shoved the man forward.

The door swung fully open, and DeWayne stumbled into the arms of the out-of-town man. He was tall, and he wore a San Jose Sharks jersey and black jeans. A gun fired, and DeWayne screamed. His body writhed in the Shark-man's arms.

Tremaine aimed carefully and fired. The top of Shark-man's head exploded, and blood fanned over the room.

DeWayne and the dead man fell to the floor. DeWayne continued to scream.

Tremaine peeked into the room. There were two beds—on the closest was an opened briefcase with papers spread about. On the other was a gun. At the opposite end of the room was a bathroom—he could see a towel rack and a painting of an owl.

A man in a black club shirt and jeans stepped out of the bathroom. He jumped for the second bed. Tremaine fired twice. Blood spattered against the far wall.

The man rolled off the bed and fell to the floor with a heavy thud.

Tremaine entered the room as a hand with a gun came over the bed. It blindly fired into the window. Tremaine dropped to the floor as the shots were errantly fired.

DeWayne screamed and writhed. His foot kicked Tremaine in the shoulder.

When the erratic shooting ended, the slide locked back on the man's gun.

Tremaine hopped to his feet. He leaped onto the bed and stood upright. It squeaked under his weight.

The man in the club shirt tried desperately to crawl underneath the bed. "Wait!" he shouted. "Wait! Wait!" His lower half remained exposed as he wriggled frantically to get away.

Tremaine shot the man in the stomach.

A howl came from under the bed.

There was never a doubt about what Tremaine would do next. He shot the man in the groin.

The howl became a screech.

DeWayne continued to wail in pain, but Tremaine ignored him.

Tremaine stepped off the mattress. He calmly dropped to his knees and took careful aim. The man underneath the bed was a frightened puppy with nowhere to go. Tremaine fired once.

But the shrieking didn't stop. DeWayne had rolled off the man in the Sharks jersey and was holding his stomach. "Help me!" he squealed.

Tremaine shot him.

The room was finally silent.

There wouldn't be much time—not with all the gunshots and the screaming. Tremaine wiped the gun with his shirt. It was Cutler's, so there wasn't any worry that his fingerprints were on the remaining rounds or the spent casings. When he felt confident that any traces of him were destroyed, Tremaine dropped the weapon on the carpet next to DeWayne.

Cutler would be able to talk his way out of them finding his gun here, Tremaine thought. The cops were at the man's house when he and DeWayne drove by only a half hour earlier. There was no better alibi.

Tremaine collected the papers from the bed and tossed them into the briefcase. He kept out one that he had seen earlier in the night. He also took a moment to throw in the cell phones of the two Vice Row Kings. Tremaine closed the case and walked from the room.

As he drove out of The Hide-a-Way's parking lot, all the lights in the various bungalows were on, and several curtains were pulled back. Tremaine didn't rev the Yukon's engine until he reached the Sunset Highway.

When he was headed for downtown, Tremaine grabbed the single sheet of paper and located a phone number on it. Then he placed a call.

Chapter 37
0408 hours PST

Corporal Kurt Botzon left the Sunset Highway and pulled into The Hide-a-Way. Several patrol cars clustered in the back, and their red and blue emergency lights bounced off the nearby building. Every bungalow had its lights on, and most of their doors were open. Patrons watched with genuine awe at the scene unfolding before them.

The dissonance wasn't lost on Botzon—the motel's name and its retreat-like setting were in stark contrast to the gathering crowd and the multicolor light show bathing its many structures.

"The Durango," Rachelle Walsh said. She pointed at the furthest bungalow.

Botzon stopped their vehicle and slipped the gearshift into Park. He held his hands in front of the heater vents.

Rachelle hopped out of the car. She was about to shut her door when she noticed Botzon hadn't moved. She leaned back inside. "You okay?"

"I'm fine."

"If you're cold, I'll handle things."

Botzon's eyes narrowed. "See you inside."

"Just saying you could stay dry." She closed the door.

Botzon hated to wuss out at that moment, but he was tired and cold. He didn't want to leave the comfort of the Denali. Yet he couldn't let Rachelle set the example. He was a corporal, and she was an officer. He was supposed to be the role model. Still, he didn't move.

There were no exigent circumstances inside the motel room. The first officers on scene had already reported the shooter had left and that three bodies had been found. Botzon and Rachelle responded because the victims were described as black males. Based on the night's events, and the weather keeping all but the most determined indoors, they had a high likelihood of tying into whatever was going on with the Dead Boys.

The hot air blowing on Botzon's hands felt good. His pants and hair were still wet, and he hadn't been warm since the team arrived at the collision on Altamont. How many hours ago was that?

He grunted and turned off the engine.

Botzon trotted through the rain to the furthest bungalow. Several male patrol officers stood around. They watched Rachelle as she moved about the tight room. Each had an appreciative grin on their face.

It appeared there were two bodies in the room—one on top of the other. However, the initial officer on scene reported three, so one was still out of view—perhaps it was inside the bathroom.

"Who's in charge?" Botzon asked.

One officer glanced at him but turned back to watch Rachelle. "Supervisor hasn't arrived yet." The officer cocked his head when she bent over to take a picture of one of the bodies. Her rear was to them.

Botzon cleared his throat. "Who was first on scene?"

Another officer raised a hand. His blue name tag signified his rookie status.

Botzon leaned in closer to read it. "Herker? This is your scene until you're relieved by a supervisor."

The rookie stood a little straighter. "Sir?"

"Remember your training." Botzon thumbed at the two officers, who quickly stopped watching Rachelle and instead focused on him. "Put these guys to work securing the scene."

"Yes, sir."

"What do you need to do first?"

Herker thrust his chin out like he was responding to a drill sergeant. "Preserve the evidence, sir."

Botzon pointed at Rachelle. "Then who is that?"

She shook her head as she moved inside the room.

The rookie looked at one of the officers he was with.

Botzon held up a hand to block Herker's view. "Don't look at them. Look at me. Who is that woman?"

Rachelle leaned near the far wall and took a photograph.

"I don't know, sir."

"Then why is she inside your crime scene?"

"Because she's a detective?"

"She's not, Herker. What's her name?"

The rookie's face whitened, and he turned to address Rachelle.

"Herker?" Botzon said.

"Sir?"

"Who am I?"

The rookie blinked several times. "I don't know, sir."

"I'm Corporal Botzon. That's Officer Walsh. We're with SIU."

"Okay, sir."

"Of course, it's okay. I just said it." Botzon pointed at the Dodge parked in front of the bungalow. "That Durango is part of an earlier shooting tonight."

"Yes, sir. I'm aware."

"That's part of the crime scene."

"Yes, sir."

Rachelle bent and held the camera underneath the second bed. When she pulled the camera back, she grimaced.

"What are you going to do about it?" Botzon asked.

"Sir?"

"You're staring at me like I'm speaking Chinese. Do

you understand what I'm saying?"

"Yes, sir."

"Then lockdown this room and secure that Dodge."

The rookie nodded. "Okay."

"We've already been over this, Herker. I know it's okay. I said it. Why is Officer Walsh still inside your crime scene?"

Herker leaned into the motel room. "Officer Walsh," he said sternly, "step out of the room."

"Inna minute."

"Now."

Rachelle straightened. She glanced once more around the bungalow, then walked out.

"Don't go back in there," Herker said. "It's officially off-limits."

"Officially?"

Herker's eyes narrowed. "That's what I said."

"Now," Botzon said, "lock it down before a supervisor arrives and climbs up your ass for failing to do your job."

The rookie and the other two uniformed officers hurried off to a patrol car. Botzon suspected it was to grab yellow caution tape. He'd been in Herker's shoes before. It was easy to get distracted on a night like this when problems kept coming like an avalanche.

Botzon moved under the bungalow's small awning. Rachelle stood next to him. They both faced the room.

"There's a dead guy under the bed," she said. "Hard to make out who he is—most of his face is gone. There's another with his back on the floor. Him, I've never seen either. Must be our out-of-town shooters. But the one next to him is DeWayne Taylor."

Botzon shook his head. "There's not going to be many Dead Boys left when the sun comes up."

"When the Giants and the Titans find out, it'll lead to more blood."

He eyed her. "You think the Dead Boys will be around after this?"

"Hard to say. We'll have to see what happens with Tremaine."

Botzon turned and faced the parking lot as a black Chevy Impala pulled in.

"Which one is this?" Rachelle asked.

In a moment, Captain Ackerman stepped out of the car.

Botzon muttered, "Great."

When Ackerman neared, he didn't step under the small awning. Rain dripped from the brim of his baseball hat. "What have we got?"

Botzon and Rachelle spread apart slightly so the captain could see into the bungalow.

"Well, Captain," Botzon said. "It looks like someone found the second set of NorthTown shooters." He pointed at the nearby Dodge. "That's the Durango we've been looking for. There are three dead inside. Two unidentified, but one of them is a known member of the Dead Boys."

Ackerman shook his head. "Three dead. How many bodies are we up to tonight?"

Botzon looked at Rachelle. "Eight?"

She nodded.

The captain stared into the small room. He inhaled deeply, then blew it out in a long, slow breath. "Looks like I need to call in another set of investigators." He turned and searched the lot. "Did I beat a sergeant here?"

"Yes, sir," Botzon said.

Ackerman eyed the line of yellow caution tape the two uniformed officers were hanging. Hecker stood nearby with the crime log.

"Looks like the guys know what they're doing."

"Yeah," Botzon said. "They were on top of it when we

arrived."

The captain smiled. "At least something worked how we wanted it." He turned to study Rachelle. "Any luck finding Tremaine?"

"We're working on it," she said.

Ackerman raised an eyebrow and shifted his attention back to Botzon. "Patrol has this scene under control. I don't think they need SIU looking over their shoulders."

"Yes, sir."

Botzon headed toward the Denali. He figured Rachelle would be close behind.

Chapter 38
0419 hours PST

Quinn Delaney stood in the doorway of apartment 312 as Geri Utley photographed Sidney Booker's lifeless body. A male teammate of Geri's stood by and followed her cues. She moved slowly about the apartment, often squatting to change angles with the camera. After snapping a photograph, Geri would consult the display screen to ensure she got the shot she wanted. If not, she would line it up again.

She wore a hazmat suit to keep additional contaminants out of the room. The hood was pulled up over her head. The suit crinkled every time she moved.

Often, Geri and Quinn would chat a bit before her team processed a scene. They had worked together for years and had developed a friendly relationship. There was none of that banter this morning. The strain of the night's events was evident—especially on Geri and her teammate.

Quinn only had his scenes to worry about—first the Emily Platt murder at NorthTown, now Sidney Booker's. The crime scene techs had multiple.

"Did the other team wrap up that murder/suicide in Fairfield?" Quinn asked.

Geri looked over the lens of her camera, and her face soured. "You didn't hear?"

Quinn shook his head.

"A drunk driver hit them in Rockford. Guess he was pissed about getting 86'd from the casino and wasn't paying attention when he barreled into them where the two highways meet. You know that intersection?"

The Coeur d'Alene Tribe owned a casino in the town of Worley, Idaho. It had been years since Quinn had gone there, but it was a beautiful destination back then.

"Is everyone okay?"

Geri nodded as she consulted the camera's display screen. "Bumps and bruises, but it knocked the van on its side. State patrol processed the collision and arrested the driver. Unfortunately, when they got the van righted, it wouldn't drive. So part of the team is securing another van to collect the evidence and get it to storage."

"Maybe it's Murphy's Law," Quinn said. "What can go wrong will go wrong."

"That's his most famous, but you know he had more laws than that one?" Geri pointed to the couch. "Put a card right there."

The male evidence tech put a yellow card with the number 4 on top of the couch cushion. Geri moved around Sidney Booker's body. She took an establishing shot of the couch and then stepped closer.

"What other laws?" Quinn asked.

Geri squatted near the couch cushion. "Like the fourth law. I think that's what we're dealing with tonight."

"Which is?"

She snapped a picture before looking over her shoulder. "If there's a chance of several things going wrong, the one that will is the one that will cause the most damage."

Quinn suppressed a smile. He hadn't heard that before, but it felt oddly pessimistic from someone like Geri. "Let's hope that's not true." His phone buzzed, and he dug it out of his pocket. "Delaney."

"Detective, it's Marshal Criddle. We met earlier tonight."

"Yeah, I remember." There was something in the man's voice that Quinn didn't like. "What's going on?"

"I just wanted to let you know Tremaine Brown is coming in."

"Excuse me?" His words were sharp, and Geri turned to face him. Even the other crime scene tech watched Quinn with curiosity.

"Tremaine called his attorney, who set up a meeting."

"When?"

"In about ten minutes."

"Tell me where? I can be wherever you need me."

"Not going to happen, Detective."

Quinn's face warmed, and he stabbed the air with his finger. "You said this was our investigation."

"Things have changed."

"Nothing's changed! We're out here investigating dead bodies. We want to know what this is all about."

"Consider this a courtesy call."

Quinn slapped the door frame. "Courtesy nothing."

"Relax, Detective."

"No, you relax. These guys have cut a swath through our town, and we want answers."

Criddle audibly sighed into the phone. "Listen, Quinn. I'm trying to help here. I could have skipped the call and left you in the dark. Take my message and pass it up the chain of command. Tremaine Brown is off the street. Your agency can stop looking for him. All the drama tonight is over."

Quinn didn't understand. He closed his eyes. "I need something more than that."

"You're a detective. You'll piece it together."

Criddle ended the call.

Quinn stared at his phone for several moments. When he looked up, Geri and the male evidence tech were staring at him. He shook his head, then walked down the hallway. Several residents lingered in their doorways. They watched him pass by.

When the elevator arrived, it stopped off-level again. Quinn stepped into the box and took it down to the first floor. He walked outside and stood in the rain.

A homeless man walked by and glanced at Quinn's feet. "Nice booties."

The blue foot coverings were soaking wet now, but Quinn didn't care. Instead, he stood in the rain and hoped the water would wash away how he felt at that moment.

A deal was struck between Tremaine Brown and the United States government. Quinn didn't know its contents or what the outcome would be. He only knew he was not getting any answers tonight.

Chapter 39
4:33 a.m. PST

"I hate being a rat," Tremaine Brown said.

U.S. Marshal Ethan Criddle reclined in his chair. "Don't think of it that way." His fingers drummed a happy rhythm along the edge of the conference table. "Consider it your civic duty."

"Easy with the sunshine, Marshal," Wanda Acosta said. "It's too early in the morning for that." Even at this hour, she wore a suit tailored to her full figure. She passed a small stack of papers to Tremaine. "These seem to be the same as we previously reviewed, but I can't say for one hundred percent certainty without more time. Given the circumstances—"

"Nothing changed except it's now my signature instead of Emily Platt's," Assistant U.S. Attorney Mike Van Dyke said. He eyed Tremaine and lightly tapped the table next to the stack of papers. He wore a Duke University sweatshirt and blue jeans. His auburn hair was mussed as if he had climbed out of bed and gotten dressed hurriedly. "It's the same agreement you worked up with Emily. Full immunity in exchange for testimony."

The four were seated in the U.S. Attorney's office at the Thomas S. Foley United States Courthouse. The building had been silent upon their entry. Not only was it the wee hours of the morning, but it was also Saturday. It was stuffy in the room since the HVAC system was off at those hours.

"What about Dontari?" Tremaine asked.

"We offered him the same deal, but it's up to him to

take it."

"And if he doesn't?"

Van Dyke shrugged. "If he's not participating in his salvation, your testimony better be a grand slam—like Game 7 World Series walk-off homer level."

Tremaine curled his lip. "I better swing for the fences, huh?"

"Did I miss something?" Van Dyke glanced from Tremaine to Wanda then back to Tremaine. His eyes narrowed. "We're not forcing you to do shit."

Wanda lifted a hand. "Watch the tone."

"Hold on." Van Dyke reached for the paperwork to stop the conversation. "You guys called our L.A. office. Not the other way around. They didn't even know you existed until then." His gaze shifted to Tremaine again. "You can walk out of here anytime."

"Your attitude isn't helping," Wanda said.

Van Dyke feigned contrition. "I'm sorry if I'm not displaying the right amount of appreciation for your client being here. The way it looks to me, I don't think Mr. Brown has many options. From the sounds of it, the ODBs know what's going on."

"Not because of us." She waggled a finger between Van Dyke and Criddle. "Because one of you has a leak in your organization."

"Maybe," Van Dyke said, "but this is Mr. Brown's problem, not mine."

Tremaine licked his upper lip but didn't look away from the U.S. Attorney.

"You see. I don't give a damn what happens." Van Dyke thumbed at Criddle. "I don't think he cares a whole lot either."

The marshal shrugged. "I'm remodeling my kitchen. I'd rather work on that today than worry about getting your client into witness protection."

Wanda leaned and whispered, "You don't have to do any of this."

Tremaine knew that. He had met with Wanda and discussed his brother's plight. The Los Angeles County District Attorney had Dontari dead to rights. Wanda suggested going to the local U.S. attorney with their offer, but Tremaine insisted they contact one in the Los Angeles area. He thought they would get a more receptive ear. They found one in Emily Platt.

When Dontari discovered what Tremaine had planned, he bucked against it. The Dead Boys had been good to them, Dontari argued. He claimed they'd been part of their family since joining during high school. Dontari refused to testify against the Originals no matter what the prosecuting attorney threw at him.

What Dontari failed to realize—what he *always* failed to realize—was how much Tremaine safeguarded him. After Dontari joined the gang, Tremaine followed him because he couldn't allow his younger brother to go in unprotected. As they moved through the years, Dontari made fewer mistakes, but Tremaine was always there to clean up the ones he did make. It got easier because Tremaine eventually rose to lead the Spokane Dead Boys.

Unfortunately, Dontari went after a friend of Detective James Morgan. That was a mistake Tremaine couldn't wash away. Tremaine banished his brother from the 509. It was the only option that could keep Morgan at bay.

That's when Dontari landed with the Originals.

Now it was Tremaine who had screwed everything up. In trying to protect his younger brother, he offered to testify against the gang. It was the only thing he had of interest for an Assistant U.S. Attorney. Tremaine believed he could convince Dontari to take a deal. So far, it hadn't worked. He only managed to mark them both as rats.

Yet, if Tremaine could offer strong enough testimony, Dontari would never have to testify. His brother could be saved without ever standing up against the Originals. He wouldn't be a rat.

Only Tremaine would face that fate.

He picked up the pen, flipped to the back document, and signed on the line above his name.

"There's a second copy," Wanda said. "They'll get one. We'll get one."

Tremaine signed the other set of documents. Then he slid all the papers and the pen to Van Dyke. The U.S. Attorney performed the same action with the documents. When he finished, he pushed one set across the table to Wanda.

Van Dyke said, "In a minute, we'll start recording." He pointed at a camera on the wall and then tapped the microphone in the middle of the table. "When that happens, I'll introduce everyone and read you your rights. We'll start the questioning after that. Most of these are preliminary, you understand. We'll loop in the Los Angeles office on a video feed. They'll have more questions, of course. Your immunity requires complete cooperation. Understand?"

Tremaine nodded.

"Do you have any questions before we begin?"

Tremaine looked at Wanda. She waited patiently for his questions, but he didn't ask any. He was simply looking for a friendly face.

Everything in his life was about to change, yet Wanda Acosta wasn't a friend. She was his counsel as long as he could pay her.

John Cutler might have been a friend if Tremaine had let him, but he used the man like the gang taught him.

Detective Morgan was never a friend. The man was a means to an end—a way to use the cops against themselves.

Tremaine Brown and the Dead Boys were no longer friends. Friends weren't supposed to hunt each other down, and they weren't supposed to turn on one another like Tremaine was about to do.

So when push came to shove, Tremaine Brown had no friends.

"No questions," he said.

"All right," Assistant U.S. Attorney Mike Van Dyke said. "Let's get started." He pressed a button underneath the conference table. "We're recording."

Epilogue

Chapter 40

John Cutler had just fallen asleep when he heard a noise. His eyes popped open, and he put his hand on the nightstand. He listened as the storm continued outside and rain smacked against the windows. Maybe it was nothing. He relaxed, and his hand slipped off the nightstand. He closed his eyes.

Someone knocked on the front door.

Cutler tugged open the nightstand. His Glock was in the desk at the front of the house. He kept a Colt 1911 in the top drawer for moments like this. His hand fumbled about in the drawer but found nothing. He pushed onto an elbow and turned on a light. The drawer was empty.

"Shit."

Cutler rolled out of bed and dropped into a crouch. He wore only a pair of running shorts, but he was alert and ready to fight. The weariness he had felt only moments before was gone and replaced by adrenaline.

Had some of the Dead Boys returned?

He padded down the back hallway into the kitchen. Cutler paused for a moment.

Would someone intent on revenge knock first? They might if they wanted to lull him into a sense of normalcy. He'd shot one man and killed another only a few hours ago. There was still blood in his basement. Right now, he couldn't take anything lightly.

Cutler hunched further and darted past the refrigerator. He continued until he reached the desk. He yanked open the drawer and tugged the Glock out. Cutler didn't bother to check that the gun was loaded—it was. He had ensured it was when he put it in the desk after the cops had left. It always had one bullet in the chamber.

His only mistake was believing the Colt 1911 remained where it had been for years. Learning from that lesson would come later. Right now, he was armed again. That potential disaster had been avoided.

Cutler moved the curtain and noticed a black Chevy Impala parked in front of his house—a cop's car. He turned and opened the door with his left hand. The Glock remained hidden behind his back.

Gary Ackerman stood in the doorway with his right hand poised for another knock. Bags were under his eyes, and his mouth hung slightly open. He slowly closed the aluminum screen door but remained outside on the small landing. "Planning to shoot me with that gun behind your back?"

"No."

"Then why don't you put it away?"

Cutler walked to the desk and put the Glock back in the desk drawer. "You can come in."

"I'll stay here." Ackerman studied the aluminum frame. "What happened to your screen? Unhappy client?"

"Something like that."

Cutler crossed his arms. He felt awkward standing in front of the fully clothed captain. The chill of the morning air crept inside his house.

Outside, the thunderstorm continued, and rain fell off the portico. Ackerman stood protected from it all. He removed his baseball hat and slapped it against the side of his leg. His silver hair was tussled. "Heard about your trouble tonight."

"You didn't come by to check, though."

"My men had it under control."

Cutler shrugged. "Yeah."

Ackerman repositioned his cap. "So, it was true. You were working for Tremaine Brown."

"I wasn't working for anyone." He didn't say it with much conviction; he couldn't. The events that occurred earlier tied him to Tremaine. With his Colt 1911 now missing, he might be even more involved. He had no idea what Tremaine might have done with the gun. "I owed a friend who asked me to keep an eye out for Tremaine."

"What friend is this?"

"He's long dead."

"Is this the first time you helped Tremaine?"

"No, but the other time was long ago."

Ackerman shook his head. "All those years we worked together, you never told me about the connection."

"I would have if there was a need," Cutler said.

"Cute." Ackerman poked at the aluminum screen door, and it bounced. "You know what I need?"

Cutler remained silent. He shivered as the cold worked up his back. He gritted his teeth and fought to stay still.

Ackerman continued. "I need you to stay under your rock. This—" He waggled a finger between them. "—doesn't change anything."

"I didn't think it would."

The captain nodded a couple of times. "Have you heard from your client?"

"He's not my—"

Ackerman interrupted Cutler by raising a hand. "Is that a no?"

"No. I haven't heard from him."

"I wouldn't expect you to. We got word he's with the feds now."

Cutler cocked his head.

"He didn't tell you? I guess he and his brother were working some deal to turn state's evidence. At least, that's how we understand it. Who knows? We could have it all wrong. We're not getting much more than that. The marshals scooped him up and delivered him to the local

U.S. Attorney's office. They had a deal waiting for him."

The shiver returned, and Cutler didn't bother fighting this one. "I didn't know."

"Tremaine was with a woman tonight who was killed up at NorthTown."

"His girlfriend."

Ackerman smiled softly. "She was an Assistant U.S. Attorney from the Central District of California. Guess he lied to you about that one, too."

Cutler's mind whirred with the news. "All the killing tonight was to stop him and his brother from turning rat?"

The captain shrugged. "We're assuming. The Dead Boys we have in custody aren't talking. Neither are the feds. Seems like you don't have much to share either."

"If I had something, I would tell you." Cutler believed he would, too.

Ackerman nodded.

"Is he going into the witness protection program?"

"Again, we don't know. Our guess is probably. Tremaine gets a new life and a chance to start over. Good for him and his brother, I guess, but we're cleaning up a mess the Dead Boys left in our streets. There are a lot of questions we don't have any answers for. Who knows if we'll ever get the whole thing sorted out."

Cutler stared at Ackerman.

"What?"

"He stole my gun."

Ackerman's expression hardened. "Tell me."

"I had a Colt in my nightstand." Cutler thumbed over his shoulder. "I only noticed it missing when you woke me up."

The captain pulled open the screen door and stepped inside. "Get dressed."

"Why?"

"Because you're filing a report." Ackerman tugged his

cell phone out of his pocket.

Cutler backpedaled a few steps. "Yeah, all right."

The captain said into the phone. "This is Ackerman. Put me back on the air. I'm going to give you a location in a second. I need a corporal for a burglary report. We need photographs and fingerprints."

Cutler turned and headed for his bedroom.

Chapter 41

Kurt Botzon pushed open the door and exited the Gardner Building. The structure sat to the west of the Public Safety Building and was the home of SIU and other programs related to the police department's mission. He headed toward his car, which was parked along Dean Avenue.

It was light outside, but the sun wasn't visible. It hid behind the brown smear of clouds still marring the sky. Thankfully, the rain had stopped. Puddles filled various potholes in the street, and water collected at clogged storm drains.

Rachelle Walsh hurried up alongside him. She carried her cell phone in her left hand. "Hey, hold up."

He turned.

"I just heard from a contact I know in the Los Angeles Sheriff's Department. The Vice Row Kings are affiliated with the Original Dead Boys."

"Affiliated how?"

"They have a working truce but check this out." She lowered her gaze to the phone. "Robbery Homicide is investigating the murder of two Kings who were CIs. They suspect the ODBs were involved but haven't figured out why there isn't retaliation." Rachelle looked up. "What do you think?"

Botzon rubbed his chin. "The Originals kill a couple of confidential informants for the Vice Row Kings, so the heat doesn't point back to them. Naturally, Robbery Homicide would look to them first."

"Naturally," Rachelle said.

"In turn, the Kings send some shooters up here to take

out Tremaine and everyone else can keep their hands clean."

"Pretty clever."

"It's *Strangers on a Train*."

Rachelle cocked her head.

Botzon waved off her unasked question. "Let Major Crimes know. I'm headed home." He turned to leave.

"Hold on."

His shoulders drooped, and his eyes felt gritty. He'd long stopped being cold, but his pants had yet to dry fully. "Yeah?"

She shook her head. "Can you believe Tremaine cut a deal?"

He grunted. He didn't put anything past gang members. Theirs was a violent world and the only goal was to survive. If the mob could use witness protection, why couldn't a street gang like the Dead Boys? It seemed like that program could use some equal opportunity infusion.

Botzon slowed. Was that racist? Surely, his ex-girlfriend would have admonished him for a thought like that, but he didn't mean for it to come out that way. He was just thinking it was always old white guys getting witness protection. Shit, he was tired.

"What's wrong?" Rachelle asked.

"Nothing."

"Seemed like you had a thought there."

"It was nothing." He glanced at her. "Where are you parked?"

"Back that way." She thumbed in the opposite direction.

He stopped walking. "Then what are you doing?"

"Want to get some breakfast?"

"Nah." His mouth went dry. "Thank you."

Rachelle jerked her head. "C'mon—my treat. We'll

head over to Frank's Diner."

Botzon's face flushed. He hoped she couldn't see the warmth spreading up his neck and into his cheeks. He looked toward his car—a Dodge Challenger.

"No, thanks." Botzon stepped backward into a pothole. Dirty water swashed around his shoe. "Shit."

She laughed. "C'mon. Breakfast'll be fun."

He wasn't a prude. He'd had girlfriends before. Many, in fact. One of them even rose to a level of a fiancée before he decided not to commit.

"Maybe some other time," Botzon said. He shook the water from his shoe.

Rachelle shrugged. "How about a ride home?"

"I'm good." He motioned over his shoulder. "I've got my car."

"You sure about that?"

Botzon turned around. It was then he noticed the passenger tires of his Challenger were flat. So were the tires of the cars next to his. Someone had walked through the neighborhood last night and flattened them all.

He faced Rachelle.

"Well?" she said with a raised eyebrow. "How're those hashbrowns sounding right about now?"

Kurt Botzon liked her. In fact, he liked her more than he wanted to admit. But he didn't want to get involved in the department rumor mill. Had they been different people and had he not been her supervisor, maybe he would have taken her up on the invitation.

"I have to pass."

Rachelle shrugged. "No worries."

Botzon didn't move as she walked away in the middle of the street. Her hips swayed exaggeratedly. He turned before Rachelle could catch him watching.

That's when the rain returned.

Chapter 42

Andrew Parker leaned back in his chair and lifted his arms above his head. The pull in his shoulders felt good. His head hurt from the exhaustion, but he wasn't going to get to rest soon. He'd felt tired often in his life—during the Army, shortly after each of his girls was born, and while on patrol—but the weariness of a detective was different. It was mental fatigue, and it wasn't as easy to push through as the others.

He looked to Johnson, who also worked on his report. His fingers sat quietly on his keyboard, and his chin touched his chest.

Beyond the Major Crimes office, the department was alive. All the lights were on, and the HVAC system hummed. Conversations buzzed in the distance.

Parker pushed his chair back from his desk and got on the floor. It wasn't a crisp movement but rather the oozing of an overworked man. He assumed the push-up position but didn't start the exercise. His stomach and back muscles tightened. Parker stayed in that static pose for thirty seconds then he began. Slowly, he descended until his chest almost touched the floor. His ascension was just as slow. Twenty-five push-ups in a controlled mannered were more effective than fifty done in a hurried, sloppy dash.

When he rose to his feet, his chest muscles remained warm. The dull headache throbbed worse, but the fatigue he'd been wrestling had diminished.

Johnson's head jerked up, and he noticed Parker rising from the floor. "You okay?"

"Push-ups."

"Good idea," he said with the enthusiasm of a disbelieving man.

Johnson shoved back from his desk and flopped to the floor. He didn't take pride in his form the way Parker did. Part of that came from Parker's military training. Johnson loved the high intensity of CrossFit, while Parker enjoyed the regimented precision of bodybuilding.

Parker's phone buzzed once—the signal for a text message. He picked it up and continued to watch his partner.

Each push-up Johnson did seemed faster than the previous one. When he reached twenty-five, the man hopped to his feet and clapped his hands. "I needed that."

Parker considered the text message then. "Well, here's something we can use. The Vice Row Kings are affiliated with the ODBs."

"Who told you that?"

"SIU. Seems the Originals are suspected for whacking a couple Kings."

Johnson flopped into his chair. "And we've got a couple dead Kings who ambushed Tremaine."

"*Strangers on a Train*," Parker said.

His partner shook his head. "I don't know it."

"Two guys trade murders. One wants his wife killed. The other wants his father dead."

Johnson shrugged. "Doesn't ring a bell." He glanced around. "You ready to call it a day?"

Parker returned to his chair and settled his fingers on the keyboard. "I'm finishing up the probable cause affidavit on Jaxson Reader."

"What's taking so long?"

"Working my report at the same time."

"Why?"

Parker lifted his thumbs as a way of a minor shrug. "Because he's the only one left standing to answer for tonight's murders. We're not getting the Vice Row Kings."

Johnson rested an arm on his desk. "Just write it enough to hold him for another day. We'll go home, get some rest, and come back at it with clearer heads."

"I don't want to do that. This guy—" Parker lifted his chin toward his computer. "—helped murder a woman tonight. We still don't know if that was intentional or not. I just want to make sure he gets what's coming."

"You're taking it personally." Johnson faced his computer. "Write the affidavit and go home. We still have a lot of work to do on this case."

Parker pulled his hands from the keyboard. His partner was right. There was more investigating to do. They still had to collate all the reports from the officers involved. That included those who investigated the collisions involved with the initial chase.

Parker and Johnson would also need to wait for the reports from the county deputies who tracked down the previous owners of the sold vehicles to wend their way through the system. On Monday, they would contact the Department of Licensing and get official copies of the sold paperwork.

And they would need to get with Quinn Delaney and build a complete timeline of the night's events. Parker wanted to disparage the man as being one of the Glory Hounds but right now he was more than carrying his weight.

To make the investigation even more complicated, the most senior investigators in the division were wrapping up a triple murder scene at The Hide-a-Way motor lodge west of town that also wrapped into this investigation.

The only one going to face any actual prosecution from it all was Jaxson Reader.

Parker set his fingers back on the keyboard.

Someone had to answer for the murders.

Chapter 43

Quinn Delaney waited for Lieutenant Brand to approve his reports.

He didn't work on any of his other open cases. He didn't have the energy. He reached for a Styrofoam cup of long-cold coffee, but he didn't drink it. Quinn remembered how the last sip soured his stomach. Yet he didn't remove his hand from it. The texture of the cup felt oddly comforting at this time of day.

So Quinn busied his mind searching the internet for news.

Football season was a month into action, but it was too early to get excited about the Seahawks. Lately, it seemed it was too early to get excited about them until the playoffs were suddenly out of reach.

A headline for one article revealed that a wide receiver for the Phoenix Cardinals was charged with raping a local college student. Quinn didn't read the article.

The Seahawks were set to play the Cardinals the upcoming weekend. Quinn was certain that reporters would talk about the implications of the player's conduct on the game but wouldn't bother to consider the emotional impact on the victim.

Quinn flicked back over to his email in hopes of finding an approval from Brand. There was none.

He stood and looked over his cubicle to the lieutenant's office. The man was there, leaning toward his computer. He seemed to be diligently reading. Hopefully, he was studying Quinn's report.

The desk phone rang, and Quinn dropped into his chair. He grabbed the receiver.

"Detective Delaney," he said.

"Criddle. Seems we're both still at it."

Quinn bowed his head and pinched his nose. The marshal was the last person he wanted to talk with. "What can I help you with?"

"Dontari Brown was murdered an hour ago."

"How?"

"How do you think? The Originals got to him. They killed one of ours in the process."

"Did you find your mole?"

"Not yet."

Quinn flopped back in his chair and looked up at the ceiling. There was a stained tile he hadn't noticed before. "Why tell me this news?"

"I thought you'd like to know."

"No, that's not why."

Criddle paused before answering. "It seemed like I owed it to you."

"How's that?"

"You were handed a shit sandwich."

"You should probably be talking with the brass about this."

"Nah," Criddle said. "The administrative types make me itch."

"Doesn't it bother you that he murdered people tonight?"

Criddle fell silent.

"We know for almost certain he killed three people at The Hide-a-Way."

"He told us about that." Criddle tapped something. Maybe a pen against a desk? "He had to, or his deal would have been voided. He also recovered the briefcase they stole from Emily Platt. The ODBs wouldn't have learned anything from the documents inside except what deal Tremaine was getting."

"The men in that hotel room weren't ODBs. They were Vice Row Kings. Hired guns brought in by the Originals to take out Tremaine."

"Look who's a detective. I told you that you'd piece it together."

"What else am I missing?"

Criddle's tapping intensified.

"Was it worth it?" Quinn asked.

"To take the ODBs down? We'll have to wait and see."

Quinn shook his head. "Hard to see how all the bodies tonight make it worth it, and don't try to give me any garbage about us being in a war. I've heard that before."

Criddle's tapping stopped. "The cost sucks, but we've got Tremaine talking. That's what matters."

"Because his brother agreed to rat, but now he's dead."

"You got it backward, Quinn."

Several seconds passed before Quinn asked, "Tremaine initiated the contact?"

"The man was his brother's keeper. That's what all of this was about."

"But Dontari—"

Criddle tapped twice. "What's done is done. Tremaine can't go back on his deal. If he doesn't live up to his agreement, he's going to face a lot of prison time for the murders he admitted to tonight. That's when the Dead Boys will get their pound of flesh."

Quinn straightened in his chair. "What did Tremaine say about the motor lodge shooting?"

"That's all you get, Detective."

"But where did he get the gun? He's a felon."

"I don't know, but it's lucky he had one, or he would have been dead earlier in the night."

"About that."

"I will tell you this," Criddle said. "The guys in the car weren't murdered. No judge or jury would ever say so."

"You don't know. You haven't seen the evidence yet."

"Detective."

"There was another Dead Boy murdered tonight—Sidney Booker. Did Tremaine go and see him? Tell me."

"*Detective.*"

"Answer me so I can quit looking."

"Detective, Tremaine Brown is helping the United States government take down the ODBs. That's what you need to remember in this situation. It's bigger than you and me now."

"You got any other good news?" Quinn asked.

"No," Criddle said. "That's it. Good luck with your investigation."

Quinn hung up.

An email arrived in his inbox from Lieutenant Brand. Quinn clicked on it. It simply read, "Nice work. Approved." He closed the email and the program.

Then he powered down the computer and went home.

Did You Enjoy the Book?

Thank you for reading *The Night of the Dead Boys* and visiting the 509! I hope you enjoyed meeting some of the recurring characters. This is a continuing series with other characters occasionally stepping into the lead role. There are two parallel series to the 509 Crime Stories—the Flip-Flop Detective and the John Cutler mysteries. I hope you'll check them out.

I'm always grateful when a reader takes time out of their day to comment on one of my novels. If you do write a review, please email me, and let me know.

I'd love to say thanks!

About the Author

Colin Conway is the creator of the 509 Crime Stories, a series of novels set in Eastern Washington with revolving lead characters. They are standalone tales and can be read in any order.

He also created the Cozy Up series which pushes the envelope of the cozy genre. Libby Klein, author of the Poppy McAllister series, says *Cozy Up to Death* is "Not your grandma's cozy."

Colin co-authored the Charlie-316 series. The first novel in the series, *Charlie-316*, is a political/crime thriller that has been described as "riveting and compulsively readable," "the real deal," and "the ultimate ride-along."

He served in the U.S. Army and later was an officer of the Spokane Police Department. He has owned a laundromat, invested in a bar, and run a karate school. Besides writing crime fiction, he is a commercial real estate broker.

Colin lives with his beautiful girlfriend, three wonderful children, and a codependent Vizsla that rules their world.

Find out more at colinconway.com.

Also by Colin Conway

THE 509 UNIVERSE

The 509 Crime Stories

The Side Hustle
The Long Cold Winter
The Blind Trust
The Suit
The Value in Our Lies
The Mean Street
Murder by Any Other Name
Black and Blue in the Lilac City
The Only Death That Matters
The After-Hours War
The Fate of Our Years
The Night of the Dead Boys
The Path of Progress
When the Wicked Rest
The Golden Witness

The John Cutler Mysteries

Cutler's Return
Cutler's Chase
Cutler's Friend
Cutler's Cases
Cutler's Bargain
Cutler's Legacy

The Flip-Flop Detective

Strait Over Tackle
Strait to Hell
Strait Out of Nowhere

OTHER SERIES

The Cozy Up Series

Cozy Up to Death
Cozy Up to Murder
Cozy Up to Blood
Cozy Up to Trouble
Cozy Up to Christmas
Cozy Up to Danger
Cozy Up to Terror

**The Charlie-316 Series
(with Frank Zafiro)**

Charlie-316
Never the Crime
Badge Heavy
Code Four
The Ride-Along

OTHER WORKS

Some Degree of Murder (with Frank Zafiro)
Tales from the Road (with Bill Bancroft)